TO
ACCOUNT
FOR
MURDER

TO
ACCOUNT
FOR
MURDER

William C. Whitbeck

THE PERMANENT PRESS
Sag Harbor, NY 11963

For information, address:
  The Permanent Press
  4170 Noyac Road
  Sag Harbor, NY 11963
  www.thepermanentpress.com

Library of Congress Cataloging-in-Publication Data

  Whitbeck, William C.
     To account for murder / William C. Whitbeck.
       p. cm.
     ISBN 978-1-57962-206-0 (hardcover : alk. paper)
       1. Law stories. 2. Murder—Investigation—Fiction.
     3. Michigan—Fiction. I. Title.

  PS3623.H5637T62 2012
  813'.6—dc22   2010019931

Printed in the United States of America.

To my wife Stephanie: always my love, always.

And for your lifeblood,
I will surely demand an accounting.
I will demand an accounting from every animal.
And from each man, too,
I will demand an accounting for the life of his fellow man.

—Genesis 9:5

As My Father Lay Dying

November, 1996

"*F*rankie," *my father says to me, using the diminutive as always,* "this business of dying is not for weaklings. Your mother knew that, but now I'm learning it the hard way."

It is evening. The nurse has not turned on the ceiling lights and the hospital room is pale and gray. The wind outside rises and falls fitfully and a tree branch taps against the windowpane with an unsteady rhythm. It has been a long dry autumn and I know that when I walk back to my car the fallen leaves will swirl and dance around my feet, parched and papery.

"You're not dying, Dad," I say. "You'll be out of here in a week."

"That's nonsense." My father sits upright in the Stryker bed, wincing at the effort. The oxygen tube partially obscures his silvered mustache, the intravenous feeding line snakes away from his one arm, but his voice is still strong. He is a handsome man and even in repose his features are sharp and regular. His cheekbones are high, his eyes a gunmetal gray. Age and illness have not yet beaten him.

"Don't you want to watch the election returns?" I ask.

"I'll pass. I wouldn't be a bit surprised if Clinton beats Dole before they turn the lights out and make us all lie here in the damned dark. I can read all about it in the funny papers tomorrow." I smile for my father, at his old-fashioned turn of phrase.

"No, Frankie, I don't want to watch television. I want to talk to you for a while."

My smile freezes in place and I shift in my chair to conceal my uneasiness. After I became a partner in his law firm, he asked me to call him Charlie, but I never could. I avoid familiarity, even with my father.

"Dad," I say, "we're not very good at talking."

"I know that," he says. "As the darkness gathers"—ever the courtroom actor, he causes a small flutter in his voice and then grimaces at his own humor—"as the darkness gathers, perhaps we can reach some understandings."

"We understand each other pretty well." It is a lie, but he need not know it.

"You don't understand me at all," my father says. Of course, he speaks only of himself. For all our time together, he knows little of me. I have never allowed him inside, and for good reason. I do not need the past coming to call, like a branch tap-tap-tapping against a forgotten window. I know all about the past. It's dead and gone.

"That's all right," he says. "Children aren't supposed to understand their parents. When they're young, they're supposed to keep quiet and obey. When they're older, they're supposed to forget. Otherwise, we'd be killing each other off with unnatural frequency."

My father, the philosopher. Can one forget without forgiving? I try to push the question from my mind.

"What do you want me to understand, Dad?" I ask, readying myself for his answer.

My father looks out of the hospital window for a moment while we listen to the whisper of the wind and the stutter of branch against glass. Then he runs his right hand through the thick white weave of his hair and says, "There was a time when your mother washed my hair once a week."

He turns back to me and says, in a different voice, "We're down to closing statements now and I'm not handling this well. But it's time to face the jury and that's you, Frankie. Just you."

He will not seduce me with this use of his own mortality as rhetoric. He wants a jury in the twilight. But it can't be me. I take a deep breath. The ammonia they use to clean the hospital's tile floors and bathrooms burns down into my chest.

"Aren't you tired? Can't this wait until tomorrow?" I keep my tone easy, nonchalant, with only a touch of impatience. Perhaps, when morning comes, he will want to forget. Just like me.

My father looks at me. But he does not relent. "I'm an old man," he says. "Do me this one favor. Let me spin out a tale before it gets too dark. There are some things we've never discussed." He pauses and we watch the shadows lengthen in the room.

"It won't be easy," he says.

"Why not?" It is a reflexive response, a lawyer's response. I regret it immediately. Why now, so late, am I asking questions?

"It's about a death in the family."

The coldness drops over me like a cloak. I do not want to go down this road, ever. I turn my face to the wall, hoping that he will give way. I know that he can be monumentally persuasive. When I was young, in the summer when school was out, the other children played baseball or swam at the nearby lakes. But I was drawn to the law and so I would go over to court for my father's trials. He was a master at telling stories to the jury. Assuring them at the outset that he would never lie to them, catching their attention with some homely parable, and then gradually weaving his client's version of the truth into the net he had cast. As the jury listened to him I did not watch their faces. Only their hands. Sometimes they moved their hands with his gestures as he paced in front of the jury box. Then I knew he had them.

Well, he won't have me. I cross my arms over my chest. My head is down, my eyes half closed. He is a perceptive man and he senses my fear and tries to dispel it. He makes a small gesture of reassurance with his right hand.

"I'm cursed with a good memory," he says. "I remember all the little victories, all the great defeats." His voice is even in the dying light and I know that he means to draw me back into the web of the past, the carefully forgotten, ever remembered past, and I will myself not to listen. But he will not be deterred.

"At night," he says, "I turn the details over in my mind like one of those Rubik Cubes, trying to fit appearance into reality. So let me start with how I came back to Lansing from the war. It was before I ever met with Lev Bernstein that night at the prison. But he was waiting for me all along the way. Like a spider in his web."

My father pauses and closes his eyes for a moment. And then he says, "Remember one thing from this, if you remember nothing else."

There is not a thing out of the past that I wish to remember, but I cannot ignore him. He is Charles Cahill. No one can ignore the legendary Charles Cahill, least of all someone who has sheltered in his shadow all these years.

"Remember this one thing," he says softly. "Everybody lies."

≡ 1 ≡

Homecoming

October, 1945

I didn't anticipate that the prosecutor would welcome me with open arms that warm October morning. But I didn't go to his office at the county building for a celebration. Only for an alibi. I had been an assistant prosecutor for all of five months before I volunteered for the Army on the day after Pearl Harbor. I doubted that Randall Hennessey even remembered me. But to my surprise, he greeted me with some enthusiasm.

"Charlie Cahill," he called out. "Home from the wars at last." There was an ancient Motorola on the credenza behind him and Harry Heilmann was calling the last game of the 1945 World Series, his voice rising in excitement as the Tigers scored. Hennessey quickly turned off the radio. Appearances were important to him and it wouldn't do for the prosecutor to be caught listening to a baseball game while the people's work languished. Hennessey circled around his desk and headed toward me, arms wide, face alight with the politician's easy smile. But he stopped when he saw the empty left sleeve of my suit coat. I had refused a prosthesis and I had not yet mastered the process of pinning the cuff back up underneath my upper arm.

"Jesus! Where the hell's your arm?"

"We gave it a proper military funeral. Randy, you haven't changed a bit," I said. I needed to move beyond the arm and curry a little favor and I knew he was sensitive about his age. It was a prudent attitude in an elected official. He had the pale skin, peppered with freckles, and the sandy red hair that characterizes so many of our clan, and occasionally the hint of a brogue softened his speech. But he was grayer than I remembered. And fatter.

"Bullshit," he said. "I eat too much, drink too much. You, on the other hand, you lost forty pounds. Bein' a war hero don't agree with you?"

"I'm no hero. I'm just a vet looking to get my job back." Hennessey's smile tightened as he motioned me toward the only chair in his office not piled with books or case files. Centered squarely on the wall behind his desk was a black-bordered photograph of Franklin D. Roosevelt, wearing a fedora and sporting that famous jut-jawed smile, a cigarette holder clenched in his teeth. Hennessey gestured toward the late president.

"I get that asshole Bigs Bigelow appointed national committeeman. And then he doesn't even get me a signed picture? What the hell's he good for?"

With that off his mind, Hennessey sat down in his mottled leather chair, propped his feet up on the mound of papers on his desk, and shook a Lucky from the pack he pulled from his shirt pocket. He lit the cigarette with a kitchen match from the dispenser on the corner of his desk and began to blow ragged smoke rings in my direction. His theatrics were the first hint that my again becoming an assistant prosecutor was by no means a sure thing. Hennessey only smoked when he had something, or someone, on his mind that he didn't like. But I didn't really care. As I said, I was only in it for the alibi.

"Well, it's not as if we don't have enough work," he said. "I filled your job with Phil McGraw. He's a good boy, one leg shorter than the other, so's the Army couldn't get him. Still and all, we can't keep up. Not with this one-man grand jury bullshit starting up. Everybody knows it's a piece of crap, but the attorney general is looking to me for some help."

His voice trailed off and he began massaging the thinning hair on the back of his head. It was a sure sign that he was actually thinking. Behind him, FDR smiled down, cheerfully, enigmatically. "What do you know about grand juries?" he asked.

Before I could answer, the phone behind him rang and he picked it up. "Hennessey here," he intoned gravely into the mouthpiece of the phone, his voice dropping a full octave. After a moment, he pulled his feet down from the cluttered desk, snubbed out his cigarette, and began taking notes on the yellow legal pad next to the phone. I looked out the window and waited. It wasn't that I was particularly calm. It was just that I was an onlooker. Watching Hennessey and watching myself. Waiting.

"All right," Hennessey said. "I'll be there quick as I can." He heaved himself up out of his chair and hurried around his desk toward the door. He was quite nimble, as many heavy men are. With his hand on the doorknob, he stopped and turned back around to face me. "Why don't you come along? There's a killing and I'm damn sure it's mixed up with this grand jury investigation."

I stared at him in amazement. "Why is that?" I asked. It was the only thing I could think of to say.

"The stiff's a goddamn state senator, that's why."

I knew nothing about an investigation. But I knew all about the senator. After all, I'd shot him.

HENNESSEY'S FIRST comment when we reached the cornfield was that the person or persons who killed the senator had no appreciation for geography. "Another hundred yards east on the Grand River Road toward Detroit and we're over the Ingham County line into Livingston. See what I mean?"

Ingham, I knew, was one of Michigan's cabinet counties. Our territorial legislature named it for one Samuel Delucenna Ingham, Andrew Jackson's secretary of the treasury. The legislature had sought to curry favor with Jackson and his cabinet to clear the way for statehood. But the good people of Michigan soon learned that politics is rarely just a matter of ceremony, even when using totems as powerful and personal as men's names. Jackson and his party were striving to maintain the balance between slave and free states, and the debate on Michigan's admission to the union dragged on interminably. Statehood came late to Michigan and Ingham County suffered under the burden not only of a failed political gesture, but also from a most obscure and ordinary name.

I knew this history, even as I knew the sequence of the alphabet and the cadence of the multiplication tables, from the inquisitions of the spinsterish teachers in the one-room rural schoolhouses I attended as a boy. I also knew that Hennessey considered the county's nomenclature to be useful for campaign oratory, but of little other immediate relevance. So I did not share my thoughts with him as we both pondered the body. For Hennessey, it was the first time.

I saw that some carnivore had chewed away at the good senator's vest and managed to penetrate the white flesh of his belly into his intestines. It was an indignity that meant nothing to him now. But I winced at the thought of some needle-toothed rodent rummaging through his mortal remains. Strangely, there was very little blood beneath his shattered head. It was as if he had been sucked dry.

We watched the state police take their measurements. For them, mystery rustled in the withered corn sheaves and whispered through the maples and poplars that lined the field, next to the barbed wire fence. It was indeed ironic that Samuel Delucenna Ingham never entered his namesake county. We had ensured that state senator Harry Maynard would never leave it. Maynard's body lay exactly where Sarah Maynard and I placed it that morning. Before I put the two bullets in his face. Before I tossed the gun into the Grand River. I had made certain of one thing. Maynard was very convincingly, very conclusively, and very certifiably dead.

The state police pathologist was a gnome of a man with an outsized, egg-shaped head perched squarely on his thin shoulders. He picked his way carefully through the dry dust of the cornfield and then squatted down to examine the body, studiously pursing his lips. He had put on this particular show a time or two before. The warmth of Indian summer lingered in the late afternoon and there was a slight bluish haze visible against the gold and russet of the trees. The yellowing corn stubble swayed and murmured with the soft, steady wind. As I watched and waited, it occurred to me again that it was ungodly peaceful in this particular cornfield. And very quiet.

Peace and quiet were not Hennessey's strong suits. He shuffled his feet impatiently and finally he knelt at the pathologist's side, next to the body. The fingers of my right hand curled involuntarily. The wait was coming to an end. "Was he shot here?" Hennessey asked.

The pathologist looked over the top of his rimless glasses and gave Hennessey a parched smile. "Here and there," he said. He pointed to the two bullet wounds in Maynard's face, one low in his forehead and the other just beside what remained of his nose. One eye was intact and Maynard looked at me with that eye, brown and unblinking, and I looked away. Lansing knew him by his face and I had destroyed that. But he was still alive in my memory. I knew what he had done and I remember it to this day.

Hennessey moved closer to the pathologist, ignoring the man's small joke. "Suppose he was shot someplace else and just dumped here," he said. "That could've happened, right?"

"I don't see how." The pathologist rose to his feet. "There's no indication he was dragged in any fashion. Two head wounds, one a through and through. I suspect we'll find the slug if the bulls"—he gestured at the uniformed policemen wandering through the field—"don't bury it with all their tramping around."

"Doc," Hennessey said. "I'm not tryin' to be difficult, but he sure as hell could've been shot down the road somewheres else and then carried out here. He can't weigh more'n one fifty wringing wet. I could lug him out here easy. See what I mean?"

"Of course I do. It would be particularly good for you if that somewhere else was in the next county. But I don't think so. Look at the position of the body. Look at the trajectory of the through and through. Look at the powder burns."

The pathologist leaned forward and for a moment I thought he might fall. But he caught himself and squinted at Hennessey in the late afternoon sun. He pursed his lips again and the wind ruffled the tufts of his hair.

"Whoever did it spread-eagled the good senator in the dirt and then shot him at close range, right in the face," he said. "I'm a little puzzled by the absence of blood, but I'm sure there's some explanation. No, I'd say it happened right here in Ingham."

"I'd just as soon you not be so fucking quick with your opinions," Hennessey said. "Fifteen minutes and the man's got it all figured out," he said to me, his face reddening and his voice rising. When properly agitated, he burned like a lit match.

"While you're at it, maybe you'd let us all in on who did it?" Hennessey was shouting now, and the policemen glanced up from their work and watched him poke his finger down at the pathologist's chest.

"I've no idea who killed him," the pathologist said. He lifted his glasses up onto his forehead and squinted again into the sun. His voice had a higher pitch, but he did not back away from Hennessey's bluster. "It looks professional to me, but it could've been the governor for all I know," he said. "Now I'd like to finish up here and go home. It's almost five o'clock." His smile flickered again and I knew he used the civil servant's cliché to anger Hennessey even further. He looked vaguely disappointed when Hennessey merely shook his head in feigned disbelief and stomped off toward his battered black Oldsmobile parked at the edge of the road, beyond the barbed wire.

"That's a fine bedside manner you've got, Randy," I said as we climbed into the rusty heat of his car.

"The man's a pure horse's ass." Hennessey cranked his window down and pulled another cigarette out of his pack. There was a row of kitchen matches stuck above the visor on the driver's side and he took one and flicked it alight with his thick, yellowed thumbnail.

"All's I ask is for him to keep an open mind on this, until the shoutin' dies down," he said. "The rockbottom last thing I need is idiot boy Marvin Altman rootin' around in a murder investigation in my county. That moron couldn't find an elephant in a fucking snowstorm and that's the fucking God's truth."

I looked at him blankly as he lit his cigarette and inhaled deeply, his head tilted back. "Who's Marvin Altman?"

"For chrissake, Charlie, he's the goddamn attorney general and now he's the prosecutor for the goddamn grand jury. You been hidin' out in a cave somewheres?"

Hennessey ground the starter down and the ignition coughed and died. He swore and jammed his foot down on the starter again. "Maybe, just maybe, now that the war's over and you heroes have all come home, I can get a car that starts," he said.

I looked out the window and nodded. The haze had thickened and I inhaled the sharp dry smell of autumn. On my father's farm, before we lost it, every fall my brother and I would rake the leaves into huge mounds. We often burrowed in the dusty, layered leaf piles after we finished, sometimes disappearing entirely from my father's view. My father always caught us, though, and ordered us to rake the leaves up again so we could burn them quickly and completely. My father would go inside to his bottle and my brother and I would tend the fires, watching the blue-gray smoke curling and dancing in the wind.

Hennessey floored the starter again and the engine groaned and hammered, but it would not turn over. "You've flooded it," I said. "Wait five minutes and it might start."

I leaned over closer to him, my side pressing against the knob of the gearshift. I kept my voice level. "By the way, how did you know it was Senator Maynard? His head was almost blown apart."

"The state police recognized him. Or what was left of him. They'd seen him before on some things. Fact is, he was sort of a regular. He liked the whores, liked 'em young. Sometimes, he'd slap them around a little and they'd complain to the local cops and the state boys would have to fix it. Anyways, his billfold was still in his back pocket with his license and his money. At least nobody robbed the bastard. It restores my faith in the criminal element."

Maybe he would go down the wrong road, I thought. *Maybe Sarah and I would be safe.*

⟹ 2 ⟸

Ironpants

October, 1945

Normally, the killing of a state senator would have made banner headlines in all the papers. When they won the World Series, the Tigers changed all that. The three Detroit papers carried the story of Maynard's death below the fold the next day. The Lansing paper featured the Maynard story while displacing its national news column with a breathless account of the Tiger victory. The paper also carried a picture of Hennessey and the county sheriff. The caption said the two men were discussing the latest developments in the Maynard case. Given the dour look on Hennessey's professionally cheerful face, the talk could not have been one that he particularly enjoyed. He had asked me to check in, and I dutifully called him from the pay phone in the lobby of the Olds Hotel. He came directly to the point.

"Judge Storey wants to see you. Be in his office in a half an hour and don't be late. He's a Republican. He expects people to be on time."

"He wants to see me? Why? I'm nothing to him."

"You're real slow for your age," Hennessey said. "You want a job, I'm tryin' to get you a job. Storey's appointed himself as the grand juror. Me, I don't see the point. Graft across the street is a fact of life, like the clap. But sure as hell Storey's looking to dump idiot boy Altman and hire himself some new lawyers. That's you, ain't it?"

I thanked Hennessey, grudgingly, and walked over to the old City Hall. Judge Leon Storey was the last man I wanted to see that day, or any other day. As I trudged up the dirty stairway to his office, I simply wanted to avoid disaster. *Act normally,* I thought. *Pretend you're not squarely in the middle of this.*

I remembered Storey as a slender whip of a man, with straight black hair and icy blue eyes. He ran his court and his life with such unbending discipline that he was widely known as Old Ironpants. I am sure he both knew and approved of the nickname. And now he was the one-man grand juror.

I knew that Michigan's grand jury system is unique. The normal citizens' grand jury of twenty-three freeholders still exists in our state. But in the middle of the First World War, the legislature passed a statute that it innocuously enumerated as Public Act 196. In fact, the statute was anything but innocuous. In the hands of a knowledgeable and sufficiently ruthless man, it could be ferociously effective. Judge Homer Ferguson had once used his powers as a one-man grand juror to put the mayor of Detroit and the Wayne County prosecuting attorney in Jackson State Penitentiary and himself in the United States Senate.

I doubted that Storey wanted to be a senator. He was a judge through and through. But I had no doubt whatsoever that he was both knowledgeable and ruthless. He was also capable of being extremely ferocious. In my few appearances in front of him before my war, I had watched him shred other young assistant prosecutors and I took care to be exceedingly well prepared. And exceedingly brief. When I walked into his chambers, he waved me to a chair. Then he lost no time in establishing that he also had a good memory. "What is your relationship to Sam Cahill?" he asked.

"He was my father."

"I remember him. He was before me several times on the criminal docket, back when I was a municipal judge. But until I spoke with Randall Hennessey this morning, I didn't connect the name with his young assistant, home from fighting the wars. Where is your father now?" His voice was without inflection. He was wearing his robe and he sat behind his desk, his hands clasped in front of him. The collar of his stiff white shirt emphasized the squareness of his jaw. He was spare, sharp, and monochromatic and he fit well into his office and his position.

"He died in 1928."

"Didn't he drink himself to death? He was a drinker, as I recall."

My control slipped and I leaned forward across his desk. "He drowned in the Detroit River," I said. "I'm sure you're not interested in the full proctology. Judge, is there some reason you wanted to talk with me?"

His eyes flickered toward my empty sleeve and lingered there, and then he pushed the chair back from his desk and walked to the corner of his office. The sun was behind the Capitol and the afternoon light slanted in through the glass rectangles of the windows, accenting the angularity of his features.

"When I came back from the last Great War, I was much like you," he said. "No respect whatever for my elders. Battle has that effect. I was in the Fifth Marines, you know."

He walked back behind his desk and sat down. His posture was so erect and severe that I could almost see the battle streamers flying. Marines dream of glory and he was no exception.

"I don't believe in the transmission of sin," he said. "My own father owed everybody in the county. He simply could not keep a job. I overcame it, but I never forgot it. Have you overcome your father?"

"There's nothing to overcome. After he died, we made our own way."

"You appear to have handled it well." Again he glanced at my sleeve and again he gave me his brief, mechanical smile. "Randall speaks very highly of you and I value his opinion. If he weren't such a damned Democrat, we might actually be friends. But set politics aside. Are you familiar with this grand jury investigation?"

"Only very generally." I did not tell him how very familiar I was with the murder. The instinct for survival is strong, even among the self-destructive. *Let him do the talking*, I thought. *He likes to talk.*

"At least you don't have any predispositions. I have been appointed grand juror"—he neglected to mention that he appointed himself—"and I intend to carry out my responsibilities. Randall may have told you that I'm not in the least satisfied with the progress Attorney General Altman has made to date."

"Yessir," I said. It was a convenient and conditioned response. I actually knew a little more. Hennessey had told me of the rumor that Marvin Altman had blocked Storey's nomination for a seat on the Supreme Court. Altman apparently believed that Storey lacked voter appeal. I tended to agree. Storey wore his rectitude like a badge. He would have been glaringly out of place in statewide politics. The black and white of his personality simply did not fit in the rough and tumble technicolor of a political campaign. He had one salient attribute, though. He remembered his enemies. We had that much in common.

"The procedure is clear," Storey said. "A judge functioning as a one-man grand juror under the statute can appoint his own assistants. I intend to appoint a special prosecutor reporting to me, not to the attorney general. I intend to appoint a full-fledged staff, working directly for him. Are you interested in a staff position?"

I could only stall. "Are you offering me a job, Judge?"

"No, I am not," Storey said. There was some asperity in his voice and he paused and bent forward to rearrange the precise array of memorabilia on his desk. When he was satisfied that everything was as it should be, he looked back at me.

"I'm asking you if you'd like to be considered for a job," he said. "I'm going to make Hubbell Street special prosecutor. If you're interested in a staff position, I can arrange an interview. I'm sure your father's somewhat checkered career will be of no interest to him."

I ignored the reference to my father. It was a response to which I had schooled myself with some effort over the years and now it served me well. "Any lawyer who wants courtroom experience would kill to work with Hubbell Street," I said. "People say he's the best trial lawyer in the state." People also said he wanted to be the next governor, but I thought it impolitic to mention that.

"Indeed. Well, now he's going to be my special prosecutor and he needs a staff. Shall I tell him you're interested?"

I hesitated. I was at the center of a crime. One slip and I would become a target of the investigation. I knew something about criminal investigations. Like landslides, they are slow to begin. But once they gain a momentum and a direction, they are next to impossible to escape. The risk was enormous and I could easily be swept away by something over which I had no control. *Keep stalling*, I thought. *Stay out of harm's way.*

"There's nothing to lose by talking," I said.

He measured out his smile. "Good. He'll be at the Olds tomorrow afternoon at three o'clock sharp. I'll tell him to expect you for an interview. Be on time." He stood up and offered up his hand. His grip was tight, his palm hot and dry. "I hope all goes well," he said.

I left Storey's chambers in a daze and stumbled down the stairway leading to the street. The back of my neck began to tighten as I weighed the chance I had just taken. My mouth tasted of old pennies, stale and coppery. Suddenly I was so stiff with fear that I leaned against the wall to keep my balance. My shirt collar bit into my neck and I began to choke, and then I sat down on the last step of the stairway. I closed my eyes to stop the whirling and I saw the cliff in the morning mist. The smell of burned flesh and cordite floated in the air and the machine guns opened up off to my left, snapping, snapping, and that frightened me even more.

I slammed my right fist down on the metal step, once, twice. But even that did not erase the remembered pain. When I opened my eyes, the yellow light filled the stairwell. I took several deep, slow breaths, but the light and the smell and the noise would not leave and I was again at sea.

≡ 3 ≡

A Morning of Battle

June, 1944

They sealed us aboard the *Prince Charles* the night before the invasion. On the morning of the sixth of June most of us were terrifically seasick. But the whiskey in my second canteen helped me along as we headed out after the first false start. Even then, even as the whiskey warmed me, I had no desire to be a hero. All I wanted to do was stay alive and reasonably whole.

Unlike the other companies, we boarded our landing craft from nets down the side of the transport. I lost my footing immediately after my first step downward onto the webbing and I hung there for a moment, suspended in the mist. Then, as the ship rolled with the choppy seas, I swung both feet forward and caught one of the interlocking strands of rope with my right boot. The spray from the waves had turned the net into a cold, slippery cobweb and the strand fell away.

I looked down between my dangling feet at the scow-shaped Higgins boat. When the transport rolled again away from the shore, I caught the net with both feet. Slowly, I unclenched my right hand, then my left, and began to work my way down the net. My rifle sling chafed against my chest with the rhythm of my descent, and the hard edge of my steel helmet cracked against the back of my neck as the transport rose and fell with the swells that swept in toward the Normandy coast.

I had to get my men down into the boat. I looked up and in the gray morning light I saw one soldier, then two, almost formless against the dark hull of the transport. They swung carefully over onto the net and then hesitated.

"Come on," I shouted. "Form on me." My voice was lost in the throbbing of the diesel engines and the pounding of the sea. But the men began to inch spider-like down the net.

When I was four feet above the heaving deck of the Higgins boat, my hands ached with the strain and I slowed my descent. The coxswain piloting the boat gestured to me urgently. "Jump," he shouted. "Jump now." I turned on one strand of rope and, when the Higgins boat rose up with the next wave, I released my grip and dropped to its deck. My rifle slammed into the back of my helmet and the blow sickened me.

"Captain," the coxswain shouted in my ear, "we're late already. You've got to get your men aboard."

I climbed up the side of the Higgins boat. As the men on the netting inched downward, I motioned to them and shouted, "Jump. Time the waves and jump."

One by one, the men dropped into the Higgins boat, their gear clanging against its steel sides as they fought to keep their balance on the pitching deck. One soldier lost his footing completely and stumbled forward into the steering assembly, catching it full in the face. The coxswain looked down at the stunned soldier and his mouthful of broken teeth.

"Don't bleed on the wheel," he said. "It makes it slippery." The skin of his face was a pasty white, but there were large circles of red below each of his cheekbones. *He's as scared as I am*, I thought.

"A lot like the courtroom isn't it, Charlie?" the man next to me said. I turned and saw Oxander, his starched fatigues soaked with sea spray and his shoulders hunched forward against the chill.

"Colonel," I said. "What are you doing here? I thought you were on the lead boat."

"This is the lead boat," Oxander said. "My transport didn't even get out of the assembly area, it was leaking so much. We'd best get moving."

The *Satterlee* and the *Talybont* circled at the rear of the transport and the rumble of their guns drowned out my shouted reply. As the Higgins boat turned in toward the coast, I heard the shells whistling overhead. When we moved closer to the shore, I saw dirty clouds of smoke and dust rising from the headlands above the narrow sand beaches. The sky was the color of lead, the shoreline a necklace of fire.

The Higgins boat rolled in the five-foot waves and a sudden gust of wind blew the greasy smoke from its engines back into my face. My stomach tightened and whiskey-flavored bile rose in my throat. I put my head down between my knees and retched painfully onto the deck, already slick with grease, and water.

"You paddy sonofabitch, you can't go sick on me now," Oxander yelled. "I need you to get those guns."

I squatted on the filthy deck and thought about the guns. The staff officer who briefed us during our endless practice runs had said that the Germans had placed coastal batteries on the promontory of Ponte du Hoc. The guns could fire directly down on the beaches on either side, beaches the Army maps now showed as Omaha and Utah.

"If we don't take Ponte du Hoc and those guns," the briefing officer said, "the Germans will destroy us on the beaches. Let me make it real clear. Take the goddamn guns and never mind the cost. They'll be plenty of medals to go around." Then he set the clock ticking. "You've got thirty minutes after the bombardment lifts." *Thirty minutes is not a lot of time in a spring storm,* I thought.

We fought through the tidal current, parallel to the coast. Behind us, the other landing craft carrying the men of the 2nd Ranger Battalion followed in a ragged line. The fighters screamed in above to strafe the beaches and cliffs. Huge fourteen-inch shells from the battleship *Texas* roared over our heads. I felt the smallest flicker of confidence. *It's going to be all right,* I thought. *Not even the Germans can live through this.*

"There it is," Oxander yelled, pumping his right arm twice toward the sky. "There's the cliff and we're only a half hour late."

At his signal, the boats began their run in to the narrow beach. I saw figures in field gray on top of the steep cliff moving through the dust and smoke, and I heard the irregular rattle of their automatic weapons fire and the whine of their slugs ricocheting off the steel snout of our boat. The coxswain lowered the landing ramp and I followed Oxander into the icy water. Gasping with the shock, I turned to wave my men forward.

Before I could shout, a mortar round exploded at the rear of the boat and the first diesel tank roared into flames. Through the curtain of fire and smoke, I saw my men slapping at the flames and I thought they might be able to beat out the fire. But then the second tank exploded and I heard the screaming and I smelled the burning flesh. Suddenly, the Higgins boat heeled over and the merciful sea swept them away.

I could not mourn them. I could only save myself. *Get to the cliff,* I thought as I drove through the waist high water toward the beach. *It's safer there.*

When I reached the foot of the cliff after sprinting across the sand and gravel of the beach, I huddled against the hard rock, momentarily sheltered. Shivering in the cold, I watched the rest of the battalion, draped with ammunition belts and carrying rope-launching rockets and scaling ladders, wade in through the surf to the beach. My whiskey courage had failed me and I was stiff with fear. I crossed myself once and then ran back onto the beach. The fire from the top of the cliff increased and Rangers fell forward, individually and then in clusters, toward the sound of the guns.

To my right, a man lay sprawled facedown over a fully assembled rope-launching rocket. He was a new corporal, his two stripes bright and clean on the sleeve of his fatigue jacket. Arterial blood pulsed from a neat, round hole punched through the back of his neck. The blood slowly stained the sand by his right shoulder. I knelt beside him and pulled him over and a gout of blood spurted from the fist-sized cavity at the base of his neck. He had another long, slanting wound on the left side of his belly, and his intestines spilled out in a yellow and red coil. But he was still alive. He curled his body inward and his hands fluttered around his viscera, as if he meant to shield himself.

I looked away from his eyes and pulled the rocket from under his body. I anchored it and then fired toward the top of the cliff. The explosion propelled the attached rope ladder and grapnel in an arc spiraling over the cliff. I pulled hard and felt the grapnel catch in the tangle of barbed wire at the cliff's crest. I grabbed the soldier by his arm, but he was now motionless, his eyes staring.

I was only a few feet up the rope ladder when the destroyers that had worked their way close in to the cliff opened up again, lashing the top of the promontory with shellfire. Chunks of earth and loose rock caromed down toward me. *Can't stop*, I thought as I drove myself up the rope ladder. *If I stop I die.*

The rockets were exploding continuously now. Through the dirt and sweat that trickled into my eyes, I saw other men swarming upward on the rope ladders that formed a lattice over the perpendicular cliff. There was movement behind the rolls of wire at the top and I pressed my face against the broken rock.

"The Krauts are cutting the ropes," the soldier below me and to my right screamed. Then the slugs rippled through his chest and blood blossomed out the back of his fatigue jacket, through the exit holes. He fell backward, slowly, gracefully, and then slammed into a rock outcropping, and pinwheeled onto the sand below. His blood seeped out immediately, a red puddle spreading fast.

Don't freeze, I told myself. *Get to the top before they cut this rope.* I scuttled upward the last ten feet, like a crawling insect suddenly exposed to the light. The twisted barbs of the wire sliced at my clothing and skin and I saw the blood spurt, but felt nothing. Abruptly, the noise died. The only sound I heard was my own panting in the echoing stillness.

I looked out at a violent, lonely moonscape, all yellow light and churned earth. Blasted out craters marched inland, with spires of smoke circling upward from them. The shelling had shattered the trees and scattered splinters of wood everywhere. Some of them were upright, like unfinished crosses driven into the soil at odd, obtuse angles. The startling white of the gashed and broken wood glinted in the shifting haze and the smell of cordite drifted in the air, as heavy as incense. Through the mist and smoke, I saw the monumental concrete bunkers. Their front apertures opened vacantly to the sea. *The Germans have pulled back and the guns are there,* I thought.

I crawled forward as two soldiers rolled over the top of the cliff and struggled through the barbed wire. "Follow me," I shouted. "The guns are straight ahead."

To my left, a German machine gun began to hammer rhythmically and the blows folded me backward into the wire. The pain came instantly, blinding, burning. I sprawled there in the wire, gasping and shaking as the blood pumped from my shoulder and arm. As the pain increased, I watched my left leg. It was caught in a loop of wire and it began to jerk with a slow rhythm, and then I lost consciousness.

The jab of the morphine shot in my thigh woke me. The drug coiled through me as the medic dusted sulfa powder into the hole in my shoulder. My left hand hung at an odd angle and I saw the whiteness of bone in my wrist. The skin around the wounds was blackened and seared, and there were deep slices in my chest and arms from the wire.

Behind me, I heard Oxander shouting into the field telephone. "You tell them the guns aren't here," he screamed. "The gun emplacements are empty. They've never even been used and I've got over a hundred casualties."

"That's not right," I said to the medic. "No, God, this can't have been for nothing."

"Shut the fuck up, Captain," the medic said. "You've got your million dollar wound. The war's over for you, just stay alive." Then the morphine numbed me and I drifted into the mist. My only emotion was the fear gnawing at my stomach.

⟹ 4 ⟸

Old Friends

October, 1945

The fear was still there as I huddled in the corner of the city hall stairway. I put my head down between my knees and tried to vomit, but I could not. I shook my head to clear it, the yellow haze began to fade, and then the smell was gone. I looked down at my right hand. It was red and raw at the knuckles and leaking blood. I stared at the blood until I stopped shaking. I knew how badly I needed a drink. In those days, liquor was my only medicine. Sarah hated it. But I needed it as much as I needed her.

I came slowly to my feet, my breathing slowed, and then I was able to walk out into the warmth of the afternoon sun. Michigan Avenue was straight and regular and in the sunlight it shimmered ahead of me to the east. Lansing's original town fathers had laid out the downtown as a series of grand avenues, with Michigan as the north-south dividing line and the Capitol as its midpoint. The town's older citizens often spoke with gentle nostalgia of the charm of the tree-lined streets and the elegance of the hostelries that arose around the Capitol in the early days of the city in the forest.

Now all the grace was gone. There were theaters and tearooms, dry cleaners and dairies, palmreaders and pharmacies, banks, bakeries, and bars. All crowded together within sight of the dome. Each jostling for space and light. Electric wires and telephone lines looped across the streets and sagged from pole to pole, black ribbons bundling the downtown into an untidy package.

The street was jammed with shoppers, civil servants, and sightseers, and the whirl of motion, the flashing colors, and the shifting of light and shadow all flooded in on me. The weather was still fair and many of the men were in their shirtsleeves, the rows of pencils in their pockets marking the state employees. The more formal ones, their doublebreasted suits signaling their professional status, often sported hats, wide felts mixing with straw snap-brims and an occasional stately homburg. Despite the continued existence of wartime controls and shortages, the women were swirls of seersucker and gabardine, with pleated skirts and crisp rayon blouses competing with floral print dresses. Bobbysoxers in their bright, soft sweaters gathered at the corners and crossings, showing their bare legs and smoking quite openly. Factory workers streamed home from the Oldsmobile plant at the shift change with their cloth caps pulled low over their eyes, their lunch pails swinging. They stepped carefully around both the girls and the cracks and potholes in the concrete sidewalks and brick streets. It was complex, crowded, and noisy. And it was home. *No fights to the death here,* I thought. *Except one.*

I inhaled it all as I walked down Michigan toward Johnny's Tack Club to meet my brother. The fear dropped back into some dark alley of my consciousness and I was able to turn the problem of Peter over in my mind. He was my only brother and so he considered himself to be an authority on the life and times of Charles Cahill. Over the years, I learned at some cost to avoid his questions and to discount his advice.

As a young man, Peter had bounced from job to job through the Depression and accumulated a fair amount of random knowledge as he worked at his various trades and professions. But his grasp of the facts of life never matured into wisdom. He was a scuffler, in and out of deals, always on the go, always on the make. His current job as a distiller's representative paid well and he had actually bought a house. The frame dwelling now reverberated with the racket of his four exceedingly active children.

Peter often ate his meals in bars, clubs, and restaurants. He solemnly explained to his wife that it was part of retaining his job. He told me in strictest confidence that it was also part of retaining his sanity. I had camped in his spare bedroom for a month and I could hardly argue. Besides, I could drink with him. It was as if we were a threesome, our father with us, glass in hand and full of good cheer. Ghosts don't talk and so I knew I could trust my father. But I also knew that I could not trust Peter. If Peter knew of something, then the world knew of it soon enough.

Johnny's was dark, crowded, and filled with the blue-gray of cigarette smoke when I entered. The images were gone and I was almost completely under control. *Stay with the present,* I thought. *There's nothing in the past that bears remembering.* I had been to Johnny's often before the war and I knew that it was ostensibly a private club. One of our hangovers from Prohibition was local option and Lansing chose to prohibit the sale of liquor by the glass, except in licensed clubs. The membership rituals at Johnny's were predictably brief. If you wanted a drink, you simply exchanged a five-dollar bill for a printed membership card. Mine was old and well used.

There was an additional benefit that came with a membership at Johnny's. Since the club was down the street from the courthouse and the police station, Johnny sensibly elected to keep his line of slot machines off the premises. He located them in the building next door, with a connecting hallway lined with autographed pictures of Michigan's sporting greats. The men of the law who took their food and drink at Johnny's appreciated his discretion. No gambling at Johnny's, they could say, buffing their rectitude until it gleamed.

I found a seat at the bar to wait for my brother. The bartender looked at me expectantly, his apron neatly cinched in front across his chest and his tie a black bow against his starched white shirt. He looked first at my bloody hand and then at my empty left sleeve, but he said nothing. Bartenders are by nature discreet. No doubt he had seen customers in worse shape.

"A martini, dry," I said. "And bring me a bar towel. I tripped and fell on the way over here."

"Got to watch yourself on those sidewalks," he said. "The city's got no money for repairs, with the war and all. You want olives?"

I nodded; and when he returned with the towel and my drink, I laid the towel on the bar and carefully blotted my knuckles against it. The spasm of pain was reassuringly commonplace. I reached for the martini and knocked it back with three long swallows and signaled for another. When I returned home to Lansing, I had decided to drink martinis. There was a certain panache to being a martini drinker. Not many returning veterans drank martinis. And I loved the astringency of the gin. It was sharp and to the point. Crystal clear in a world of subtle shades of gray. There was no pain to drinking martinis. Just a slow release, a falling away from myself. It was the best of all medicines. When the bartender brought the second one, I cradled it gently. It was always nice when old friends welcomed you home. It lent stability to the world.

Johnny's was a favorite with the city's lawyers and politicians, and through the cigarette smoke I saw Hennessey seated with three of his cronies. He gave me a hearty wave that I promptly returned. *Be of good health*, I thought. *I need you alive and remembering just where I was when they found Maynard's body.*

My brother bustled up, late as usual and slapped me on the wrong shoulder, again as usual. If he saw me wince, he paid it no mind.

"You gotta stop looking so worried," he said. "It'll make you old before your time." Peter grinned at me and motioned to the bartender who directed a stream of Schenley's into the double shot glass he placed in front of my brother. A tall glass of water and ice magically appeared, but Peter ignored it and tossed the shot back with a snap of his wrist. "Gimme another and a beer chaser," he said to the bartender.

"How does he know what you're drinking?"

"I work for the guys who make it by the barrel. The more Johnny sells over the bar, the more the Liquor Control Commission sells to Johnny. And the more I sell to them. You think I'm going to drink somebody else's booze? Let's eat, I'm starved."

The bartender raised an eyebrow to me and I drained the tumbler. No need to let my one remaining relative drink alone. My brother, the big spender, folded a bundle of ones on the walnut bar and we picked our way through the crowd to a vacant table. The linens were snowy white and the glassware sparkled. After we ordered, we chatted, aimlessly, carefully, about life in the small city. It had to be that way with Peter. Finally, he leaned forward and said, "What'd Old Ironpants want?"

"What do you mean?" I could not keep the surprise out of my tone. I thought only Hennessey and Storey himself knew of our meeting.

"Oh hell, everybody knows Storey's pissed off at the attorney general. So pissed off he went and hired Hub Street to take over the corruption investigation. What'd he do, give you a job? Maybe on account of your disability?" The waiter brought our meals and I was silent as he moved around the table.

"He didn't give me a job. How did you know I'd seen Storey?" I asked when the waiter finally left. I kept my voice level. If Peter thought this was all brotherly banter, it might dampen his curiosity.

"I got my sources." He was alight with the sheer pleasure of so conclusively showing me up. "Take it. The pay's not bad and it sure beats the hell out of workin' for a living." Peter gestured at the waiter for another round while I leaned back to digest both my dinner and his remarks.

"Pete, just what is it you do as a distiller's rep?" I asked, mainly to divert him.

"I sell booze, just like Dad. Only legally. Every crate I sell to the Liquor Control Commission, I get a percentage from Schenley's. You just gotta know the buyers on the staff out there at the Commission. But if you treat the guys right, you can make some money. Plus, I'm out on the road a lot pushing the product. And I can run my little deals on the side."

"What kind of deals?" I had him going and I wanted no more talk of grand juries.

"Well, take the strawberry business," he said. "I was doing a helluva business in strawberries before the goddamn government took the price controls off. I'd hire a truck and take off early Saturday morning over to the lakeshore. After the war started and the controls went on, all's a farmer could get for his strawberries was the government's ceiling price. But I'd take my truck right out to the guy's farm. Right out to where he was down there in the dirt pickin' them damn strawberries. I'd give him the ceiling plus four bits a crate on the side and he'd be grateful for it. Then I'd take a night run over to Chicago or maybe back to Detroit. I'd sell them strawberries to the grocers at fifty cents a quart. Hell, I was grossing maybe six, seven hundred bucks a run. After I paid the freight for the truck and my driver, I might put some real money in my pocket."

Business bored me. But even I could see that Peter had devised a new variation on an old profession. He was a strawberry bootlegger.

"Dad would have been proud of you. Where'd you get your money in the first place?"

"I told you, I got my sources. Course, the sonofabitch always wanted his piece. Just like with everything," he said. "Hey, here's the persecutor."

Peter stood up and shook Hennessey's hand, grabbing the man's elbow as he pumped away. "Sit down, have a drink. Schenley's is buying." Hennessey extracted his hand from my brother's grasp and pulled a chair over to the table.

"Thanks for your good words to Storey," I said. Again, I marveled at my own composure.

"You gonna take the job?"

"I haven't been offered a job," I said. Peter was listening with great interest and I chose my words carefully. "I'm going to talk to Hubbell Street tomorrow. My brother, the insider, tells me everyone in town knows he's going to take over the grand jury investigation from your friend the attorney general."

Hennessey grunted. "He's no friend of mine. I hope Storey gives him a royal screwing. Storey's a tough guy. Guy like that, you get crosswise with him and you're out on your ass."

"I'm not even in. I can't very well be tossed out," I said. And then I paused for a beat. "What's going on with the Maynard case?" I immediately regretted the question. It was too casual by far.

"We got a lead on a jealous boyfriend. Maynard was squiring this guy's lady friend around a lot in the last couple of months." Hennessey stopped and looked around the bar, for effect. "Thing is, maybe he picked the wrong babe. The boyfriend's in with the Italians. He sure as hell could have hired it out or done it himself. We found Maynard's car parked down in the weeds off that back road and they're going over it for prints. They won't find much, not if it's professional. You see where I'm going with this?"

I nodded again. Jealous boyfriends and unidentified professionals were just fine with me. Hennessey could wander down that road for as long as he pleased.

"Got anything else?"

"When the state boys went through Maynard's office over at the Capitol, they found a whole stack of dirty magazines. You know, young girls and that shit."

Hennessey's mouth twisted with distaste. He was a notorious prude about matters of the flesh. It was rumored that he and his wife took their pleasures only in the missionary position. Prosecutions for sex crimes in Ingham were almost nonexistent. Hennessey simply didn't want to hear the testimony. It was another piece of good luck for us and I risked one more question, the obvious one.

"I thought Maynard had a family," I said.

"He did, wife and a daughter. Wife's a knockout. Beats the hell out of me what he was doing runnin' around with some gunsel's girlfriend and goin' to the whores at the same time. He should've stuck to his wife, nice and safe. 'Course, maybe she wouldn't have him."

Hennessey glanced over at my brother. "Petey, why don't you go get those drinks." My brother was clearly disappointed. But he was no fool. He got up from the table and walked over to the bar. He quickly fell into conversation with the bartender and I saw him lay another five on the bar for the drinks. Peter watched himself in the gleaming mirror behind the bar and occasionally he smoothed his hair back or adjusted his tie, until he was momentarily satisfied with his own good looks.

Hennessey leaned forward and put his right hand on mine. Suddenly his voice was hard and precise, without a trace of the Irish.

"Every damn thing I just told you is true. And that'll be the story around town by tomorrow morning, thanks to Petey. But the thing is, I got witnesses who put you at Maynard's house the morning he was killed. Now why would that be, Charlie?"

"I don't even know where Maynard's house is," I said. There was no panic in my voice. I was breathing deeply and slowly, just as they had taught me at the hospital. I did not move my hand from underneath his. I looked straight at him without blinking. But there was no sound around me. No buzz of conversation, no clatter from the kitchen, no shouted food orders from the waiters. I was alone with Hennessey.

"Don't fucking lie to me," he said. "I don't give a damn where you were. Right now, all's I care about is that Storey's hired Hubbell Street. That dimwit Altman's going to be out on his ass. There's going to be a big investigation on this corruption shit. And that's a big problem. That's the only thing I care about. I don't care about you, I don't care about Maynard, I don't care about who's going to be the next governor. None of that. All's I know is, I hate surprise parties in my county and this one's headin' in that direction. So you're going to be my surprise party insurance policy. If Street offers you a job, you take it, no arguments. Then let me know what Street's up to once a week. That way, they'll be no surprises. And nobody else gets hurt. You got it?"

It was a long speech for Hennessey, the words like a river moving slowly through the fog. I floated on the current, without conscious thought. When he finished, I asked only one question. "What about your witnesses?"

"They'll stay my witnesses, nice and quiet. The police won't know a thing. Be a good little messenger boy and you'll be just fine. Cross me and you're looking at a murder charge. Now smile pretty and let's get your fool of a brother back over here."

I nodded. It was all I could do. Hennessey stood up and swallowed half his drink. There was a light sheen of perspiration on his forehead. Otherwise, though, he looked curiously normal. Not at all out of place. But his eyes were avid and voracious. Like a fox. I had just seen the essence of the man.

Then the moment was over and Hennessey waved cheerfully at Peter. "Sit down, Petey," he said, after my brother made his way to our table. "I was just leavin'. See you later, Charlie. If you get the job with Street, give me a call." The brogue was back and he was the good, bluff prosecutor again. Everyone's next best friend.

As if I had turned up the volume on a radio, the sound came back to the room. But I was still floating in a haze. I stared at Peter and struggled for some commonplace thing to say, some way to cover the panic. He was my brother and I could tell him nothing, show him nothing.

"You're sure throwing your money around tonight," I said, finally, banally. "Did you find it under a rock?"

"A little grease for the wheels is all. I take care of the bartenders, they push my brands. Anyways, it's not my money. It's other people's money. That makes it easier to spend."

Peter smiled happily at his good fortune. He was overjoyed that he could satisfy his taste for business and for bourbon simultaneously on someone else's nickel. In a shimmer of conscious thought, it occurred to me that we were both truly our father's sons. Sam Cahill had not been a man to dwell on the past. And at that moment I simply wanted to obliterate it. My hand hurt, my head ached, and the fear was there, fully formed. All I sought was oblivion. And I knew one sure way to find it. I put my arm around my brother's shoulder. "If you're buying, I'm drinking," I said.

⩵ 5 ⩵

The Man Who Would Be Governor

October, 1945

The next afternoon, I had a pounding hangover and no semblance of a plan of action when I met Hubbell Street at the Olds Hotel. But I was determined to stay within myself and equally determined to have nothing to do with a grand jury investigation. Street was known as an absolute killer in the courtroom, but his heavy, rugged face was open and obvious. His nose had a leftward slant, the result, he later told me, of a collision with a wayward elbow in a backyard football game in his youth. His head was large and ponderous, leavened in its solemnity only by a boyish shock of brown hair that fell down over his forehead almost to his eyes. He was my height and he outweighed me by at least fifty pounds. But he had a solid, comfortable look and he exuded vitality. His suit coat was thrown over a chair, his shirt sleeves were rolled, and the bottom points of his open vest dangled over his belt when he ushered me in to the suite of rooms that the grand jury was using as its offices.

"Rest your coat," he said. "It's hot."

"I'm fine," I said, even though I wasn't. I might be there, but I wasn't fine.

"Have some water," he said. "It's good for almost everything that ails you." He gestured to the full water pitcher that sat on the bureau, packed with ice and glistening with beads of condensation, and I filled one of the tumblers from the tray. The windows were open and the venetian blinds snapped and clattered between the cotton curtains with their ruffled tie-backs. The warm October wind blew softly into the room and I began to sweat. The coffee table was piled with transcripts and red rope folders, one of which Street used as a fan when he sat down across from me.

"You're a farm boy?"

"Yessir. My father had a truck farm outside of Lansing."

"My dad was a farmer too. Over near Lake Michigan. We grew the best peaches in the county."

Street propped his feet up on the coffee table and fanned himself. "You sure you don't want to take off that coat? You look a tiny bit hot," he said.

I shook my head. The man's easy informality was so seductive that I instinctively tried to preserve some sense of distance between us. I desperately wanted him to pass me over for the job. *Make yourself as drab and routine as possible*, I thought. *Perhaps he would judge me of little value.*

He gestured toward my left arm, without embarrassment. "That bother you?"

"Nossir. I think it worries other people more than it worries me." It was the truth, but I hoped it would jostle him into thinking about how poorly a man with only one arm might play out before a jury.

"Good. A lot of boys are coming back like you. We just have to get used to it. So it becomes commonplace. Do you like the law?" He had quickly changed the subject and I wondered how much artifice there was to the man. Maybe he was interested in me, not in spite of my missing arm but because of it.

"Yessir, I do," I said. I kept my voice properly respectful.

"Ah hell, don't call me sir. It reminds me of the Great War. Worst experience of my life. I enlisted, all full of piss and vinegar. Then I was stuck in New Jersey for eight months and all I did was play cards and clean latrines. To this day, I can't stand either poker or privies." There was the smallest note of theatricality in his alliteration. It was not the first time he had used that particular anecdote.

"No, I mean do you like to go to court? Do you like to be on your feet with the judge and the jury?"

"I haven't really done that much of it," I said.

"You'll love it. When you win, it's like being with a woman. Only it's better. You bare your soul, you lay it all out there in front, and you shout and scream and beg and plead and stamp your feet. Finally, they open their legs and whisper yes. Then there's just nothing like it." He paused and grinned at me.

"Of course, when you lose, you die."

There were three packs of gum on the table and he opened one and methodically stripped the shiny foil off the individual strips and crammed them into his mouth, one after another. "I've sworn off cigarettes," he said. "The doc says they do funny things to my vocal cords. Makes me so hoarse I can hardly talk. Who wants a lawyer who can't talk? It's a walking contradiction in terms."

He chewed away for a moment and then he stood. "I won't beat around the bush," he said. "You've got a good record, law review at Michigan and all. Plus, Randy Hennessey likes you and Ironpants thinks you've got guts. The thing is, I need help on this"—he gestured at the stack of transcripts—"and I need it right away. I'm offerin' seventy-five a week plus per diem. That's a hell of a lot more than you'd make over with Hennessey." He extended his hand. "Let's shake on it."

The only thing I wanted was out, out of anything to do with Harry Maynard's murder and I hoped the fact that I knew Maynard's wife would end the charade. "I've got a problem," I said. "I've met one of the people in the Maynard matter. Sarah Maynard. She asked me for some legal advice last summer when I was in the hospital and I counseled with her. I may have a conflict."

He dropped his hand. "Are you her lawyer now?"

I hesitated. "No. But she may think I am."

"What are you worried about? I used to represent a couple of guys Altman waltzed around, but I'm sure as hell not representing them now. Besides, as far as I'm concerned, at least right now, the Maynard thing is a local matter. Let Hennessey handle it. I've got other fish to fry."

He sat down and crammed another stick of gum into his mouth. "Just out of curiosity, what kind of legal advice did the Maynard woman want?"

"She was having marital problems. She was thinking about a divorce."

"Forget it, you're fine," he said, and my mouth again began to taste of pennies. "Damn, it's hot. Let's go down to the bar and have some beer."

We took the elevator down to the hotel's front bar. It was late in the afternoon and the room was already jammed with lobbyists and legislators. The side door was propped open to provide ventilation and an overhead fan droned away. The bar had the baroque aroma of stale beer and new sweat that characterizes most establishments where the drinking and the deals are done simultaneously. The hotel had only a tabletop beer and wine license. In those days, nobody drank wine and so the bartenders worked the taps feverishly to keep their customers supplied.

The room buzzed with a dozen conversations as Street worked his way forward, with me in tow. He often stopped to shake hands or to speak with those he knew, and he always positioned his body close to theirs, crowding them in the friendliest possible way until they stepped aside. He used his hands often, gesturing expansively, grasping an elbow for emphasis as he talked, slapping a shoulder in derision when he joshed a senator about his expanding waistline. He treated the wives and girlfriends, and there were many more of the latter than the former, with genuine courtesy, holding their hands for a long second and leaning forward attentively to hear their voices above the shouts and the whispers. When we finally reached the bar, every person in the place knew that Hubbell Street had arrived.

"When the legislature meets, no man's wife or property is safe. Our good governor should have remembered that before he called another special session," Street said. He motioned to the bartender, who carefully placed a pack of cigarettes next to a heavy glass ashtray on the bar.

"You're in trouble when the bartender knows what you want before you even tell him," Street said. He shook a cigarette out of the pack and looked at it appraisingly.

"One more can't hurt," he said. As he lit the cigarette, I saw the dark yellow stains on the first two fingers of his right hand.

After we ordered our first two beers, he put his arm around my good shoulder and spoke directly into my ear. "Take my offer," he said. "I'm starting down a long road here. I don't know how the hell it will end up, but it'll be one sonofabitch of a ride. Why not chance it?"

"I'll think about it," I said. I was very careful, very much the young lawyer weighing his choices. "I appreciate the offer, but it's not what I had in mind when I came home. I'll let you know tomorrow."

Leaving the bar was more difficult than entering it. The lobbyists were in constant motion, circling the legislators like hounds braying after foxes. Often, groups of men left together for the hotel's upstairs rooms. Up there, both the liquor and the women were hard, plentiful, and free. Street repeated his passage, stopping frequently at tables to talk, appearing now to be on a first name basis with everyone to whom he spoke. He paused at a large table in the corner where three men sat. The man in the center had fine white hair, thinning somewhat so that the pinkish skin of his scalp showed through at the part. He gazed steadily up at Street, then nodded to him. In a pleasant, quiet voice, so low that only Street and I could hear, he said, "Governor."

Street stood looking down, his hands jammed into his pockets, and the two men were locked in silence amid the noisy blur of conversation in the bar. Then the moment passed and when we finally reached the door, Street turned and waved cheerfully at the assembly.

"You know," he said to me as the door swung closed, "you could empty a twelve gauge in there and not harm an honest man." He shook another cigarette out of the pack he had slipped into his pocket.

"Don't tell my wife," he said. "She'd kill me."

"Who's the man in the corner?" I asked.

"That's Wade Fleming. He likes to call me governor. He thinks it's funny."

He turned to the elevators. "I'm going upstairs for a bit. I've got all kinds of health problems. If I don't get laid every two or three days, I get these awful headaches." He grinned at me and strode away, loosening his tie.

I had a bellyful of beer and my mind under control when I walked to my brother's house from the bus stop. Once Street offered me the job, I had no choice. I had to accept it. If I turned it down, Hennessey would surely know and then Sarah and I were surely lost.

When I reached the house, Peter handed me a plain white envelope, without a stamp or postmark. "This was under the door when Helen came home," he said.

I had no idea why, but someone had decided I was important enough to threaten. Hennessey wanted me next to him, but now I had my way out. The note was handwritten, and it was an absolute gift. Just one sentence: Stay away from the grand jury.

⇒ 6 ⇐

Toy Soldiers

October, 1945

I met Street early the next morning for coffee at the Olds. He wasted no time. "Well, are you ready to join up, for God and country?"

I showed him the note. Certainly it would be enough. Certainly he would see me as compromised. Certainly he would now turn to someone else.

The dining room was not crowded. The waiters in their white jackets fidgeted at their stations and Street toyed with the note. He carefully turned it over by the corners, tapping it with a blunt fingernail.

"Whose prints do you think are on this?" he asked, finally.

"Mine, certainly. My brother's and his wife's on the envelope, but they didn't handle the letter itself. Whoever sent it, if they're careless."

"I don't think we can count on careless. We'll get it out to the state police lab after I show it to the judge. I'm meeting him at eight to get sworn in. You in or out?"

So much for certainties. Street had hesitated only for a moment and then plunged ahead. Had he waited, had he considered the circumstances, had he thought it through, then it all might have been different. But he was a man in a hurry and the only certainty now was that I was in the middle, with nowhere to turn. "You've got yourself a lawyer," I said. Hennessey thought he had me and now so did Street. I was surprisingly calm about it all. The fear would come later.

"There's one thing you should know," I said to Street as we walked out the front door of the Olds. "Randy Hennessey wants me to keep him up to date on the investigation. He probably still thinks I work for him." I made it sound as innocuous as I could. What Hennessey really wanted was an informer on Street's staff.

"Let me take care of that," Street said. "Randy's not really smart enough to play a double game. I'll tell you what to give him. Keep it general. He's not much of a stickler for details. Unless it's his own ass on the line." *Maybe that's exactly where it is,* I thought. *And mine as well.*

City Hall was just a short block from the hotel, but the weather was changing and it was a dark, wet morning. When we reached the front steps, we were both damp and flushed from our sprint down Capitol Avenue. The lobby was filling up with a sluice of morning city workers, lawyers lining up for their cases, uniformed deputies herding prisoners from the county jail into municipal court for their preliminary investigations, vagrants seeking shelter from the rain, and ordinary, if somewhat confused, citizens.

When we reached Storey's chambers, the swearing-in was predictably brief. The judge's court reporter dutifully transcribed our solemn oaths, then scuttled out of the office, glancing back over his shoulder at Street and me.

Storey turned toward Street. "How will we handle the public announcement? The attorney general may contest your appointment and I want to be ready for that."

"I don't think Altman's going to contest anything," Street said. "I had a nice chat last night with Sergeant Maloney of the state police detail. It seems the attorney general was just a wee bit less than candid with you, Leon."

Street paused and leaned forward across Storey's desk, "Maloney says Maynard was naming names," he said. "Until I talked with Maloney, I thought the Maynard killing was just something out there in left field. Now I think Altman lied to you when he said Maynard was clean. When we hit him with that, he'll go peacefully."

It was like a bolt of lightning across an evening sky, a jagged shard of light that froze me in place. Sarah had never hinted that her husband was involved in any sort of corruption. She despised him. But she had not thought of him as a crook. *Street will go after this*, I thought. *He'll be all over it and he won't let it go*, I thought. *And I'll have to be right there with him, trying to keep Hennessey at bay every step of the way.*

Storey sat like a rock, staring straight ahead, his face still and composed. His hands were in front of him, palms on the desk, and I could see his nails whiten as he pressed down on the polished wooden surface. Suddenly, he raised both hands and slammed them down, with a crack like splitting wood. The squad of kilted Scottish soldiers on the corner of the desk collapsed in disarray.

"I will not be lied to," he said.

"There's this too, Judge," Street said and handed him the note. Storey sat as still as his fallen soldiers while I explained the circumstances of its delivery. Beside me, Street examined his signet ring, but he made no mention of Hennessey.

When I finished, Storey turned to Street. "Hubbell, let there be no mistake. I'll not be lied to. And I'll not be threatened. I want Altman before me under subpoena by the weekend."

Street stood and walked to the corner window. The Capitol was just visible through the slanting rain. "Mind if I take my coat off, while we think about this?"

The judge shrugged. His hands were again on his desk, fingers again pressing down. Street walked away from the window, shed his coat, and began to turn the judge around.

"Leon, I've learned the hard way you can't back a rat like Altman into a corner. All's he can do then is bite you on the pecker. We need just two things from the attorney general. First, we need him to get out of our way. Second, we need him to give us whatever he got from Maynard."

"Colorfully put, Hubbell. As usual. What exactly do you suggest?"

Street kept his voice soft and level, just a lawyer chatting with his client. "I say you write him a nice letter telling him his services as prosecutor are no longer required. I say I'll deliver that letter to him and then we'll have a little chat about Harry Maynard." He grinned at Storey. "Oh, and I say that I'll have a subpoena in my pocket, returnable Friday, just in case he doesn't care to be reasonable. What do you say?"

The barest hint of a smile crossed Storey's face. He reached forward and righted his toy soldiers, making a small show of weighing Street's advice.

"We'll do it your way, this time," he said. He straightened his tie, rose from his desk, and marched to the door, flags flying. "You prepare the letter. Get it out immediately."

The rain had stopped, but the gutters were overflowing and the streets were streaming as we walked back to the hotel. "Can we trust Altman to tell us what he got from Maynard?" I asked, while we picked our way through the puddles. I was careful not to mention that the Maynard killing was suddenly not a side-show. Street had decided to make it part of the main event. If I showed the slightest hesitation, he was sure to wonder why. The only hope for Sarah and me lay in pretense. Against all odds, we had to preserve the artifice of normality. A slip, a false word, a knowing look and we would be found out.

"Hell, no," Street said. "I don't trust that shitheel any further'n I can throw him. We'll interview him over here with a court reporter taking down every word. That way he can't deny it later."

Street stepped off the curb at the corner and was up to his ankles in dirty water. He shrugged and laughed. "One pair of lace-up shoes. That'll look just great on the state expense account," he said. "Anyway, I don't want to start parading witnesses in front of Ironpants until we're ready. He'll start sending them out to the county farm if he doesn't like their answers. We need information, not a bunch of contempt citations."

My first day on the worst job I could possibly have had and Street already had it wrong. I didn't need information. I needed a drink.

7

First Blood

November, 1945

As Street predicted, the attorney general chose prudence over valor and did not dispute the appointment of a special prosecutor. We interviewed him in the Olds at the suite of rooms reserved for the grand jury. The chenilles and pretty prints were gone, as were the beds, dressers, and coffee tables. We had replaced them with steel desks and filing cabinets, each painted a utilitarian green. The only vestige of the previous regime was the water pitcher, crammed with ice. We had also commandeered a corporal's guard of investigators from the state police and I had actually found several secretaries who could type. It was a remarkable accomplishment in the fiercely competitive white-blouse market in postwar Lansing and I was predictably proud of it. I was happy to be the good deputy, immersed in details and out of the line of fire. The Altman interview changed all that.

Street greeted Altman warmly and showed him to a deep leather wingback. It was the only comfortable chair in the room. They were both former county prosecutors and they spent the next half hour trading war stories, topping each other with their great victories and their disastrous defeats. They were like two fighting cocks circling the ring and eyeing one another before the fray. Altman, with his beaky nose, blotchy skin, and the wattles lining his chin and neck, had a decidedly roosterish look. He also had a nervous cackle of a laugh.

Finally, Street glanced down at the large gold timepiece he pulled from his vest pocket. "Good Lord, it's three o'clock," he said. "We'd best be getting started. Marvin, I've got a steno here to take a transcript. It's just for the record. When he types it up, you can sign it and it'll serve as your statement. That way, there's no confusion between us lawyers. The law can abide damn near anything but confusion." He laughed and signaled me to summon John Danto, Storey's court reporter. I ignored Altman's squawk of protest and promptly showed Danto to his chair.

As Street had directed, Sergeant Maloney walked silently in behind the court reporter and stood with his back to the door of the suite. Maloney was a hard case, a streetwise deputy sheriff who had moved up to the state police and spent ten years as a plainclothes detective before he was assigned to the grand jury detail. He was a spare, silent man who went to Mass early each morning. Then he turned from the sacred to the profane with a face as smooth and unrelenting as a piece of polished stone. His tough Irish face was empty of expression. He had the blank, patient cynicism of the policeman who has seen it all before. He was totally absorbed with the condition of his fingernails, running his thumb over the edge of each nail and then buffing them across the sleeve of his blue serge suit.

When the steno was settled, Street launched immediately into the preliminaries. "This is the time and place for the taking of the statement of Marvin Altman, attorney general of Michigan," he said. "Mr. Altman is a lawyer and has waived the right to have counsel present. Is that correct, Mr. Altman?"

Altman nodded his head once. The blemishes on his face and forehead were suddenly more pronounced. Absently, he began to pick at the dry, red skin on the back of his left hand.

"I'm afraid the court reporter can't hear you when you nod Mr. Altman. Have you waived the right to counsel, yes or no?"

"Yes," Altman said. His voice was little more than a whisper.

"Please speak audibly so the court reporter gets every word. Have you waived the right to counsel?"

"Yes, goddamnit, get on with it."

Street began to pace as he took Altman through the jumps, his education, his work experience, and his duties as attorney general. With each question, he increased his dominance over the smaller man. And with each answer, he further converted his friendly interview into a full-fledged deposition. When Street paused for a glass of water, Altman's voice had again dropped to a whisper.

"Off the record, please," Street said to the stenographer. "Marvin, you're a little dry. Would you like a drink?"

"You sandbagged me, you prick. If you don't finish this thing up, I'm walking out."

Street made a courtly bow. "Let the record reflect that Mr. Altman is anxious to proceed and gracious as always. I have just a few more questions. There is one witness we cannot interview and that is Senator Maynard. When did you last talk with the senator and who was present?"

I leaned forward without thinking and then I caught myself. *Show them nothing but lawyerly interest*, I thought.

Altman shifted in his chair. There was a tiny bubble of blood forming on the raw skin of his hand. "I talked to him around the end of September, first of October. Maloney was there and Bob."

"And who is Bob?"

"Bob Howard, my driver. He knew the senator. I thought that having him there would make Maynard feel more comfortable."

Street stopped pacing and stood directly behind Altman's chair. "What did you discuss with Senator Maynard?"

Altman struggled back into the well of the wingback, craning his neck to look for Street, but the special prosecutor remained directly behind the chair. The afternoon sun glared through the window from the west. Earlier, Street had drawn up the venetian blinds completely, chuckling to himself. Altman now attempted to shield his eyes with his reddened hand, without success.

"Well, we went over his committee assignments. The bills he worked on. Who he talked to." Again he turned his head, squinting. "That sort of thing."

Street leaned over the chair and spoke directly into the attorney general's ear. His voice was suddenly so soft that the steno strained forward to hear. As if on cue, Maloney straightened and walked over to the window, directly into Altman's line of sight.

"I have it on good authority that Senator Maynard told you he took bribes," Street said. "That he sold his vote on a number of occasions. Is that correct?"

Altman looked at Maloney and then down at the floor. "No, no, he didn't say that, exactly. He said he'd been reimbursed for his expenses. He said he'd gotten paid for giving speeches. That's not a bribe, that's not against the law. Don't make something out of nothing." As if to counteract Street's shift in tone, Altman was now shouting.

"Oh, I think it's something," Street said. "And exactly who did Senator Maynard say made these payments to him?"

Altman shifted again in his chair. "Off the record?"

"On the record, sir. On the record."

"He may have mentioned Lammers, Otto Lammers. Among others." Altman reached into his pocket for a handkerchief and used it to blot the blood on the back of his hand.

Street paused for just a beat and then went at Altman with a volley of questions. His voice was no longer soft as he drew out the details of the relationship with Lammers. After he drained the man, he sat down on the corner of my desk and took off his coat and loosened his tie.

"Just one last question, Mr. Altman. Bob Howard, your driver. Has he been chauffeuring anyone around recently? Besides you, of course."

"He may have. I think he's given Wade Fleming a ride a time or two."

"And just who is Wade Fleming?" Street's voice was soft again.

"You know goddamn well who he is, Street. No, strike that. He's the state treasurer and there's not a thing wrong with giving him a ride home. Not so long as it's reimbursed. Which it was."

Street smiled gently at the attorney general. "I'm not a bit worried about the reimbursement. I'm worried about what passed from Bob Howard's mouth to Wade Fleming's ears. Sounds to me like Fleming knew everything the grand jury did, regular as clockwork." He motioned to Danto who flipped his book closed and left the room at a half trot. Street pulled out his gold watch and shook it vigorously.

"It can't be six o'clock, can it?" He was all innocence.

"Street, you make something out of this Fleming thing and you're asking for trouble. He beat you once. He can beat you again." Altman heaved himself out of the deep trap of the chair.

"Marvin, let me tell you a story." Street's voice was warm, his face open with friendship.

"My grandfather was a sheriff years ago and his one big adventure was a train robbery. He chased the boys who did it across half of Ottawa County. When he caught 'em, one of 'em put up such a fuss that old John shot him twice in the leg, just to quiet him down. Then he sort of helped himself to that boy's gold watch."

Street rubbed his timepiece against his shirtsleeve. "It still keeps good time."

Altman headed for the door of the suite, his wattles shaking as he walked. "You're a cocky bastard. You're dead in this town. I'll see to it," he said.

Street shook his head sorrowfully. "Marvin, you didn't let me finish. There was a little public outcry after Grandpa John shot his train robber. More than a little, actually. So much that he had to retire from the law enforcement business permanently."

Altman was still caught in the deep trap of the chair and Street looked over at him again. "With the testimony you just gave, you may want to start thinking seriously about private practice." He said it as evenly as if he were announcing the time of day.

"HAVE YOU ever seen a dream walking?" Street asked. Most of a fifth was gone and he was in a mood to talk as we rehashed Altman's testimony that evening. "I've been lying in the weeds for Fleming for years. Altman just gave us motive for the Maynard murder. Could it actually be possible that Fleming got rid of Maynard because he was about to spill his guts to the grand jury?"

I knew that it was not possible. But I said nothing. Street was having a conversation with himself and I saw no reason to intrude. I would be delighted if he wanted to pursue Wade Fleming, even though I knew it to be a fool's errand. If Fleming was in the spotlight, then perhaps Sarah and I could remain off stage. Sometimes random fortune smiles down on the most unlikely of beneficiaries. And it was an absolute blessing that Street had a score of his own to settle. Circumstance makes strange bedfellows.

"If that bastard's involved in this, we're in for a ride. Fleming's the prince of darkness," Street said.

He jammed a stick of gum in his mouth and chewed it slowly, reflexively. "He's been indicted three times and never seen the inside of a jail cell," he said. "I went after him once when I was Kent County prosecutor. The next thing I knew, I'd lost in the primary. The *primary*, mind you. Lost to some potlicker from his pet law firm who'd never tried a case. Fleming put out the word that I was going to run for governor. People didn't like it. They like their prosecutors to concentrate on county business." The shock of defeat was still evident across the years.

"Let's not dwell on it," he said, finally.

Point him in that direction, I thought. "If we go after him and get him, it'll be all over the papers," I said.

"The thought never crossed my mind." Street grinned at me. "Yessir, a man could do something with that." He paused for a moment. "I want to know what Hennessey's got on the murder. But he's such a busy man there's no need to bother him. Use Maloney and get a copy of the state police report."

I chose my words carefully. "Remember that Hennessey asked me to keep him informed on where things are going over here," I said.

"And Charlie, that's just what you're going to do. Only let's just see where we stand first. Then you and I can figure out what you're going to tell our Mr. Hennessey. There's no reason to get his Irish up prematurely over me dreaming about Fleming."

MALONEY DELIVERED the state police file to my office at the Olds the next afternoon. He volunteered no information as to how he obtained it and I asked no questions. I turned to the autopsy report and it was a punch to the stomach. Alone in his lab, away from Hennessey's bluster, the state police pathologist had done his work. In a few sentences, he had destroyed my attempt to turn Maynard's killing into a gangland-style execution. The shots to the face had been post-mortem. There had been only a small amount of blood out there in the cornfield for the simple reason that Maynard was already dead when I shot him. In his cramped cursive script, the pathologist added a parenthetical for the lay reader to the effect that dead men do not bleed copiously.

Then he came to the last point, the fatal one. The cause of death was a fractured skull and three broken vertebrae in the neck, probably inflicted by a blunt instrument, perhaps a metal tool or farm implement. I read that sentence twice and the fear crept in to gnaw at my bones.

After a long, long while, my head finally cleared and I was able to pick up the file again. I found the police write-up of their interview with Sarah. She had told them she had been with her mother all that morning on the day of the murder. There was a notation that the mother confirmed Sarah's story, down to the last detail. The state police trooper who did the interview added a postscript. Sarah Maynard bore a remarkable resemblance to Rita Hayworth, he said.

The rest was bits and pieces. The first trooper on the scene had spotted Maynard's car parked off the dirt road on the edge of the cornfield, just where we had left it. The trooper was a good cop and he noticed another set of tire tracks. But the police cars that swarmed around the Maynard vehicle promptly obliterated them. *They can't track Peter's car*, I thought. The report also said that the interior of Maynard's car was devoid of fingerprints, other than his own. The door handles contained no prints whatsoever. It was an indication to the crime lab techs that they were wiped clean.

There was a full dossier on the Maynard family. If Harry Maynard's death had been a complex, bloody affair, his life was as plain as the dusty Indiana towns of his youth. When he ultimately made his way to Lansing, it was as a reporter for the county's weekly paper. Assigned to the capital beat, he at last found his vocation; and when the incumbent finally drank himself to death in the last, great days of Prohibition, Maynard upset the hometown favorite in the Republican primary and then walked home in the general election. Six years later, he was a state senator.

The only clipping concerning Sarah was that of her wedding announcement. The office was deserted and silent. As I stared at her picture and cradled my head with my right hand, I heard the ticking of my watch.

The smudged text of the announcement said the bride was born in Lansing and attended Michigan State College until she met and married Maynard. He was ten years her senior and then in his first term as a state representative. The wedding photograph was of a dark-haired girl, her eyes cast downward in the formal style of portraiture.

I stared at her picture. Then I leaned back in my chair. I closed my eyes and remembered how I lost my arm. And found a woman like no other. All in all, I thought it to be a fair trade.

8

Salvation

Summer, 1945

In my time at Percy Jones veterans' hospital, I was suspended in a gauzy, white cocoon. I measured out my days and spent my nights overwhelmed by terror. The German slugs had slammed through my collarbone, smashed my shoulder, and almost severed my left hand at the wrist. The doctors put me in a body cast, from my neck to my waist, with only my right arm free. The plasma bottle hung above my head. Whenever I awoke, my first glance was at that bottle. If it still hung there, then I knew I was still alive.

The pain was insidious, starting slowly at first as the drugs wore off, and then building as the hours passed and the lights shimmered. I floated on it, like a sailboat suspended on the crest of a wave. Waiting, praying, for the sound of the nurse's heels clicking on the tile floor as she made her rounds with the drugs. With them, I could sleep. But I always awoke in the yellow light with the taste of pennies in my mouth. The missing guns were there with the dead. And the fear. Slipping in quietly in the night. Watching me from a corner of my mind.

As the wounds began to heal, the doctors cut the cast away from my left shoulder and arm, and insisted that I exercise the stiffening limbs every day. I screamed as the nurse moved the arm forward and back. I might have been a cripple, but at least I had a voice. Ultimately, the nurse gave me a wooden dowel to bite down on when the manipulation began. But then one day, she would give me no more of the drugs. The surgeon gave me the news.

"Your arm has to get better or we're going to have to take some of it off," he said. "There's considerable infection in your wrist and that bothers me. But we'll try to wait it out." Then his voice softened. "I'm more worried about what's going on in your head. I've never had a patient who screamed so much when he was asleep and said so little when he was awake. It's classic shell shock."

"You worry about my arm. Let me worry about my head," I said.

His eyes narrowed. "Suit yourself. Good luck. You'll probably need it."

And so I waited. In the spring of 1945, Roosevelt died and I overpaid an orderly for a pint of whiskey so that I could properly mourn the president's passing. Less than a month later, Germany fell and they carted us in by bus to Battle Creek—we called it the Cripple Creek express—and the local tavern owners put every second drink on the house. By that week's end, the orderly was bringing me my pint every evening when he went off duty.

But the liquor never got me through the night. I would awaken gasping in the stillness of the early morning hours with my head pounding and my heart racing. Through the haze, I saw the Rangers fall forward on the sand of that hard, empty beach, but I felt no remorse at their deaths. I saw the corporal's life spill out, but I had no pity for him. I saw the empty gun emplacements through the swirling haze, but I could summon up no anger over how meaningless it had been. But the fear was always there, jaws open in its death's-head grin. All I could do was huddle in the darkness, hoping that the yellow light would fade.

I was actually relieved when the surgeon made his final visit. At least he had the courtesy to get on with it. "Captain," he said, "the infection in your wrist is going deeper. It's down to the bone and it's spreading. We think that's why the therapy isn't working, but we don't know for sure."

"Is there anything you do know for sure?"

"We're going to take your arm off below the elbow. Either that or you're probably going to die here."

"I'm not sure it matters."

"The hell with that," he said. "Nobody's died on my watch and you're not going to be the first. We'll operate tomorrow morning."

"Enjoy yourself," I said.

As such things go, the surgery was a success. But my recovery was not. My left arm was gone at the elbow. But the fear remained. Trotting along behind me like my own faithful shadow, grinning. And with that came a growing disregard for my own well-being. It was difficult to shave with my right hand and I did so with less and less frequency. Until the dressings were removed, I couldn't use the showers, and when the nurse came by for my sponge bath I would often wave her away. The discipline was lax in the officers' ward and the other patients quickly learned to leave me alone. My favorite orderly resumed his scheduled deliveries. He knew a good customer when he saw one. I ate very little. When I visited the bathroom, I would occasionally stare at myself in the mirror for a long while and wonder if the pallor and the pouches under my eyes were permanent. It finally occurred to me that I didn't particularly care.

IT WAS a bright summer morning when Sarah Maynard walked into the ward in her Gray Lady uniform. She was so vibrant that she stood out like a burst of color in the sterile hospital whiteness. She was tall and straight and whole, with a blaze of silver in her gleaming chestnut hair. There was a richness about her that I could scarcely comprehend. I could not imagine that she would have the slightest interest in some death-haunted cripple. But she stopped by my bed and looked at me carefully.

"Your hair's dirty," she said. "You should wash it."

I stared off into the middle distance behind her and said nothing. She glanced down at the chart hanging from the end of the bed.

"It's Charles, isn't it? Cat got your tongue, Charles?"

I sat up and pulled the blankets away and swung my feet over the side of the bed. "Lady," I said, "I've only got one goddamned hand. Just how the hell do you think I can wash my damned hair?"

"I thought you were an educated man. Do you always swear so much?"

"It's an art form," I said. "And what do you know about my education?"

"Everybody in the hospital knows you're a lawyer. Just sit there and mind your manners."

She walked off toward the orderlies' room, radiating heat, with every man's eye on her. When she returned, she had a white-enamel basin half-filled with water.

"Lean forward," she said, and she produced a bar of yellow laundry soap from the pocket of her starched apron. With great vigor, she began to scrub my hair, totally ignoring my muttered complaints. When she finished, she looked at me critically.

"I don't suppose you have a mirror and a comb?"

"In the drawer."

"Well, are you completely helpless? Let's see how you look. I'll hold the mirror and you comb your hair. It's a fair division of labor."

The lieutenant in the bed next to me was choking back his laughter and I felt like a childish fool. But I complied. When I was done, she smiled at me.

"See how easy that was?"

"Don't mock me, lady," I said.

"I'm not mocking you. I'm talking to you. I assume you know the difference?"

I stood up and she spun away, walking toward the door at the end of the ward, leaving only a slight hint of her perfume behind her. It smelled of lavender mixed with honey. She turned back at the door.

"I'll be here on Wednesday," she called to me. "Do you think it's possible that you could shave by then?"

With that, the lieutenant beside me began to laugh aloud. He had a steel plate in the back of his head and I knew I couldn't punch him, so I poured the basin of soapy water over his mid-section. He just grinned at me.

When she swept into the ward the following Wednesday, I was sitting up in the bed, freshly shaved and combed. She worked her way down the corridor, very deliberately stopping to talk with each man before she got to me, drawing it out.

"You might pass for a human being," she said when she finally reached my bed. "But it's still an open question. Do you want something to eat?"

"I don't have much of an appetite."

"The nurses say that you might eat more if you drank less. Are you totally committed to pickling yourself or is it just some sort of Irish ritual?"

"It's an ancient and permanent compunction, not to be taken lightly," I said. I realized that, for some perverse reason, I actually enjoyed talking with her. It wasn't simply her shocking beauty or her obvious intelligence or the way she carried herself. Strangely enough, it was the sharp edge of her humor. I realized that I had not laughed aloud since I made my way up my Norman cliff.

"I brought you a book, one of Hemingway's. It's a war story, about love. You can start the first chapter while I'm getting you something to eat. Who knows, it might elevate your mind."

When she returned with the tray of soup and sandwiches, the book was on the nightstand, unopened. "I see you're not interested," she said and turned away.

"Wait. Of course I'm interested, but I've read that book. Actually, I've read it twice. Stay and talk with me for a while."

She leaned over the bed and whispered in my ear. "Charles," she said, "I thought you'd never ask."

AND THAT was the way it began. As the summer inched toward fall, the discharges from the hospital accelerated and we were often able to spend full days together in virtual solitude, walking through the hospital grounds, talking without artifice and without reservation, laughing at the improbability of it. But of course, I had to ask. It was the only thing I could do. We were sitting on one of the white wooden benches in the hospital's side veranda. I reached across her for her left hand. The one with the wedding ring.

"You're married," I said.

"My husband hasn't been married for years. And maybe I'm not either."

"Why do you stay with him?"

"Because of our daughter. But now, she's terrified of him. She won't stay in the same room when he's home for dinner. Not that he's home that often. Why do you ask, Charles? Do you have some reservations about married women?"

"I don't care a damn."

"Then neither do I. And the hell with Harry Maynard." She smiled at me, her mouth slightly open. "This is a very public spot, Charles. Surely you know somewhere in this huge building that's a little more private?"

I had walked the hospital endlessly during my convalescence and I knew every inch of it. After we found an empty ward in the east wing, we made our way quietly down the long corridor toward the private room at the end. The blinds in the ward were pulled. But the afternoon light slanted in and the dust motes floated softly in the air. When I shut the door behind us, she turned to me. Then we were on the bed. My robe and hospital pajamas were easy to remove. But her clothing took longer and she laughed as I fumbled with the buttons.

"I've never done this one-handed," I said.

"It's a learned skill. I'm sure it will come to you." She stroked my scars, murmured, and I was lost in her.

Afterward, we lay entwined on the hospital bed, and in the stillness I thought I could hear her heart beat, steady and slow.

"You're taking this very calmly," I said.

"Well, I certainly didn't know I could look at the ceiling in so many different ways. Did the earth move for you?"

"Life imitates art. But I think it was the bed. The bed definitely moved," I said.

"You're such a romantic."

"I'm an anti-romantic. I think of it more as a matter of anatomy." It was a lie and she knew it. My hand was on the bed next to her face and I could feel her smile.

"Want to dance naked in the afternoon sun?"

"I'm a lousy dancer. I'd step on your feet," I said. "Besides, we have to think of our reputations."

" 'I could not love thee half so well, had I not loved honor more.' That's what the poet said."

"It's hardly a question of honor," I said. "Primarily, it's a question of survival."

She smiled again in the shadowy light. "Yes, you are a romantic. Forget about survival and romance me again." And so I did. I knew that I could refuse her nothing.

"There's only one question," she said, afterwards.

"I know you're going to spoil the suspense and tell me."

She moved her hand slowly, delicately, across my lower abdomen. "Of course," she said. "It's simple. What are we going to do about my husband?"

9

Pointing the Way

November, 1945

Street jarred me out of my reverie. "I'm the only one around here allowed to daydream," he said. When I pushed the file at him, he thumbed through it methodically. He stopped when he reached the section containing the interviews of Sarah and her mother.

"You know her, don't you, Charlie?"

"She's the one I told you about. The one I talked to last summer."

"Any chance she's involved in this?"

"No," I said. I kept my voice entirely normal. Street had tried enough murder cases to know that family members are always the first suspects.

Street nodded thoughtfully. "Let's have lunch with her," he said. "Maybe she's just a looker. Like that cop says, Rita Hayworth and all. But still and again she might know something about her husband's business."

The fear was there in an instant. I tried to stall, but Street was insistent. I trudged back to my office and when I finally reached Sarah on the phone, there was a second, an eternity, of silence. Then, her voice improbably calm, she quite reasonably suggested that the three of us meet at the country club.

"This is a small town and my neighbors have big eyes and bigger mouths," she said. "If I'm going to be seen talking with Hubbell Street, it might as well be in the most public place there is. Don't worry, Dad's a member. I'll use his account."

We talked for a bit about what she might say to Street. To lead him the next step down the road he so obviously wanted to travel. It would be very easy, really. Or at least that's what I thought.

Street and I were already seated when she came in through the dining room toward us. In an era of heavy rouges and lipsticks, she wore little obvious makeup, perhaps as a complement to the obligatory black of her clothing. Her carriage was erect and proud. She had an air of controlled vitality, like an athlete in repose before the race begins. When she was seated at our table, I noticed again the narrow blaze of silver hair, vivid against the russet. *She's a feast of a woman,* I thought. And I remembered the taste of her.

"Please don't get up," she said when she reached our table as we struggled with our chairs. "Charles, it's good to see you again. And is this the famous Hubbell Street?"

Street inclined his head and took her hand over the table. He was all charm and courtly gestures, and there was no trace of the country lawyer as he turned the full force of his attention on her. I felt as if I were seated at another table, in another room. I listened to them as they talked, from a distance that was as real as my imagination.

"It's the buffet for me. And you, too, Charles?" she asked, turning finally to me. We made our way through the formal dining room to the long banquet tables at the north end of the club. Michigan State College had resumed its football schedule that fall and the school's colors were splashed throughout the room, extending even to the green and white motif of the linens at the buffet. The tables were jammed with food. A pale pink sliced ham and a blood red prime rib of beef. Steaming vegetables and cold fruit. Baskets of sliced bread and rolls. Hot soups and cold consommés. Bowls of tossed green salad and platters of gelatin molds. An entire sweets table of cakes and cookies, pies and puddings. It was a huge, rich confusion of food, and Sarah and Street attacked it with genuine relish. I walked silently, awkwardly, behind them as they loaded their plates.

"You'll have to excuse me, I love good food. I don't care who knows it," Sarah said to Street. She glanced back at me and her eyes were gleaming.

After we ate, Street began to edge the conversation toward the business at hand. He watched her steadily as he probed. Finally, he asked a direct question.

"Mrs. Maynard, do you know how much money your husband made a year?"

She had chosen poached pear for dessert and she sliced it with her knife, inspected it carefully, and then devoured a bite. "No, I don't," she said. "Should I?"

"Not necessarily. It's just that your family lived well. You've got that big house in East Lansing. An automobile. Club memberships." Street looked around the dining room. "A state senator makes three dollars a day."

"Well, of course, my father helped us out after we were married. The house was his wedding present. And Harry was the executive secretary of the horseracing association. They paid him a salary when the legislature wasn't in session."

"Any other sources of income?"

"I don't really know. Harry had his business ventures. People were always stopping by the house. But we never discussed any of that."

Street looked at me and then at her again. "Charlie here tells me you came to see him last summer about a divorce."

Before I could speak, she smiled at me, a flash of light. "I didn't exactly go to see Charles, Mr. Street. I was a Gray Lady volunteer at Percy Jones. I knew he was a lawyer and I asked his advice."

Her voice was measured, practiced, as she speared the last of the pear with her fork. "It's no secret that Harry and I were having our differences," she said. "I hoped that we would resolve them. But I wanted to know how difficult a divorce would be. Charles told me that it would be quite difficult, quite public, given Harry's position."

"Were you aware that Senator Maynard was seeing other women?"

"Yes," she said. "Do you see other women, Mr. Street?"

Street shifted in his chair and his control slipped, but only for a moment. "Of course not," he snapped. He tapped the nail of his forefinger against the water glass and there was a small, silvery chime in the silence. Then he laughed and leaned forward across the table. The sleeves of her dress came only to her elbows and his hand rested lightly on her bare forearm, but she did not move.

"Mrs. Maynard," he said, "a pretty woman like you can always make a country boy feel like a dolt. I apologize. All I'm trying to do is find out whether your husband's death had anything to do with the grand jury and this corruption business. Do you think it did?"

She looked at him without expression. "I don't know. Harry and I weren't talking a great deal. He was out of the house much of the time. When he was home, he was either meeting with people in the den on business or sound asleep in the other bedroom, next to my daughter's room."

"Did you know any of the people who came by?"

"I knew Otto Lammers. We went to high school together. He was always around. Some of the other legislators would come."

She paused for a beat and I waited. Then she gave him what he wanted. Just as we had planned in our little telephone conversation.

"Wade Fleming, the state treasurer. He was there several times with those people who drive him around."

Street tapped the glass with a slow rhythm and again there was the clear ting of good crystal.

He's taken the bait, I thought. *Now he's got Fleming squarely in his sights.* The mystifying part was that everything Sarah had said was true. Down to the last detail.

"Thank you Mrs. Maynard," Street said. "Is there anything we can do for you? This must be a difficult time."

"Just find out who killed my husband. My daughter thinks of it all the time and it's affecting her schoolwork. Her teachers say she is very withdrawn at school. When she's at home, she spends most of her time up in her room. I'm hoping she'll get over it, but putting an end to all this waiting would certainly help."

"Can we drop you off somewhere?"

She rose from the table and signaled to the waiter for the check. "I have one of my father's cars. And he's buying." She paused for another beat. "What a pleasure to see you again, Charles. But under such different circumstances," she said. There was the flash of her smile as she turned away. She walked across the room, stopping several times, bending over the tables to talk. Her dress tightened across her hips and the warmth rose inside my groin. Street drummed his fingers on the table. But his eyes were like mirrors and they did not leave Sarah Maynard.

"Fleming doesn't have people who drive him around," he said, after she went through the door. "He has goons. Do you know anything about the Purple Gang, Charlie?"

I said that I did not. It was another of my lies. I knew a great deal about the Purple Gang. During Prohibition, they'd shot the man who drowned my father.

10

Brotherly Love

November, 1945

"Fleming's thugs are Purples. Everybody knows it," Street said as we drove back down the river road from the country club toward the heart of the city.

"They worked for Fleming after Lev Bernstein and the rest of them went to prison for the Collingwood killings in '31." He edged the car over to the side of the road and sat back, tapping his fingers on the wheel. The clean light of October had given way to a sullen November gray, and the bare arms of the trees shifted and creaked in the wind.

"It's Fleming. He's at the center of it," he said finally, and he tossed the brown shock of his hair back out of his eyes. "This time I'm going to nail his ass."

Sarah had done it, I thought. *She'd put Wade Fleming in the same room with the late, great senator. It might be enough.*

Street swung his massive head to the right and faced me directly. "Do you know the secret to police work? It isn't brilliant deduction. It isn't great crime labs or any of that crap. It's simple. You gotta have a squealer. Now, who's our squealer? Who's the rat that's been at the cheese?"

I knew his questions to be rhetorical. He had already picked his prey. "Little Otto Lammers," he said. "We're going to squeeze little Otto until we turn him. And then he's going to rat out Wade Fleming."

He put his hand on my shoulder, like a father. "You know this town. Who's been close to Otto Lammers? Who's close to him and who hates him?"

I looked at him steadily. The wind had died down and the only noise in the quiet of the car was his slow breathing and my own. All I had to do now was to move him along, on down the road to which Sarah had pointed him, toward a corrupt conspiracy. It was just another half-step.

"His brother, Bert," I said.

BERT LAMMERS practiced law the hard way, down at the street level. He hustled constantly for the table scraps from the court system after his regular clientele of pimps and prostitutes deserted him for other, marginally more reliable counselors. For years, Otto Lammers had used his older brother as an errand boy. One of his errands was to see legislators who swilled too much whiskey home safely to bed. And then to roll them out again in the morning to vote according to instructions.

The next day, leaning against the bar at Johnny's, Bert Lammers gave Street the lever with which to turn his brother. "He never should've made me clean up their puke like that," he said. "I'm a lawyer, not a nursemaid." He hunched forward and lowered his voice. "You know, Otto was the man in the gray suit."

I remembered the phrase. Before she died, my mother had clipped a brief story from the *Lansing State Journal* and sent it to me in England with a note about the workings of democracy. According to the clipping, an obscure state representative was indiscreet enough to state on the floor of the House that a man had approached him to ask what it would take to keep a particular small loan bill in committee.

A brief and unusual silence had fallen over the assembly. Then the sergeants at arms hustled the representative off the floor into the speaker's office. When he emerged, he read a statement to the knot of reporters that had formed in the hallway. Unfortunately, he said, he did not recognize the man and could not describe him. He did recall that the man was wearing a gray suit. If he ever saw that suit again, he would certainly be able to identify it.

"James Blewer, he's the state rep who shot his mouth off," Street said to me the next day. "He decided not to run last year, maybe with a little friendly persuasion. But he's still around. Works for the Highway Department. It's time to start taking a few pawns. Let's get Blewer over here in front of Storey."

I delivered the subpoena to Blewer myself. I carried it in my left side pocket, under my topcoat, and when he stepped around from his desk, I pulled it out and jabbed it at him with my right hand. He backed away, his hands at shoulder level with his fingers slightly curled, and I almost asked him for his name, rank, and serial number. Instead, I simply dropped the folder subpoena on his desk.

The Highway Department was growing steadily as the state swung into its postwar road-building program, and the bullpens in the old State Office Building were lined with rows of metal desks bunched closely together. Behind each desk sat a state employee, endeavoring to look occupied. They watched me curiously as I threaded my way back to the door. When I closed it behind me, I saw Blewer through the lettering on the glass, still standing behind his desk. He was a small man, so forlorn and solitary that even in the ordered clutter of that office he looked as if he were about to vanish.

STREET WAS at him immediately the next morning and Blewer shifted in the metal folding chair in which he was seated, fumbling with his answers, twisting his hands in front of him. In those years, regular grand juries normally convened in a closed courtroom. The proceedings were secret, but the ritual of question and answer was somehow less foreboding when it took place amid the familiar symbols of secular justice.

Storey, however, was the one-man grand juror. He could take testimony anywhere and so he chose to use the jury room next to his chambers. Jury rooms are designed to be efficient, not comfortable or reassuring. This one was no exception. It was cramped, severe, and airless. The only grace note was a deck of worn playing cards with which the jurors would occasionally amuse themselves when the judge sequestered them during arguments of law.

Street and Storey were not overly concerned with the law that day. After Blewer muddled through his account, Street slapped the flat of his hand down on the plain wooden table in front of him. Blewer jumped and so did I.

"Let me see if I understand you," Street said. "Your testimony is that you were standing there in the cloakroom? A man you didn't know just walked up to you? And then he offered to buy your vote in committee?"

John Danto looked up from his steno pad and waited patiently for Blewer's answer.

"We may have talked some first," he said, finally.

"What did you talk about with this man you didn't know?"

"We talked about the bill. Whether it was going to come out of committee or not. Then he asked me what it would take for me to vote no in the committee. You know, with the doors shut. But I told him my vote wasn't for sale."

Blewer looked away from his twisting hands at Storey. "Judge," he said, "I'd only been over there in the legislature for a year. I didn't know how things were done. I just stood up in the House and it all came out. And then the roof fell in." He lifted his hands in supplication and suddenly I believed that this dim little man was actually telling the truth. He was simply too commonplace to be a crook.

Naturally, I was wrong. Later, after we indicted him in another of our cases, he took immunity in trade for his testimony and spoke freely. He made his little speech in the House, not because a bribe was offered but because it hadn't been. "I saw everybody with their money and I wondered where mine was. So I thought I'd raise a little hell," he said, and he had lifted up his hands with the same feckless look of innocence, surprise, and surrender.

Street knew none of this when we first brought Blewer in. But his instincts were good. "And you still say you don't know this man in the gray suit?" he asked.

"I'd never met him. I wasn't in his league."

Street leaned forward. "So you knew who he was?"

Blewer looked over at Storey again. "Maybe I did. I said something when I shouldn't have. I didn't know what I was talking about. I don't want to say anything else. I've got a good job now. I can't afford to lose it."

Street gestured at the court reporter. "Off the record," he said and he turned to Blewer. "Listen to me, you miserable little shit. Do you know what we can do to you? We can send you out to the county farm and I don't think you're going to like hoeing sugar beets when it gets cold. I did it when I was a kid and my hands still hurt from the frostbite. You won't like the sleeping arrangements much either. There's only so many beds and sometimes you gotta double up and you know what that means. Why don't you just tell us who this mystery man is and get it over with?"

Blewer shook his head. Storey stood abruptly, all black robes and blue ice for eyes. "Mr. Blewer," he said, "I find you to be evasive. In my experience there's nothing like thirty days of uninterrupted meditation to improve a man's memory. I'm holding you in contempt. You're going to jail. If you wish to purge yourself, you can do so at any time. If not, we'll see you back here in a month."

Storey gestured at his steno. "John, call the deputy and we'll put this on the record in open court." He marched out of the jury room with Blewer trailing miserably behind him.

I turned to Street after the door closed. "He's no good to us in jail," I said.

"The hell he isn't. That's where he's the most good. The word'll get out we're serious here. I don't need him to finger Lammers. I just need people to think he's going to. Storey gave me the axe and I'm sure as hell going to swing it."

"What am I going to tell Hennessey?" I asked.

"Not a damn thing," Street said. "What's he going to do? Kill you if you don't call him?"

11

Little Otto

November, 1945

We raided the duplex Otto Lammers owned in Lansing the next day. It was an easy thing to do and the obvious next step. We waited carefully until we saw Lammers leave. Then we served our subpoena on his tenant and, as we hoped, he simply handed us the key to the front door. Lammers' wife had left him and the house was a shambles. We raced through it, piling papers into the cardboard transfer cases to which the state police are so partial. It was mainly debris, letters from his creditors, unpaid bills, marked-up legislation, yellowed newspaper clippings, and empty file folders, the stale detritus from the loose fall of his life. But we took it all.

Street had earlier leaked the fact of our visit to the papers and Bert Lammers, to whom his brother unsuspectingly turned for counsel, railed on cue about our high-handed, utterly illegal search. By pre-arrangement, he said nothing about the one item of value we found.

It was a worn pocket ledger and it was enough. Otto Lammers may have lived in chaos. Perhaps because of it, he sought to keep a record. It was an accounting, tangible enough to hold onto when the doubts came calling. Real enough to show that he was a man of stature, not a squalid little influence peddler. It was just tears, he said later, just tears in rain. But for us it was enough.

His accounting, the ledger of his existence, was a listing of the payments he made over the years. He categorized every entry by bill number and by legislator, with an annotation of his source of funds. For the 1944 session, he carefully prepared a term sheet, estimating the price at which he thought he could buy a vote, in committee or on the floor. He had set out the names of over half the sitting members of the Michigan legislature in his little black book.

"You know," Street said to me as he leafed through the ledger, "they're crazy. You'd think they'd have the mother wit not to write it down, but they always do. Maybe they think God's going to come down and ask 'em how they spent the money. They want to have it all written up, nice and neat."

He was quiet for a moment, staring at the ceiling. "Here's what you do. Get subpoenas out on every small loan company that shows up in here. Get their books, get their records, and get them over here. They're all from Detroit. They'll like the drive."

"What about Lammers?"

"We'll leave him alone for now. His brother says he's ready to deal. So we'll let him think we don't need him. I'll make sure Rachel knows when the small loan boys start coming in."

Rachel Loeb was one of Street's new friends in the press. She covered the capital beat for the old *Detroit Times*. When her editors decided that Storey and Street were news, they added the grand jury to her assignment. Storey bored her. But she found Street fascinating. The fact that she had landed a big story in a profession where women and Jews were rarities didn't lessen her interest in her prime source one bit. She had black hair cut short and swept back like a boy's, and she wore her skirts short and her blouses tight. Soon she and Street were having dinner and drinks alone in his suite at the Olds on a regular basis. When we began to parade the small loan company officers through Storey's jury room, we sat Rachel Loeb outside the door. Before we issued a single warrant, their trials were already underway.

But we needed Lammers for the warrants. We had loan company officers admitting that they had retained Lammers. We had their canceled checks to him, accumulating to an even ten thousand dollars. We had the same officers referring to the cash-and-carry legislature. We even had one man stating that the money flowed to Lammers to buy votes. We had the black book. But we had no one to authenticate it. We had conspiracy, but we didn't have bribery. Otto Lammers was the only person who could give us that. Our investigators were disheartened and Storey was apoplectic. But Street only laughed.

"This case is already over," he said. "My little birdie Bert Lammers tells me so."

Again, he was right. After Rachel Loeb wrote her last story on the secret grand jury proceedings, complete with authoritative quotes from conveniently anonymous sources, Bert Lammers called Street. When the two brothers presented themselves at our offices, he wasted no time.

"Otto wants to make a proffer of testimony," he said.

"Is that right," Street said as he began his slow walk by the window. "Hell, Otto, you're free as a bird. We haven't charged you with a thing. So tell me, where's your gray suit?"

Otto Lammers was a dapper little man. But he looked more than a little worse for wear that day. The weather was turning sour again and the combination of rain and sleet had soaked through his topcoat. His starched white collar was wilted. The moisture beaded on his forehead. Even his dark, precise mustache seemed smeared. His eyes, though, they were extraordinary. They were deep and midnight black. And they glistened like small glassy bits of coal stuck in the pallor of his face. Lammers looked at Street with those eyes and smiled in a stiff, embarrassed way.

"I don't own a gray suit," he said. "Gray suits are for bankers."

Street smiled right back at him. "That's not what your friend Blewer says."

He turned his back on the two brothers and ran his hand along the top of the sill of the hotel window. "Maid service's lousy here," he said. "Makes this a dirty business." He looked up at Lammers from the grime that soiled his hand. "Let's get to the nut cutting. What've you got and what do you want?"

Bert Lammers started to speak, but Otto cut him off with a single gesture. "I want immunity for my testimony on the small loan bill. Bert says my wife's going to clean me out. The house and everything. So I want a place to live. And a stipend. I don't work for free."

Street's voice was so low that Lammers strained to hear it. "And what do I get?"

"You get it all." Lammers' eyes glittered against the chalk of his skin. They darted back and forth between Street and me. And then to his brother, then down to the floor. Always in motion. But his voice was calm.

"You get the names and dates," he said. "Who I paid. And how much. Right out of the black book. You get me on the stand." Lammers leaned forward. "You get everything you want, Street. You get your convictions. And that means you get your headlines."

= 12 =

Signatures

November, 1945

And so the deal was done. We moved Lammers into the Olds and started running the checks through the state police detail, six hundred a month. Within a week, Storey issued twenty warrants, six to finance company officials and the rest to sitting legislators. We arraigned the defendants and after they bonded out, we set the preliminary examinations before our grand juror, now transformed with the blessing of the Michigan Supreme Court into an examining magistrate.

"Lammers likes you," Street said to me on the day before the first prelim. "He's scared shitless of me. But he likes you. Let's keep it that way. You handle the examination. Just walk him through it, nice and gentle. Besides, Storey likes veterans."

He's taken leave of his senses, I thought, but I did not argue. *After all, who could suspect an industrious assistant prosecutor, laboring away at the people's work? No one but Hennessey and I would have to deal with him later.*

Lammers was so smooth that I began to worry about how well this debonair man, with his oiled black hair and his dancing eyes, would play out before a jury of farmers and housewives and mechanics. But when he was playing only to Storey, he was fine. He answered my first question with a grandiloquence that went well beyond anything we had rehearsed, and I saw Rachel Loeb and her cohorts in the press, jammed into the jury box, struggling to keep up.

"In this state," Lammers said, "bribery was a way of life. Whether you liked it or whether you didn't like it made no difference. You had to do it. There was a point where logic and reason no longer served to obtain results. They wanted money and I gave it to them."

The defense lawyers were on their feet, but Storey gaveled them down and he allowed me enormous latitude as I took Lammers through his testimony. The details were the dry dust of political corruption. The small loan bill was a sandbag, thrown in without a prayer of passage. It was so draconian that it brought the small loan companies galloping to Lansing with their checkbooks at the ready.

Lammers had been a willing clerk of the works and he used the toilet in the basement of the Capitol as the place for the payoffs. One by one, the legislators filed in for their money. One by one, Lammers paid them, in the dark. The stench was so bad, he said, that he wrote the checks out in advance, to save time. The legislators called him the baron of the bathroom.

When Lammers finished and I offered the black book as an exhibit, the crowded courtroom was still. Storey ordered a brief recess, and when he returned to the bench we had three pleas in hand. Then I finished the preliminary examination with a handwriting expert from the police lab.

"Mr. Arnold," I said to the witness after I qualified him, "I'm going to show you twelve canceled checks that we've marked as exhibits. Have you seen these checks before?"

"Yes sir," Arnold said.

"Describe the circumstances for the court."

"You asked me to compare the endorsements on these checks with the signatures on certain other documents."

I picked up a stack of papers from the counsel table. After the court reporter marked them as exhibits, I showed them one at a time to the expert.

"And are these the documents to which you're referring, Mr. Arnold?"

"Yes sir, they are."

"Can you identify them for us?"

"Yes sir. They are the oaths of office that the members of the state legislature executed when they were sworn in," Arnold said.

"Do the signatures compare?"

"Yes sir. The signatures on the canceled checks are the same as those on the oaths of office. When these men swore to uphold the constitution."

With that, Storey had little difficulty finding probable cause and he immediately bound all of the defendants over for trial. Rachel Loeb's story the next day reported that the legislature had developed a full-blown case of the grand jury jitters. But if the men under the dome were nervous, Otto Lammers was petrified.

After we walked out of the courtroom, Street threw his arm around the lobbyist's shoulders and said, "Now that you've got the hang of it, you and I are going to have a little talk about Harry Maynard and Wade Fleming."

Lammers looked at me and I looked back. Right into his shriveled soul. "I'll see you in hell first," he said.

= 13 =

Unlawful Flight

November, 1945

In late November of 1945, R. J. Thomas, president of the United Automobile Workers, and the Reuther brothers took their union out on strike against General Motors. On the same day, Otto Lammers disappeared from his rooms at the Olds. The two events were entirely unrelated, but I remember them in tandem. Both appeared decisive and yet in the end neither was. They were only beginnings.

For the union, the strike opened in militancy and closed in compromise. Walter Reuther promised a winter of industrial warfare. But in the spring of 1946 he settled for a wage increase, eighteen and a half cents an hour. Two weeks later, he was the president of the largest union in the country and Thomas was only a memory. Otto Lammers, though, was not so fortunate. He left Lansing to escape Fleming and Street and he returned in irons to face them both.

The strike wore on in Lansing that winter like an aching tooth, with an occasional sharp flash of pain right at the nerve when a striker lost his home or his savings. Each afternoon the paper printed an encouraging story. But each evening the pickets walked their slow circles in front of the struck plants, stomping their feet against the cold and slipping out of line to rub some warmth into their hands over the barrel fires. They knew little of formulas, less yet of ability to pay or of Reuther's demands for a look at the books, nothing at all of corporate conspiracy.

A few of them may have actually believed the president of General Motors when he later denied that he had traveled to New York, first class, to draw up a plan for breaking the unions. He said that he met with the steelmakers, the meatpackers, and the electronic manufacturers over lunch merely because they were all looking down the barrel of the same gun. There were no agreements, he said. It was just an honest and frank discussion of how everything was going to hell, he said. It was too bad, he said, that the same group couldn't make decisions for the country.

Otto Lammers had been even less forthright with us about his meetings with Maynard and Fleming. He was there, he told us, when they discussed legislation to reduce the license fee for Michigan breweries and distilleries. He was there when Fleming said that the governor supported the bill. He was there when Maynard agreed to be a sponsor. It had all been very straightforward. And very honest.

"This wasn't the small loan boys getting sandbagged," he said. "This was high level. When Fleming put his group together to back the bill, I jumped at it. It was a step up for me."

Street shot his hands forward, pinning Lammers against his chair. "You're a liar," he said. "You want me to haul you before Judge Storey? You want to go through this bullshit under oath? You want to face a perjury charge?"

"You put me under oath on this, I'll take the fifth."

"Wrong constitution, Otto," Street said. "This is a state court. You refuse to answer, we grant you additional immunity for any crimes you committed involving Maynard. You know all about immunity. If you don't testify, you'll be swinging a hoe out there in the cold in Mason during the day. And at night you'll be swinging on the business end of some con's dick. You want that, I can arrange it. You'd probably like it."

Street's voice was quiet, but with each sentence he shoved the little man further back against the chair. Lammers didn't struggle. He simply stared straight ahead and his incandescent eyes blinked once with each shake. At the corner of one of his eyes there was a single tear.

"I gave you what you wanted," he said. "Nobody cares about Maynard. Let him lay. Fleming's boys would bash my head in just like Maynard's if he heard I was talking about him. I've done some things. So have you. So has Charlie here. But nothing to deserve that. I'll give you the bank bill. I'll give you the horseracing bill. I can even give you the doctors. But not this one. I'm asking you. For Christ's sake just let this one alone." Lammers brushed the forefinger of his right hand against his cheek and then under his nose. His face was still damp and he dabbed at it again, irritably.

I took a shallow breath and started to rise from my chair. I had no idea what I was going to do. But I could not sit there watching that man's fears leak out like quicksilver. I was surprised at myself. After my morning in the yellow mist, I had thought my capacity for compassion entirely gone.

Street hesitated. And we lost Lammers. "All right, Otto," he said. "Charlie thinks I'm being too hard on you. Talk to Bert about it. Then come back and talk to me. Just don't think I've got what I want. I want Fleming and you're going to give him to me."

Lammers walked quickly out of the room. The next day he disappeared. We located him within two weeks in Chicago at the Palmer House, where his brother had placed him. But he was beyond our jurisdiction. When I reached him by telephone, he refused to listen either to our promises or to our threats.

"We have to do it the hard way," Street said to me after I failed to move Lammers in the final heated phone call. "We'll get a federal warrant."

The procedure was an intricate, stylized governmental dance. As the strikers shuffled in the cold around the Oldsmobile plant, we filed our papers and circled Lammers according to the law's precise and measured cadence. The U.S. Attorney in Detroit was an old adversary and an older friend of Street's and he took the case before a federal grand jury. Within days we had an indictment against Lammers for unlawful flight to avoid giving testimony. The FBI arrested him in Chicago and shipped him to Detroit for arraignment.

Maloney and I were waiting when little Otto stepped off the train, his topcoat thrown over the handcuffs linking him to the FBI agent. He sat quietly during the ride to the old Federal building in Detroit and the transfer after his arraignment went smoothly, according to plan. He spoke only once on the way back to Lansing. He leaned over toward me in the back seat and whispered so that Maloney could not hear.

"The Detroit cops've got a guest," he said. "Name of Vanik. He's an old friend of Fleming's boys. You should talk to him. Maybe we can all still come out of this."

⇒ 14 ⇐

Shorteyes

December, 1945

The Detroit police were toying with Nathan Vanik like cats with a ball of yarn. They batted him around the circuit from one station house to another. And with each midnight move he would give them a new thread of information.

It was a game with a predetermined result. The cops knew that eventually they would have all of Vanik. They knew his fear of prison was as paralyzing as it was justified. Vanik was a child molester. A shorteyes. The prison suicide rate among shorteyes approached one hundred percent. But he wasn't in prison yet and for us, he was a godsend. By profession he was a wheelman and he had once worked for the Purples.

I first saw Vanik at the old Beaubien police station. The young street bull who led me down to the basement holding cell that was Vanik's home for the day was not a tolerant man. In Vanik he saw an archetypal combination of religious difference and sexual deviancy.

"Sit down, jewboy," he said as we walked through the door and Vanik slumped immediately into the chair that sat at the center of the small room. The light bulb overhead was unshielded and it hung down from the ceiling over Vanik's head. The cell had a sharper smell than the rest of the building. It was the pungent, salty stench of sweat and ammonia and fear.

"He's all yours, Mr. Cahill. If you can take him," the patrolman said as he pulled another chair up behind Vanik. On the floor next to him was a large Detroit telephone book.

Vanik looked at me expectantly. He was a vessel, waiting to be drained or filled at my choice. I wanted both and I had to be sure.

"Nate," I said, careful to establish my dominance, "how long did you work for the Purple Gang."

"Ten years," he said. "From '21 to '31, until Collingwood."

"What did you do for them?"

"Like I told the boys here, I was a driver. I drove Lev Bernstein and the Keywells around. What'd you think?" The policeman slammed the thick telephone book into the right side of Vanik's head. Vanik rocked forward with the blow. But he did not make a sound.

"Little kike's got no manners," the patrolman said. He had exactly the expression of a man describing an unruly dog.

"Do you know Wade Fleming?" I asked.

"I know his boys. I used to drive them around on jobs, after Bernstein went to prison. Tell him not to hit me like that."

The patrolman swung the telephone book again and this time he knocked Vanik from the chair. I went over the chair after the cop, and wedged the thumb and forefinger of my right hand up under his chin below the hinge of his jaw. I cut off his breath, just as the Rangers had taught me.

"You goddamn Nazi," I shouted at him and then I shoved him hard against the cement wall. For a moment he looked as if he would come back at me. But he thought better of it and stumbled toward the door.

"I'll be back with the lieutenant, you cocksucker," he said.

With that, I had Vanik completely. And with him came the case against Fleming's two bodyguards. Yes, he said, he drove them often over the years. In August of 1945, he drove them to Lansing, not once but twice, to case a hit on a politician who was talking too much. Yes, it was Maynard, and indeed they once stopped on Maynard's street to get a close look at his home. But they left hurriedly when Maynard's wife and daughter came out on the porch. Yes, he would testify, for immunity and for relief from the Detroit police.

"No prison time. That's all I want, no prison time," he said, and I agreed immediately. As I walked to the door, he called after me. "I'm only half Jewish," he said and my stomach churned. Incredibly, I now knew that the Purples were circling around Maynard before I got to him. Another piece of the conspiracy fell into place and I wondered again at our good fortune.

The patrolman was waiting for me outside the basement room. "Did I do okay?" he asked. He had the blind, faithful face of an acolyte. And the build of a furniture mover.

"You did fine," I said, "just fine. We did real well, you and me. Where can we go to get a drink? I'm buying."

= 15 =

Peter's Turn

December, 1945

Street looked at me quizzically the next morning. "*In vino veritas*, Charlie?"

I tried to divert him, but he would not be deflected. Perhaps he saw in my diluted guilt an empathy with the enemy that he could not permit. Perhaps he was simply irritated. But he did not know me. And he could not know my true motives. We had Fleming in the middle of the murder. *If we can turn Otto Lammers, we can put Fleming in charge of it,* I thought. That was exactly where I wanted him to be. And so did Street. He had his reasons and I had mine.

"Not truth," I said. "Comfort perhaps. But not truth."

"I don't understand you." Street shifted into his prosecutor's voice and there was a sharp edge to his tone. "You get all moral on me when I raise Lammers' blood pressure a little, but then you work Vanik over like a piece of meat."

"It had to be done. You said so yourself."

"I know what I said. This is no church social. It's a criminal prosecution and we're gonna win. To make these cases, we have to break people. It's the only way we'll ever get Fleming. You'd do well to keep that in mind when you start pickling yourself over scum like Lammers and Vanik."

I did not debate him. Rather, I left him for my brother. My apotheosis. My nemesis. Peter was in the hospital and the doctor who called me said that he might live. And that he might not want to.

When I reached the emergency room, the same doctor stopped me at the door. He recited the litany of my brother's injuries like a priest chanting the liturgy, formal, stylized, and fearful. "Right leg fractured, tibia and fibia. Both kneecaps shattered. Broken ribs. Fractured jaw. Broken nose. Whoever worked him over wanted to cripple him," he said, and he looked at my empty sleeve with unembarrassed clinical interest.

"Can I see him?"

"He's sedated, but he's coherent. The police were here. But he wouldn't talk with them. He said he wanted to see you. We've splinted his legs. We can't cast them, though. They're too swollen. We had to tie his hands to get the catheter in."

The doctor opened the door for me and as I walked into the darkened room, he added the benediction. "They dumped him off on the front steps of the hospital. Like someone delivering the mail."

Peter lay on his back. The splints that framed each leg made him look like a boy on stilts. A boy who had fallen straight backward into a carefully prepared hospital bed. His knees were like soft purple balloons and they filled the center of each narrow box. His face was raw and misshapen, puffed so grotesquely that his features were all but lost in the swollen red pulp. His hands were tethered with strips of white sheeting to the metal rails that framed the bed. He was breathing slowly. And each time his chest rose, his hands twitched reflexively. He stared straight up at the ceiling. When he spoke to me he squeezed his words out, drop by painful drop.

"Untie my hands," he said.

"I can't. The doctor says you shouldn't move at all."

"Untie my hands. Please."

"I can't," I whispered, so quietly that I hoped he could not hear my voice shaking.

"I want to touch my face. How's my face?"

"Your face is fine," I said. "What happened? Who did it, Pete?"

"Fleming and his boys. Hennessey. And Bernstein. And some other guy, looked like a gorilla. They were all laughing about how Bernstein had to get back to prison. I got to brag-ging. I told Fleming how I'd sent you that note. Told him I could still fix things with you. I was just tryin' to get in good with him. Fleming told his boys to straighten me up and then the other guy hit both my knees with a tire iron. When I went down, Hen-nessey leaned over me. Said to tell you this is what happens to Cahills who can't follow instructions. He started kicking me. And then I passed out. But I don't think he stopped kicking me. He liked it."

My brother ran his tongue over his broken teeth. "I fooled you with the note, didn't I?"

"You sent me the note?"

"Yeah, I thought I'd scare you off. Thought I'd show Fleming. Guess I really showed him."

I stared at my brother, the big tipper and the big fixer. "What were you doing with Fleming?"

"Got my job with Schenley's through him. Got my orders through him. Everybody knows he owns the Liquor Control Commission. Every month he gets a quarter of my gross. Every month. I've only been late a couple times. He laughed about it. Said I was a good credit risk. He even lent me money for my little deals."

I couldn't touch him without hurting him. I patted the pillow beside his head. "I'll get Fleming. And I'll get Hennessey. I'll get the cops and we'll get the bastards." I had forgotten for a moment about Harry Maynard's killing. Peter was my only family and now Fleming had smashed him. Fleming may not have been a murderer, but he was the closest thing to it and I wanted him dead. And I wanted Hennessey in the next grave. I had not done his bidding and he had taken his revenge. He had sent me a message and now my brother was a cripple.

Peter struggled briefly against the sheets and then he turned his head toward me, his breath whistling thought his shattered mouth.

"No!" he said and his eyes were frantic. "You do that, they'll kill me for sure. That Bernstein's the boss of the Purple Gang.

He'd cut his own brother's throat with a smile on his face. And Hennessey'd be right there to put the boot in."

The nurse came in then, clucking with concern, and I got up to leave. I was almost to the door when Peter called out to me.

"Charlie," he said. "I'm sorry about everything. I never meant to hurt anybody. What's gonna happen to me now?"

I turned back to him. "You'll survive," I said. "That's enough."

Consequences

November, 1996

*T*he doctors have performed a minor operation on my father, drawing out a quart of reddish liquid that has collected against his chest wall. He says that he feels much improved and he fights them constantly, demanding an explanation for every procedure and questioning every opinion. He is a difficult patient when he is in a good mood, impossible when he is out of sorts. I am sure that when the doctors retreat from his room in the intensive care ward their muttered comments cannot be flattering. Ever the trial lawyer, my father simply ignores their irritation. Or he patronizes them so outrageously that they respond in anger and then he laughs at their lack of control. The nurses love him. They constantly bend the rules on his behalf and he accepts their favors with grave courtesy.

"Frankie," he says to me, "why don't we just kill the doctors? Let the nurses run the place. They're so much more competent."

I am amazed at his composure and I slip into flippancy. "Would you like to contract it out or just do it yourself?" I ask.

He snorts. "You're too bright by half. And you've no respect for your elders. Living alone has that effect. Why don't you move in with someone new?"

It is my turn to snort. "I like my sleeping arrangements just fine," I say, but I am not at all at ease with this topic. Julie and I have been apart for months. I rarely think of it, but when I do, the odd mixture of relief and panic I felt on the day she left returns to me. She wanted far more than I could give. When I couldn't explain it, that drove her further from me. Our relationship slowly turned into a long, cold winter, untouched by spring. I was frozen into silence and she took that as a continuing rebuff. When she finally could take no more, she left without a word. I am alone now. It is sufficient. But sometimes at night I ache for Julie and her slow hands and soft mouth.

I try to shift the topic again. "Uncle Pete has been asking about you. He wants to come and see you. The doctors say it's okay."

He hesitates and I think that he does not wish to confront the reality of his brother's condition. But I have misunderstood him.

"Peter is always welcome," he says. "I hope the hospital doesn't upset him. He's an old, old man and not a happy one."

He is right, as usual. Uncle Peter's golden years are filled with defeat. Even the smallest slight—a chance remark, a glance on the street—will send him careening off on a reckless, drunken binge. When his children track him down at the hospital or the city mission or the city jail, he is always filthy. Always penniless. And always angry. Against all advice, they give him money for food, for clothing, for rent at the furnished rooms into which he drifts. He hoards it obsessively for the next bender. Then it is gone. They despair of him, as do my father and I. But we cannot reach him through the layers of his bitterness.

When he arrives after my phone call, the small squeaks that the rubber tips on his canes make against the floor punctuate his slow shuffle into the darkened room. His face is wizened, lumpy, and flushed, and his cheeks and chin are covered with a graying stubble. I cannot see in this bowed, desolate wreck a trace of the handsome young man my father has described.

"Fine figure of a man, ain't he?" Uncle Peter says to me and he jerks his thumb toward my father. I help the old man to the chair beside the bed. He lowers himself into it, places the canes across his lap, and squints in the half-light.

"When you getting out, Charlie?" he asks. His voice has a reedy, insistent quaver to it. I am suddenly aware that he is relishing my father's weakness.

"I'm sure it will be some while," my father says. His tone is ironic, for he has sensed his brother's pleasure. "You're looking well, Peter."

My uncle's head snaps up and when he speaks, his voice rises sharply. "Don't tell me I look good. I never look good." He raises both hands to his face. Then he lets them fall back down to his knees in a gesture that is both accusatory and despairing.

My father shifts in his bed. "Forgive me. I was only trying to be pleasant." His voice is gentle as he continues. "We were talking about Lansing after the war, when the world was young. I was in hopes of generating some understanding in Frankie here of what it was like."

Uncle Peter turns to me, mollified, and his shattered face brightens. "You know what I remember? I remember VJ day. Charlie was in the hospital over in Battle Creek, but I was all right then and I marched down Michigan Avenue with the rest of them. Right up on the steps of the Capitol. A bunch of spades were playin' some of their jazz on a flatbed truck. But you couldn't hear them for the noise. Church bells and fire sirens and cars honkin.' We just marched around like kings. Then everything went to hell."

"Things are always going to hell," my father says. "But we've had long lives, Peter. Against all odds."

"Yeah, but yours meant something. After they crippled me up, it was just one damn thing after another and every one of them a piece of shit."

He stares at me and I bow my head. I have my own memories. It is best not to revive them.

My father saves me. He reaches his good hand out to his brother, his mirror. They chat for a time, but then my father tires and he says, "Frankie will call a taxi to get you wherever you're staying these days."

When I return, my father is quiet for a moment and then he says, "After the first war, the French had a parade each year to celebrate their great victory. The veterans would march down the Champs-Élysées and they saved the places at the front of the *parade for the broken faces, men whose faces were destroyed by war. Peter never fought a war, but he's a broken face. Without a parade."*

"Has he always blamed you for what happened?"

"He blames me because I kept going when he could not. We both knew that Bernstein and Hennessey worked him over. After that, Peter walked through life with a sign on his back that said, throw me overboard."

My father turns his head toward me. His face is a mask. "Time stretches out when it's running down," he says. "And you spend a good deal of it just remembering. You're not thinking less of me that I waited this long to tell you what I remember?"

He pauses. But I make no response. The dam within me is holding. I will listen to everything my father says. But he will get nothing from me.

"You're uncommonly quiet this evening," he says. "Well, at least you're present at the reckoning."

He stops and the room is silent. Then he turns the clock back again.

"Will Storey issue a warrant against Fleming?"

Street grinned at me. "Hell, Storey wants Fleming's ass worse'n I do," he said. "Fleming blocked his nomination to the Supreme Court. The real question is, will he agree to try this case? No grand juror's ever done that. But there's nothing in the statute to prevent it. If I can try all three of those shitheels in front of Storey, I'll send them to Jackson prison and we'll play 'em off against each other until one of them talks. Then we've got our murder case."

Street had the wrong murderers, but his plan was daring and the key to its initial success was Otto Lammers. We filed another set of immunity motions; and when Sergeant Maloney brought Lammers to Storey's cramped jury room, Hamilton Richards was waiting for us. He was a long, leathery man with a narrow face like a riding boot. He wasted no time.

"I've advised my client not to testify and to request that I be present during all of this," he said to Street.

Street laughed at him. "Lammers has immunity for this case. Storey won't recognize the privilege for secret testimony. And he sure as hell isn't going to let you into the grand jury room. I sure hope your boy's developed a taste for that crowbar hotel out in Mason. If he crosses Storey, his sorry ass is going back to jail for contempt. You look sidewise at Storey, you'll be out there sitting right next to little Otto."

Richards pushed his jaw up at Street and his words had the sharp ring of authority. "I know you've got Storey all nice and primed," he said. "But you threaten me or my client again, I'll take you before the State Bar."

The corridor in front of the jury room bustled with the usual mixture of lawyers and loiterers, but the buzz of their conversation fell off suddenly with the crack of Richards' voice. To my left at the end of the hall, I saw John Danto, Storey's court reporter, watching intently. His face fairly glistened with curiosity. Street leaned over to Richards.

"Go fuck yourself," he said. "You think you've got a charge, bring it."

He turned to me. "Take little Otto into the jury room. I've got a phone call to make."

Lammers and I waited in the jury room for over an hour, and every fifteen minutes John Danto shot his head through the side door to announce that the judge was getting very impatient. Richards had coached Lammers well, for he refused to respond even to my most innocuous questions about the Maynard case. To pass the time, we turned to politics. It was the common denominator of discourse in a town where all the other games of chance are considerably less rigged.

"What do you think? Is the governor going to run again?" I asked.

"Why not? He won going away in '44 with Roosevelt on top of the ticket. If he can buck that, he'd be crazy to pass up a sure thing next year. And Jim McReynolds is anything but crazy. Besides, who's going to beat him? Your friend Street?"

"Street's never said a word about running for governor."

"He's been running for years. He just didn't know for what. This grand jury thing's getting him a lot of attention. He's got a shot at McReynolds in the primary next year if he gets Fleming ahead of time. Why else do you think he's so impatient?"

Before I could answer, Street swept into the room. He was cheerful and hearty until Storey arrived with Danto in tow. Then he was all efficiency.

"State your name for the record," he said to Lammers.

Lammers turned to the judge and his eyes began their curious dance. He took a slip of paper out of his pocket and read from it carefully.

"Your honor, I request that my counsel be present for this examination."

"Denied," Storey said. "State your name and get on with it."

"Your honor, my counsel has advised me to refuse to answer any questions on the grounds that my testimony may be used against me in the federal prosecution pending in Detroit. Therefore, I respectfully refuse to answer."

Storey looked at Street expectantly and the special prosecutor answered on cue. "This court has granted the witness immunity for any testimony he may give in the Maynard matter. Mr. Lammers' testimony is under seal. It can't be used in the federal case. I ask the court to allow Mr. Lammers to consult with his counsel, and when he returns to direct him to answer my questions under pain of contempt."

Storey nodded at Lammers and the little lobbyist walked to the door. His head was down and his feet were shuffling.

I leaned over to Street. "Why'd you let him go?" I asked.

"I've got something out there for him in the hallway. Maybe he'll think again about brother Richards' advice when he sees his next cellmate. Have a look."

When I walked out of the jury room, I saw Lammers huddled next to Richards against the far wall at the end of the hallway. But he wasn't listening to his lawyer. He was staring at the man who was seated on a metal folding chair halfway down the corridor, handcuffed to two uniformed deputies. The man was grossly fat, with huge rolls of flesh cascading down his neck and chest to the enormous bulge of his belly. His skin was a moldy white, a sharp contrast to the blue of his prison uniform. He had a fringe of dirty blond hair tufted above his ears and circling behind his head. He smiled at Lammers and half closed his eyes, making a clucking, kissing sound. Each time he heard that noise, Otto Lammers flinched.

I walked back into the stuffy jury room and sat down next to Street. He sensed my unease immediately. My own fate was in this man's hands, but I could not conceal my instinct to turn away, to avoid the naked immediacy of his threat. Street stood and looked straight at me, removed his suit coat, and snapped his braces as he spoke.

"Ends and means, Charlie," he said. "You'd best learn the difference. If you can't, then I'll pass you the puke bucket."

I did not respond and we waited in silence until Lammers returned. He sat down across from Street and folded his hands in front of him on the table. His face was stiff and composed, but the whites of his eyes flashed like those of a nervous colt. One leg bounced with a steady, jerking motion against the floor.

"Have a nice chat?" Street said to him.

"You know I won't go back to Mason with that faggot out there. Keep me out of jail and I'll take a chance with you today. But today is all. You've got to promise me that none of this will leak. Fleming and Hennessey can't know."

Street leaned forward and pumped Lammers' small hand. "We'll take it one step at a time. You've got my word on that," he said and then he paused. "Besides, you'd be Romeo's second choice. He likes working with farm animals." Street yelled at Danto through the side door and the court reporter hurried back into the room, followed by Storey.

"I think we're ready to proceed," Street said to the judge. And then he began to squeeze the testimony out of Lammers. There was no art to it. Nothing but a steady constriction. With every answer, Lammers shrank further into himself.

"Have you ever had a discussion with Wade Fleming about buying votes on the liquor legislation?" Street asked, after he finished the preliminaries.

"Yes. Fleming had a war chest from the distillers and the brewers. We decided who we needed to buy. We went over it all at Maynard's place last summer. I took the House. Maynard took the Senate."

"Who was present at these discussions?"

"Fleming and Maynard were there. And Fleming's two body-guards. Abe Lefkowitz and Izzy Shrieber."

Street followed up quickly. "What are their actual names?"

"I don't know for sure. Maybe Abraham Lefkowitz. And Isadore Shrieber?"

"Do you know who they are?"

A smile flickered over Lammers' still face for just a moment. "Hell yes. I know exactly who they are. They're from Detroit and they're what's left of the Purple Gang."

"Did you ever meet with Fleming after the grand jury investigation started this fall?"

"Just once," Lammers said. "He came over to my place with Lefkowitz and Shrieber. Said he'd heard Maynard was singing to the grand jury. Said he was going to have Maynard taken for a ride."

"And what did that mean?"

Lammers looked straight at Street. For once, his shifting, slanting eyes were absolutely still.

"Fleming meant to have Maynard killed," he said. "That's what he meant. And now Maynard's dead."

We've got it, I thought. *We've got enough to convict Fleming. And Sarah and I would be safe.*

Sweet Charity

December, 1945

Street arranged to have the conspiracy warrants for Fleming, Lefkowitz, and Shrieber issued on a Saturday, and he held a press conference at our offices in the hotel that afternoon. Despite his promise of secrecy to Lammers, he was determined to go ahead. "It's simple," he said to me. "Storey will issue the warrants on my say so and Saturday's a slow news day. This way I'll be all over the Sunday papers and we'll worry about the evidence later."

He was right. The small room was crowded with reporters. For the first time I saw stringers from the national press mixed in with the regulars from the capital beat and the political writers from Detroit. Street sat behind a long wooden banquet table that we borrowed from the hotel for the occasion, amid a tangle of radio microphones with their black umbilical cords linking him to the world outside.

"It was amazing," he said to me later. "It was like I was sitting there in the kitchen talkin' to mama and the kids. I wonder if that's how Roosevelt felt."

I told him I didn't know. I didn't tell him that we were too poor after my father's death to afford a radio and that I had never heard one of the president's fireside chats.

When the press conference was over, Street was brimming with good cheer. "The Charity Ball's tonight here at the hotel and the mayor's reserved two places for me," he said. "The missus is at home. Why don't you and I go stag?"

"It's formal. I don't own a tux," I said.

"Wear a sincere blue suit. You're a veteran. You can get away with murder." He said it without a trace of irony.

Street may have been a man of many talents, but as a social arbiter he was an absolute disaster. Of the one hundred males at the dinner dance, there was only one in a blue suit, whether sincere or not. I promptly concluded that I needed only a little manure on my shoes to round out my appearance.

Street soon deserted me for Rachel Loeb and I headed for a corner, out of the light. The ballroom was decorated for Christmas and a tall, stately evergreen stood in the center of the dance floor. It was bedecked entirely with scarlet ropes, ornaments, and bows, and it sparkled cheerfully with a hundred white lights. Frosted wreaths coiled around the orchestra platform. The long mantle at the far end of the room was crowned with crystal candelabras lit with fire and glowing softly. The orchestra had not yet begun to play and couples circled around the buffet and swooped from table to table, laughing gaily at words I could not hear. It was a world I had never known. And rarely had I felt more alone.

"Do you like it, Charles?" she asked and I turned to Sarah, there in the shadows. She was wearing a long gown of forest green with offsetting silver lamé threads. Her shoulders were bare and her chestnut hair was piled high, the white streak sharp as a blade. Her eyes were alight and I thought again that her mouth was the softest red I had ever seen.

"It's very pretty," I said. "I thought we'd agreed we wouldn't see each other until this thing is over."

"You agreed. I didn't. I don't see why we can't at least talk. I'm a respectable woman. You're a very respectable man. Besides, we're both here with somebody else." She smiled at me and I shivered at the thought of her fingers and her whispers and the dust motes in the air at the hospital, floating slowly down around us.

"Who are you here with?"

"Are you jealous, Charles?" She threw her head back and her laughter pealed out. "Don't be. I'm here with my father. You're going to meet him. Right now, before you lose your nerve."

She tucked her arm through mine and pulled me across the dance floor to her table. Her father was a slender, dark-haired man and when he rose to greet us, she said, "Dad, this is the lawyer I mentioned. Charles Cahill, this is my father, Joshua St. Clair."

St. Clair had a reassuringly firm handshake. He wore a starched, well-stuffed white dress shirt with a coal black bow tie, and he was sufficiently polite not to look too long at my suit. "I understand there was an announcement today about the killing," he said to me.

"Yes, sir. Judge Storey issued conspiracy warrants."

"For Wade Fleming?"

"Fleming and two of his employees."

"Can you prove he did it?" Sarah asked. She had not lost her talent for getting directly to the point.

"We don't have to prove he did it. We only have to prove he conspired to do it. I think we can prove that," I said. She nodded once at me and smiled. She understood perfectly.

"Good," St. Clair said. "I've never liked Fleming. He gives honest businessmen a bad name. I hope you put him in jail. Harry was not my favorite son-in-law. Sarah knows that. But to be so brutally murdered . . ."

"Stop it, Dad," Sarah interjected. "This is the first time I've been out to anything social since it happened. Don't spoil it for me."

She turned to me and cocked her head to the side. "Charles Cahill, the band's playing and you're going to dance with me. Isn't he, Dad?" St. Clair shrugged and I was trapped.

She was a graceful dancer and somehow she managed to accommodate my clumsy foxtrot. But I still felt like an awkward, drab farm boy as we bumped and jostled the other couples on the crowded dance floor. To accommodate my empty left sleeve, she put both her hands on my shoulders and that brought her very close to me. I breathed in the smell of lavender and honey. I remembered the taste of her and the words she had murmured to me.

"It's working, isn't it? Your Mr. Street actually thinks Fleming was involved," she said.

"Otto Lammers testified that Fleming was going to have your husband killed. You and I, we just got there first. But there's Hennessey. Hennessey knows something."

I hesitated. I was talking too much, even to her. "This is not a very good idea," I said, finally.

"You mean people will think badly of me? That I danced the night away right after the grand jury indicted the men who conspired to kill my poor husband?"

I felt a tap on my shoulder and it was Hubbell Street. "I doubt anyone could think badly of you, Mrs. Maynard," he said. "Charlie, let me cut in. I want to talk to Mrs. Maynard about the trial."

As I turned to go, he pulled my head down and whispered in my ear. "I just got a call from one of Fleming's lawyers. They've waived preliminary examination. We're going to trial. We're going to get Fleming and those Purple Gang hebes. Hennessey probably knows about it already, but call him anyway so he doesn't feel left out."

He whirled away with Sarah. I found my own way out into the cold. And then, for reasons that I could not fathom, I was a boy again, staring into the night. Caught up in the past, the Purple Gang, and my father's last run.

≡ 18 ≡

In the Market

August, 1928

Mistakes had marked Sam Cahill. Mistakes and bad luck. Of course, for him, the best drink was always the next one. And there always was a next one. But he had worked hard at our farm, rising before dawn and pushing himself through the day, often without noticeable effect. His fields were no more rocky than those of his neighbors, but he smashed his plow at least once each spring, or broke the axle of his wagon, or caught his harrow in among the fence posts and barbed wire. He drove a pitchfork halfway through his foot one summer and spent the rest of the year fighting off tetanus, mainly with blended whiskey. Our neighbors, stolid Germans all, took pity on our small family and brought in the crops while my father lay in the back bedroom, wrapped in blankets and shame. In Prohibition he saw an opportunity and he became a puller.

After the Great War, Canadian wartime prohibition had expired and those Canadian companies holding charters from the federal government in Ottawa could again legally manufacture the full range of intoxicants, just as the United States clamped down the lid on its own production. Canadian breweries and distilleries were quickly in full-time operation. The flow of beer, wine, and spirits across the Detroit River, the strait that separates the province of Ontario from the state of Michigan, soon became a torrent.

The product poured over the black stretch of water in fair weather and foul. It came in fake funeral processions, with every car packed with whiskey. It came by boat in the choppy waves of summer and by car over the chopped ice of winter. Often by airplane and sometimes by submarine. By the bottle, by the case, by the barrel, by the trainload. Fully eighty percent of all the liquor that moved into the United States during Prohibition coursed through the narrow neck of the Windsor-Detroit funnel. There were 25,000 illegal saloons in Detroit, including scores of school pigs that sold whiskey only to young children. Little Harry's, Pinky's, and the other speakeasies on East Jefferson did a roaring business and they did it day in and day out. There were no holidays in their line of work.

It was into this cauldron that my father plunged. His concept was by no means original. He would buy, quite legally, in Canada. Then he would pull his commodities quickly and quietly across the river in a small boat and sell them, quite illegally and quite profitably in Lansing to the hotels, speakeasies, and blind pigs that ringed the Capitol. Our farm was the cover for his new enterprise.

During the summer months, we would husband our small crop of tomatoes, cucumbers, peppers, and melons until we had enough for an early morning run to the Eastern Market in Detroit. Occasionally, we might actually sell some of our undersized produce to a gullible housewife. But the experienced shoppers passed us by without hesitation and we would idle the day away, sitting on upended crates and watching the rich urban stew as it bubbled around us.

My father was mainly concerned with sneaking a pull from the bottle in his back pocket, but I was fascinated by the diversity of dress and dialect, the mixture of the customs and culture of the old world with the clang and the clatter of the new. Poles from Hamtramck shouldered impatiently in front of downriver Hungarians. Bearded Jews bartered with hard-handed Italian stonemasons. Negro domestics filled their shopping bags with fresh fruit and vegetables for the evening meals they prepared for their employers out on the Gold Coast. Gypsies with their flashing vests and their flashing hands worked their way through the crowds, and I would delight in watching them pick the pockets of the unwary.

The market would empty in the evening. My father and my brother, then in his early teens, would rattle off in the darkness, leaving me to stand a forlorn watch over our unsold goods. They would row the lugger across the river. Just a man and his boy out for some evening exercise. Then they would make the purchase from my father's supplier, known to the trade only as King Canada.

The return trip was the difficult part. Since my father was usually well gone by then, Peter would row the small boat back with the oars carefully muffled. The Prohibition Navy was a motley collection of police pugs, bored customs officials, and raw Coast Guard recruits. They were both corrupt and inefficient and they rarely apprehended the small time operators. The real danger came from the pirates and hijackers who operated from the downriver Barbary Coast. They were pitiless hoods that my father managed to avoid through a combination of patience, guile, and caution.

After the two smugglers returned from their evening's adventure, I would hop aboard the ancient truck and Peter would drive slowly back home. Our cargo would clink and jounce in the back under the canvas tarpaulin and my father would mumble to himself in his drunken half-sleep.

When I was not in school, I would often make the rounds with my father as he plied his trade in Lansing. Hotels were among his biggest customers and the stop at the old Downey was my favorite. Legislation was passed in the lobby, governors and senators were made and unmade in the bar. With Prohibition, the drinking moved upstairs and I would sit quietly in one of the leather chairs in the foyer, my feet dangling in front of me over the green marble floor, while my father transacted his business. I did not view him as a criminal. In those years, he was my only hero.

My father's business, however, was not one that favored heroes, particularly those who drank too much. As Prohibition wore on, the free market of the crossriver trade gave way to a net of cartels, complete with assigned territories and complex commercial rules. Lev Bernstein and the Purple Gang were at the center of the web, operating out of the back alleys and crowded tenements of Detroit's east side. One of their early victims said they were as purple as spoiled meat. When there was movement on the web, whether it was bootlegging, extortion, insurance fraud, or hijacking, the Purples felt it and responded. With over five hundred murders to their credit, they were particularly good at discouraging competition.

On a sunny Saturday morning as we were setting up our stand at the market, my father was given the opportunity to work for the Purples. Their proposal was a simple one. For a reasonable twenty percent off the top, my father could continue with his business under their protection. Lev Bernstein delivered the invitation personally. I had no idea who he was. But I watched him as he talked with my father. Perhaps it was because he was so unremarkable. He was slim and of medium height, with thick black hair and brown eyes, flecked with amber. He wore a crisply starched white shirt, open at the neck, and a pair of gray trousers with sharp, cleanly defined creases. He looked for all the world like a bored young mailman, making his rounds.

When my father finally declined his proposition, Bernstein merely nodded and walked away toward a Cadillac sedan parked on the side street next to our stand. The driver opened the car's rear door for him and he sat down in the back seat quietly and looked straight ahead. My father remarked that he appeared to be a very polite man. A sensible man. A businessman, like any other.

That evening the two smugglers came back from their run without a cargo. King Canada had refused my father's money, without explanation and without regret. The situation was the same with the other major suppliers, and my father ultimately was compelled to work his way through the labyrinth of inlets and coves that lined the Canadian side of the river.

He began picking up odd lots from the small operators who backed their trucks down to the water's edge and sold to all comers. The transactions were conducted swiftly, since the Canadian coast was notoriously dangerous. The parties counted the money out and loaded the cases into the boat in a matter of minutes. The sellers often made side arrangements with the hijackers and signaled them by flashlight when a boat carrying a full load was on its way across.

My father knew the risk. But he persisted. His fear of another failure outweighed all other fears. When he and Peter left me at the market, he would squeeze my shoulder, take a swig from his bottle, and walk to the battered truck without looking back. I would run behind the truck until it turned onto the street and disappeared into the darkness.

Then I would wait, huddled in a blanket against one of the warehouses that lined the market, until they returned, wet and exhausted from the pull across the river. I would run to my father and he would hold me again. But his face would be set and tired and his mumbles would turn to moans on the slow drive west to our farm.

One August evening, they did not return. I stayed silently at our stall all night and all the next morning. When panic finally overwhelmed me, I sought out the fattish beat cop who patrolled the market. He was sitting on a folding kitchen chair in the shade of one of the warehouses. In front of him was a card table piled with food, his spoils for the day. He ate steadily as he listened to me. When I finished, he looked at me for a moment. Then he simply waved me away. Ultimately, though, he agreed, in exchange for all of our produce, to drive me to the old Beaubien police station. And there I found my brother.

Peter sat on a long wooden bench at the front of the station. He was alone and the flood of police business eddied around him. He clasped his arms over his chest and rocked back and forth with a slow deliberate rhythm. When I sat down next to him, he glanced at me once with no movement of his head and then he looked up at the tin ceiling. His voice when he finally spoke was as parched and fine-grained as sandpaper.

"Dad's gone," he said. "I'm supposed to wait here until they find him, his body."

It was as if a door had swung shut, out of my sight and hearing and now I could only push at it, childishly. When Peter began to talk, he spoke without inflection or pause. With each word, that door became more firmly shut.

The run to Windsor had been routine. So was the pickup. But when Peter rowed the lugger out into the river for the return trip, a sleek dun powerboat roared suddenly out of the fog and cut its engines alongside the lugger. The man at the wheel wore a silvery gray suit and a matching fedora. His voice hung on the mist as he ordered my father and brother to load the cases of whiskey into the larger boat. My father dropped one of the cases, but the man only laughed at his drunken clumsiness.

After they finished, the man in gray emptied his tommygun into the wooden rowboat at the waterline. When the boat finally sank, my father clutched at Peter and began to thrash in the darkness of the river, alcohol and panic fueling his struggles.

"At first I thought we'd make it easy," Peter said. His voice was now a curious singsong, and he looked up at the ceiling while he rocked.

"Then I started to get tired and I swallowed some water. I let go of Dad just for a minute to rest, and he grabbed me and we both went under. I couldn't get behind him and I couldn't see. He was kicking and I was kicking and then he just stopped. Maybe I hit him down there."

He gave me another slanting, sideways glance. "I had to. Otherwise we'd of both drowned," he said.

I knew then that the door would never again open and I began to sob. I had loved him so and now he had left me. But no one in the station paid me the slightest attention and after a short time I stopped.

My father's body washed ashore the next day on Peche Island. My mother took the bus to Detroit and we all drove home together. The three of us were jammed in the front of the truck and my father was wrapped in the tarpaulin in the back. His body was beginning to bloat, and the skin of his face and hands was puckered and whitish gray. We buried him quickly, and Peter and I never again spoke of the circumstances of Sam Cahill's death. But the Irish sickness, that was there with us both. An old and treasured family friend. Always there. Always welcoming. Always comforting. *Until now,* I thought.

⇒ 19 ⇐

The Winter Wind

January, 1946

It took the federal jury exactly ten minutes the following week to find Otto Lammers guilty of unlawful flight to avoid testifying. And it took Hamilton Richards less than half that time to decide to take an appeal. He came right to the point.

"I'm not letting Lammers testify against Fleming," he said as we walked down the steps of the Detroit federal building into the steady wind. "I can convince any fair judge that with an appeal pending we could win, his jury testimony could still be used against him," he said.

Street pulled the collar of his chesterfield up around his neck and bent forward against the wind. His hair was ruffled and he stamped his feet on the icy sidewalk. "It'll be a cold day in hell when Storey buys that argument," he said.

Richards looked at him oddly. "Seen this morning's *Free Press*?" Street shook his head. "Justice Viney died yesterday. Storey's the odds-on favorite to replace him. The governor said he'd make the appointment within a week. You're going to have a new grand juror, once Storey goes up to the Supremes."

The sky to the west was a flat gray. Small hard pellets of snow slanted down through the canyons of concrete and stone and formed a delicate white lace on the dark fur collar of Street's topcoat.

"A Canadian clipper's coming," he said to Richards. "Those storms start way up there in Canada and come piling down here across the lakes. Interesting to think about all that power coming out of all that emptiness and then ending up caught between all these tall buildings like the rest of us."

"I don't need a weather report," Richards said. "You've got your indictments in the Fleming case. But Lammers isn't testifying at that trial. No good judge will permit it."

Street blew on his hands. I could see him back on his father's farm. Leaning into the wind as it forced its way in across Lake Michigan. Trudging through the morning chores. Stomping his feet against the stiff ground. Cupping his hands to his face for the brief warmth of his breath. Farmers hate winter, I know, and in particular they hate the storms that howl in to block the roads and trap them in their drafty barns and farmhouses. A farmer lives for growing things. In winter, it is only chapped hands, empty fields, blowing snow, and endless repairs. In winter, the farmer lives with naked trees. He lives with the frozen corn stubble poking through the snow cover. And he lives with the winter wind. Wailing and whistling and winnowing out his soul. Farmers hate the wind because it is always there, cold and cruel.

"Let's get the hell out of this weather," Street said and we tramped down Randolph, dodging hurrying pedestrians and swirling sheets of newspaper, shielding our faces from the blowing dust and the sting of the driven snow. Richards remained behind us on the steps of the courthouse.

As Maloney pulled our car up alongside us, Street cupped his hands and yelled back to Richards, against the wind. "Who said anything about a good judge?"

WHEN WE reached Lansing, we made our way through the building storm to Storey's chambers. He was as uncompromising as the west wind. "I've already talked to the governor," Storey said. "He's offered me the appointment to the Supreme Court and I'm going to take it."

Street slammed his fist down on the polished mahogany of Storey's desk and the toy soldiers lined up in their tight formation toppled forward, casualties of war. "Shit, Leon, you can't do that," Street said. "McReynolds and Fleming are right out of the same chamberpot. The governor knows I'm onto this Liquor Control Commission thing. Who knows, he may even be involved himself."

"That's preposterous. Governor McReynolds is above reproach. I've known him for years."

"So have I," Street said. "He was a great secretary of state. Every year he made exactly the right decision on what color license plates to have. As a governor, he presided over all this crap, while guys like Charlie were getting shot to hell. What makes you think he wants it all to come out now?"

Storey rearranged the precise array of objects on his desk. His ceremonial gavel and lacquered letter opener. His polished brass pen set and leatherbound calendar. The carefully framed picture of his wife and daughters. And the tightly shut cigar humidor. He ignored the fallen soldiers and dismissed Street's argument with a stiff smile.

"That's enough, Hubbell," he said. "This is my only chance for the Court. I'll help you all I can from there. But I'm not turning it down just so you can hang Fleming and McReynolds."

Street seized the opportunity, just as we had discussed on the long ride back from Detroit. "I don't need your help from the Supreme Court," he said. "I need it right now. Appoint a trial judge now for the Fleming case. One I can live with."

"What about Judge Stellinger?"

Harris Stellinger was Ingham County's other circuit court judge. It was a delicate point and one that Street had anticipated. "Fleming knew there'd be a Supreme Court vacancy and he knew the governor would appoint Storey," he had said to me earlier as we thawed out on the drive home. "Hell, he probably set it up. That's why he was so quick to waive the preliminary examination and go right to trial. He knew Storey'd be long gone. We gotta have the right trial judge."

"You were ready to argue that a grand juror can try his own cases. Why not Stellinger?" I had asked.

Street snorted. "Harris Stellinger's a hole looking for a dough-nut. He couldn't judge a cookie-cutting contest. He'd prob-ably buy Richards' self-incrimination argument. I've got to have

Lammers' testimony to get Fleming. I may have to live with Stellinger as the grand juror. I sure as hell don't have to live with him as the trial judge in the Fleming case. I want a hanging judge."

"I just know you've got someone in mind."

"Damn right I do," Street had said, and he rubbed his hands together in mock glee. "I want Stanislaus Thaddeus Syzmanski." He had rolled the words out lovingly. "He thinks the constitution is like the bible. You don't read it. You just hold it to your chest and mumble the words along with the preacher. Every prosecutor loves St. Stainless."

"There's an inherent conflict in having a grand juror try his own cases," he now said to Storey. His tone was solemn and sincere. "Judge Stellinger's got to be the new grand juror. This investigation's too important to be compromised." As Street leaned forward across the desk toward Storey, he picked up the small soldiers in their painted Scottish kilts and reformed them into careful rank and file.

"No, I was thinking Judge Syzmanski from Detroit would be perfect," he said. "He tried some of the cases coming out of the Ferguson grand jury and he did a fine job. He's fair and he's got a good legal mind." Street glanced at me and I looked down at the floor, then up at the ceiling.

Storey hesitated and then Street played his trump. "There's one other thing. We both know there's been a leak since the day this got underway. I finally got Maloney to tail the guy I thought was doing it. Maloney saw him giving copies of the grand jury transcripts to one of Fleming's goons."

"Who is it?"

Street walked slowly over to the window and watched the snow filter down. "John Danto," he said. "Your court reporter." He said nothing at all about Hennessey.

Storey's face crumpled as he saw his dreams of glory vanishing in the storm. He knew that if there were even a rumor that his own court reporter was selling secret grand jury testimony, his appointment to the Supreme Court would be only a wish and a memory.

"What do you propose we do?" he asked. His voice was as tight as his face.

"Not a damn thing. Your replacement will get John. I'll feed him some dummy stuff to pass along to Fleming. It'll keep him off balance."

Street walked back to his chair and sprawled out, linking his hands comfortably behind his head. "Unless of course you want to go public with this," he said. He was so elaborately casual that there was only a momentary flash of steel.

"I don't think that would be wise under the circumstances. I'll get Syzmanski appointed as the trial judge in the Fleming case. Then we'll be done with this whole sorry mess," Storey said.

Street reached into the pocket of his suit coat. "I took the liberty of preparing an order before we came over," he said. Storey reddened only slightly as Street slid the typed page over the orderly expanse of that broad desk. He signed and dated the document quickly.

"I look forward to the day when you appear before me when I'm on the Court," Storey said.

"So do I, Leon. So do I." Street folded the order and handed it to me. Then he patted his suit coat pocket. "Particularly since I've got a signed statement from your little Johnny boy right here for safekeeping."

As we walked to the door, I looked back at Storey. He jabbed methodically at his small soldiers, batting them over one at a time. We passed John Danto in the corridor and Street gave him a friendly smile.

"Good to see you, Mr. Street," Danto said.

"Good to see you too, John. I think the judge may want to talk to you. Don't worry though. You've got a friend in court," Street said. He patted Danto once on the shoulder. The little man bobbed his head and scurried into Storey's chambers.

"Life's a puzzle and timing is all, don't you think? Now we can feed every damned lie we can think of to Fleming through Hennessey *and* Danto," Street said as we walked down the stairs and out into the storm. "Maybe it'll confuse him some. You know, Yeats was right. Sometimes you can't tell the dancer from the dance."

⇒ 20 ⇐

Stainless

January, 1946

From the beginning, the leaders of Ingham County worried that Lansing might come to dominate the everyday workings of their oddly named county. At first, almost by accident but then by design, they maintained Mason, a tiny farming community southeast of Lansing, as the county seat. It was in the Mason courthouse that Judge Syzmanski determined to hold the Fleming conspiracy trial. In part, a desire to remove the trial from the influence of the capital may have motivated him. No doubt he was also acting out of simple self-interest. The Mason court was free of the peeling paint and the unreliable plumbing of the downtown courts. When Syzmanski had first come to Lansing in February, he looked around the crowded, shabby lobby of City Hall and shook his head. "Reminds me of Detroit," he said. "Great place for a murder."

The Mason courthouse, by contrast, was a model of rural probity. It was a twentieth-century temple of civic virtue, somber and solid in the classicism of its Doric columns, carved stone garlands, and gray mansard roof. A bronze eagle soared over the dome, and the clock that faced out onto the public square was stopped perpetually at noon. Huge varnished doors on the ground floor protected those who transacted the people's business from the wind that whistled across the flat farmlands surrounding the county seat. Judge Syzmanski took the circuit courtroom on the second floor, where the lawyers generated the only wind. He was a sturdy, proper man with graying hair, apple-red cheeks, and guileless brown eyes. He was endlessly patient and unfailingly pleasant. And he combined the soul of an inquisitor with a brain of the thickest oak.

Hamilton Richards was in trouble from the beginning. "Your honor," he said, "we're here on my motion to restrict any questions of my client to matters that do not involve the possibility of self-incrimination."

Richards made the mistake of pausing to glance at his notes and the judge broke in immediately. "But Mr. Lammers has been given immunity in this case. How can he possibly incriminate himself?" Syzmanski's voice was reassuringly clear and strong as he beamed innocently at Richards.

"The immunity extends only to this case. A federal jury convicted Mr. Lammers for unlawful flight to avoid giving testimony. We've filed an appeal and that conviction can be reversed. A new trial might be ordered. Then the testimony he gives here in the Fleming trial could be used against him in a new trial down there."

"It's all pretty confusing, Mr. Richards. And pretty remote." Syzmanski blinked gently and then turned to Street. "What does the special prosecutor have to say?"

Street lumbered to his feet and ran his fingers through the tousled mop of his hair. Then he spoke to the judge as he would to a cherished boyhood friend. And he kept it simple.

"Your honor, the fact is there's just no logical connection between the testimony that Mr. Lammers will give in this case and the charges in the federal case. All the U.S. Attorney had to do down there in Detroit was establish that Lammers was a material witness in this case. Then he had to show Lammers fled the state to avoid giving testimony. That took about two minutes. Even if a new trial is granted down there, no testimony that Lammers gives in this case against Fleming can change anything. How could he possibly incriminate himself?"

In fact, the law was strongly against us and Street knew it. The privilege against self-incrimination is one of the law's great shibboleths, a constitutionally enshrined prohibition against forcing a man to convict himself with his own words. Its roots are in the revulsion against the fire and iron of the ecclesiastical courts of the dark ages. Now we look back with horror on the scorched flesh, mangled joints, and broken limbs that marked the tortured passage of heretics back to the true faith.

Had Syzmanski been a scholar, he would have recoiled from Street's argument. And our case against Fleming would have collapsed that morning. Fortunately, the judge was on the side of the angels. "Mr. Richards," he said, and his eyes twinkled with good humor. "I'm going to deny your motion. Mr. Street will prepare the order."

Richards was on his feet immediately. "Will your honor grant an adjournment so I can appeal?"

Syzmanski stood. His face was full of grace. "No adjournments. This case is going to trial."

He swept down from the bench. The folds of his black robes masked his comfortable bulk as he shook hands with the lawyers. "Good to see you today, boys, good to see you," he said to each of us. His grip was firm and his fixed smile was positively cherubic. His skin was like translucent porcelain, only somewhat cracked by age.

"You gotta like Stainless," Street said to Richards as we left the courtroom. "Back when I was on the defense side, I used to go before him down in Detroit. He'd just kill me, but he's just so damn likable about it."

Richards put his hands on the polished rail that circled the open rotunda. "I hear Fleming's got a copy of Otto's testimony before the grand jury. You said there'd be no leaks. You promised him he wouldn't have to testify in open court against Fleming."

Street look up at the pastoral scenes painted on the frieze below the domed ceiling. "You ever notice the Spirit of Liberty looks like a cheerleader? Big tits and nice legs?"

He took a step closer to Richards and his voice hardened. "I never promised Lammers he wouldn't have to testify. I said we'd take it one step at a time. What the hell do you think we're paying him for? And I'd be real careful about how cozy I got with Wade Fleming. That man's got friends that'll swat you like a fly."

"I'm not afraid of Fleming. But Lammers is," Richards said. "He says you promised to protect him. But you're going the exact other way. I hope you sleep well at night."

"The sleep of the just. Tell your boy that Romeo's still waiting for him over there at the county farm. Thinks Otto would be a nice little Juliet. Now, all's Otto got to do is put on his show one more time. Then we'll let him retire. Like Lou Gehrig."

"Lou Gehrig's dead," Richards said. "I want to keep Lammers alive." He walked down the cast-iron stairs and out the towering oak doors into the winter wind. We watched him through the clear glass until the twilight obscured him.

⧿ 21 ⧽

Trench Warfare

January, 1946

We feared another Depression that winter. But the economy was actually building up under our feet toward an enormous explosion of postwar production. It would be an upheaval that would shatter the old political and moral contours and remake the topography of our lives. Through it all, the moving force would be the government that had vanquished our foreign enemies and would now make friends of us all.

Hubbell Street had a profoundly different view of the government. He was preparing to make the wonderful, dangerous state government that dominated our city an additional defendant in our conspiracy trial. I had no objections. All I wanted was to live out my life with Sarah, safe and unnoticed. And I wanted Fleming and Hennessey and their men to pay for what they did to my brother. The two tied nicely together and I had no scruples about methods. If Fleming went down for the wrong crime, there would be some rough justice to it. And that would be justice enough.

"It's simple," Street said to me as Maloney drove us through the snow back to Lansing. "This case'll be a trial within a trial. I'll try Fleming for conspiracy. But what I'm really trying him for is murder and corruption. I'll try him for murdering poor old Harry Maynard while he was corrupting the Liquor Control Commission. I'll try him for buying votes on the liquor legislation. I'll try him for selling the people's government to the highest bidder. The defense'll object, but it all goes to motive."

"Motive's irrelevant in a conspiracy case." I sought to slow him down, if only to assure that his ends and mine were equally served.

"You're a walking damn advertisement for the Michigan Law Review. I know that and so do Fleming's lawyers. What I'm counting on is that Syzmanski doesn't know shit about the law. Or if he does, he's forgotten. Or maybe he's just too damn dumb to care. Whatever one it is, all I've got to do is put this stuff before the jury. If Vanik and Lammers deliver, I'll get the convictions and that's all that matters."

I saw my brother's broken face and broken life and I remembered well who had beaten him so savagely. "What about Lefkowitz and Shrieber?" I said nothing of Hennessey.

"I'll try them for every job the Purples every pulled. The jury'll think those little yids are worse than Al Capone. And they'll be right."

He turned to me and turned the heat up a notch or two. "One thing I want you to do every day of the trial. Pick up Sarah Maynard every morning and take her home every night. Put her right behind the rail, on our side. In her widow's weeds. I want the jury to see her cry."

"She'll never do that," I said. *We can't do that,* I thought.

"The hell she won't. I've already asked her and she's agreed."

He had missed my point, but I did not correct him. "Why not Maloney or someone else from the state police detail?"

"You're her wounded hero. She asked me to have you drive her. It was the night of the Charity Ball. When I pitched her on being at the trial." I could see Sarah's smile. How convenient that Street had arranged for us to be together every day. How perfectly proper. And how incredibly dangerous.

WHEN WE reached the hotel, Street turned to the business at hand. In anticipation of the Fleming trial, Syzmanski had enlarged the venire, the pool of prospective jurors, to one hundred fifty citizens and we had received the list of names. There was one man, with the unlikely name of James Sixtas, who concerned us. He had phoned Street, full of righteous indignation and claiming that a pair of men in Wade Fleming's hire had questioned him.

"How do you know Sixtas?" I asked Street.

"Jimmy Six? I beat Hennessey on his kid's breaking and entering. Little matter of a couple truckloads of mattresses from a furniture warehouse. Greeks have a sense of obligation. Jimmy's returning the favor. Fleming's boys are lucky Jimmy didn't do a number on them right there in his front yard. Let's just pretend we don't have that jury list yet. Jimmy's not off limits until we get it. Give him a call and get him over here."

When Sixtas arrived, he told us he had actually invited Fleming's legmen into his home and served them coffee. "They think I'm one of them Mustache Petes," he said to Street. "I'm insulted by them. That Sangster, he used to be a cop."

"What did they want to know?"

"They ask me how old I am. Where did I go to church. Who did I vote for. They say they're investigators for the court. But I know better."

He had straight thick hair, streaked with gray, a proud hooked nose, and a black suit shiny with age. His face was brown and deeply lined. "They give me a paper," he said and he handed Street a copy of the *Lansing Reporter*, a weekly political gossip sheet. I saw the headline: "Political Witchhunt."

"One other thing," Sixtas said. "They ask me if I know Senator Maynard. I tell them no. But I remember him. He was the one who always wanted little girls."

After Sixtas left, Street tapped his fingers lightly on the metal of his desk. "Did you ever try his produce?" he asked.

"He's a grocer?"

"Sort of. He runs a string of cathouses. That's how he knew that cop. Jimmy was probably giving him the run of his place down on Turner Street in return for some protection. And I'll bet that's how he knew Maynard." I said nothing at all. I knew all I needed to know about Harry Maynard.

"This thing's a sideshow," Street said. "You handle it. Get a show cause and go after Sangster for contempt."

"Do you want a new jury panel?"

"Hell no. I hope every person in the jury pool read the damn thing. Think ahead, Charlie. They've set me up for some great voir dire. If I don't like the answers, I can challenge for cause and save my perempts. Wade Fleming's just given me a little present for Valentine's Day. I sure as sweet Jesus don't want to send it back."

Street was describing the elaborate trench warfare that takes place before the beginning of every jury trial. Jury selection is combat and peremptory challenges are the queens of battle, lethal and precious. They can be used any time during the selection process without explanation. But once used, they are gone. In the Fleming trial, each of the three defendants would have fifteen perempts and we would have the same total. They were an asset we would use only at the crucial moment.

By contrast, challenges for cause are foot soldiers. Their supply is inexhaustible. But their effectiveness is limited. Few judges are anxious to rule a prospective juror unfit to carry out the law's oldest function. By approaching the veniremen in advance of the trial and creating a possible prejudice, Fleming had apparently armed us with a weapon, a showing of cause for removal from the jury that we could use at our discretion and with telling effect.

As STREET instructed, I dutifully secured a show cause order from Syzmanski, directing Roger Sangster to appear in court to show the judge why he should not be held in contempt for seeking to prejudice the prospective jurors. The hearing was a short one. Sangster took the stand, swore his oath, and gave his name. Then he refused to answer any of my questions.

Syzmanski blinked, smiled, and leaned forward across the high oak bench. "Did you bring your toothbrush, Mr. Sangster?"

"Sir?"

"I hope you brought your toothbrush because you're going to need it." Syzmanski slammed his gavel. "Thirty days, contempt of court," he said.

One of Sangster's former officers, now assigned to Syzmanski as his bailiff, led Sangster off into the holding pen. He looked back toward the courtroom. His eyes were wide and staring, like those of a steer being led into the chute at the slaughterhouse. But there was no help coming for him. Once he was a cop and now he was going to jail. He knew what was in store.

I was packing my briefcase, awkwardly, when there was a light touch on my left shoulder. I turned in annoyance and it was Wade Fleming. He was shorter than I. Compact. Honed. Machined. His hair was beautifully barbered and his double-breasted sharkskin suit clung to him. His mouth was full, almost sensual. His upper lip, on the right side, had the thin line of an old scar.

When he spoke, his words were slightly slurred. But his voice was low and mannered. And he lifted that lip in a smile twisted with permanent contempt. "Tell Governor Street I said hello. Tell him it won't be so easy from here on in," he said.

I saw my brother's face. "Tell him yourself, Fleming. You'll be seeing a lot of him." I turned to go and again there was that light touch.

"So much anger," Fleming said. The slur was more pronounced. "It was only business with your brother. He was a fool to deceive me. Ask your friend Hennessey. And tell Street that I'm tired of this stupidity. I've hired a new lawyer. You'll both like him."

He brushed his hand across my shoulder. "Nice suit," he said. "Was it the same one you wore to Sarah Maynard's house that morning?" His smile broadened and the slanting line across his lip was red against his skin. His teeth were white and even, just as Peter's had been.

Initial Skirmishes

January, 1946

My head throbbed and my stomach churned when we picked Sarah up the next day for the opening of the trial. At best, I was a badly hung-over lawyer. At the very least, she was the model of the grieving widow. Her hair was caught back in a severe bun and crowned with a black pillbox and a matching veil. Behind the fine black netting, her face was pale and composed. Sarah waved to the girl in the window of her home and then waved off my apologies for the condition of the car. It was one of our unmarked state police vehicles and I hadn't had a chance to clean it. Maloney was in the driver's seat, inspecting his finger-nails, and I gestured to him.

"I brought the sergeant along to keep us company," I said. With Maloney in the car, I couldn't say anything about Fleming. And that was fine. The fear and the sickness were so strong that I could think of nothing at all to say.

"You're right on time and ever so proper," Sarah said to me. "Can we stop and say hello to my mother before we go?" I nodded, and we drove the five blocks to the spacious Tudor home that Joshua St. Clair had built for his family in a quiet East Lansing subdivision. When we pulled into the driveway, she placed her gloved hand on my shoulder.

"Wait here. I'll be just a moment," she said. I watched her walk up to the house through the slush that covered the driveway. Then I watched the branches of the oak trees sway and shift in the wind. They too were dressed in widow's weeds.

"How is she?" I asked when she returned to the car.

She looked at Maloney, then she looked at me and shrugged. "This was a bad day. Let's go. We don't want to be late for my grand entrance."

She turned her head toward the window while we drove to the court in a heavy silence. The courthouse was jammed, and when we entered there was the anticipated stir. Syzmanski's bailiff had turned the small civil jury box into a bullpen for the press, and Rachel Loeb gave me a knowing grin as I maneuvered Sarah into the seat we had reserved for her squarely behind the prosecution's table. Fleming, Lefkowitz, and Shrieber were seated with their battery of lawyers to our right. They did not look up as I walked around the rail into the arena. When Street arrived, he made a great show of solicitude for the widow, winked at me, waved at Rachel Loeb, and then dropped his battered briefcase on the counsel table with a solid thump. He was clearly ready.

As Syzmanski took the bench and we took our seats, one of Fleming's lawyers stayed on his feet. "May it please the court," he said. "I have a preliminary matter. The defendants have recently retained additional counsel. I would like to move his admission *pro hac vice* to practice before this court for the duration of the trial." I winced at the Latin, but Syzmanski beamed. He was no doubt the product of a parochial education.

Fleming's lawyer gestured to the far end of the crowded defense table. I leaned forward, for all I could see was a row of seated men. Then the seat at the end moved out of the phalanx and I realized that it was a high-backed wheelchair. Seated in it was an erect, broad-shouldered man in a dark blue tailored suit. His trousers were carefully folded back beneath the stumps of his legs. Just below the knees. He looked up at the judge and said, "Joel Haricot for the defense, your honor."

Syzmanski immediately called us into chambers for a conference. It was the standard reaction of a startled judge. As we gathered up our documents, Rachel Loeb leaned over the rail to Street.

"Who the hell is Joel Haricot?" she asked.

"Christ, Rachel. Don't you read the papers? He's the top goddamn mob lawyer in the country and if you quote me, you're buyin' dinner."

I knew of Joel Haricot. Most lawyers knew of him. He had lost his legs and won the Silver Star in the First World War, and he fought his courtroom battles with the same relentless ferocity as he had fought the Germans. He handled only criminal defense work and he was absolutely committed to his clients. They generally shared only two traits. They always expected to pay big fees. And they always expected to walk free, out of the front door of the courthouse, at the end of the trial. Haricot rarely disappointed them on either ground.

When we were seated in the office that Syzmanski had borrowed for the trial, the judge looked at Street over the square rims of the glasses he wore when he was not on the bench.

"Do you have an objection if Mr. Haricot is admitted for this case?" he asked.

"No, your honor. I've sat on the same counsel table with Joel before. It'll be a privilege and a pleasure to have him on the other side," Street said. He leaned over to Haricot's chair and shook hands warmly. The two men were frozen there for a moment. Street slouched forward and Haricot sat straight as a sword. Then the battle was joined.

"I understand there's a problem with the jury panel," Haricot said. "I suggest we just start over with a new panel and remove any possible taint. I'm sure Mr. Street will agree."

It was Street's turn to look startled. "Nossir," he said, "nossir, I damn well don't agree. We can't get a new panel until the next term and that'll delay the trial for months."

Haricot cut in. "I have today filed a number of motions, dealing with that matter, among others," he said. He gestured to one of the lawyers standing behind him who silently handed Street an inch-thick pile of documents.

"Your honor, we contend that Mr. Fleming and the other defendants cannot possibly receive a fair trial. There has been

extensive publicity throughout the state that the special prosecutor has inspired largely to create such prejudice that no fair,
impartial trial can be had," Haricot said.

Street was on his feet and braying, but Haricot would not
be deterred. "There has been misconduct by the prosecution. They've coerced testimony. They've purchased testimony.
The special prosecutor and the grand juror have worked in
tandem to achieve their own political interests. Judge Storey has
received his reward and Hubbell Street still pursues his. He has
timed this trial to coincide perfectly with the filing date for the
Republican primary for governor."

"That's a goddamn lie," Street shouted. "Anybody who wants
to be governor of this state is crazier'n you are."

Syzmanski threw up his hands. "Gentlemen, no personalities, no personalities, please."

He clasped his hands in front of his ample stomach and
leaned back in his chair. "It's very warm in here and I want some
time to think," he said. "We'll take a recess for the rest of the
morning. Then you can argue your motions on the record." He
flipped his hand at us in a gesture of dismissal.

WE PORED over Haricot's filing in the small lawyers' room off
the courtroom. There was an affidavit from the young Detroit
policeman describing my interview with Vanik. There was an
accounting of the expenditures of the grand jury, including the
payments that flowed through the state police to Otto Lammers.
There was a verbatim transcript of Street's press conference,
with his references to Fleming and the Purple Gang underscored
in red. And there was a carefully indexed set of newspaper arti-
cles and editorials praising the special prosecutor and excori-
ating the graft that he had uncovered. Street looked up from the
mass of documents and sighed.

"You know the definition of conscience?" he asked. Then he
answered his own question. "Conscience is the small voice in the

middle of the night that says somebody may be watchin'. Well, somebody sure as hell was watchin' us."

"Do you think Syzmanski will buy it?"

"Hard to tell. Stainless likes things simple and this sure ain't simple. He may sit on it a while."

Street heaved himself to his feet and when the judge gaveled the court back into session that afternoon, he proceeded to defeat his own prediction. After Haricot made his case, Street argued for two hours. He never glanced down at a note as he prowled in front of the counsel table. He never conceded a point. And he never missed a beat. He laughed at Haricot's political arguments. He blasted his affidavits and he disputed his accounting. When Street finished, he had Stanislaus Thaddeus Syzmanski. He had him cold and he had him convinced. During Haricot's rebuttal, the judge leaned back in his chair. His eyes were half closed and I knew we had won.

"Mr. Haricot," Syzmanski said. "I'm going to deny your motions, deny them all. I'll see you all tomorrow morning for the jury pick."

⇒ 23 ⇐

High Court

January, February, 1946

But we were not in Mason the next day to pick a jury. We were in the chambers of the Supreme Court of Michigan to pick up our case. Haricot's men had served us early the next morning with his papers and they were startling. He sought a year's delay in the trial, a change of venue, and Street's disqualification. He wrapped the whole package together with an application for the extraordinary writ of mandamus, the lightning bolt of judicial command tossed by a high court at errant trial judges who wander into error and abuse. The Supreme Court had granted Haricot's emergency application for leave to appeal and entered a stay of the trial while the appeal was pending. But the justices did not rule on the substance of his motions. Most remarkably, the court set oral arguments for February 1st, only three days hence.

Street was not at all amused. "Haricot expected to lose his motion at the trial level. He was planning all along to take it up to the Supremes. Before Syzmanski even ruled, Fleming had it wired for them to grant leave," he said.

Like all other members of the judiciary in Michigan, the justices of the Supreme Court are elected officials and they mix the oil of politics with the water of the law on a regular basis. In those years, there were eight justices and four of them were beholden to Fleming for their nominations. Indeed, it was widely believed that the Republican nominating conventions were actually held in Fleming's hotel suites. Storey, now ensconced as a sitting justice, would be required to recuse himself because of his prior involvement with the case. If we lost the other four Republicans, we were lost as well.

"I don't know how well I can brief this thing in three days," I said to Street.

"You keep wantin' to play by the rules," he said. "They'll never read the briefs. This one's pure politics. If they think Fleming's on his way down, they'll let it go to trial. If they think he's still strong, we're fucked and fucked again."

He lunged for the phone. "I'm going to see Storey. *Ex parte*'s a game I can play better'n Fleming."

Street said later that his meeting with Storey was like skating on a frozen lake in January. The ice, he said, was smooth as glass. And Storey had good reason to fear the cold breath of scandal. If his new colleagues found prosecutorial misconduct in a case he had supervised as the grand juror, it would be beyond embarrassment for him. It would be anathema.

Street said that he tactfully avoided mentioning John Danto's admissions. He merely laid Danto's statement on Storey's desk with his other papers.

"You should've seen Ironpants try to read that thing upside down," he said. "He damn near broke his neck."

With very little additional prompting, Storey had volunteered to circulate the transcript of Lammers' grand jury testimony among the justices. When Street returned, he was in high good humor.

"Haricot's gonna be tryin' me for cuttin' a few corners," he said. "I'll be tryin' Wade Fleming for conspiring to kill a man. I should win that one."

The argument before the court was all hushed civility and elaborate charade. Appellate courts do not see the blood and the dirt of trial by combat. The high drama and the low comedy of the arena are lost in the dry pages of the transcript. These courts sit above the battle. They deal with thought, not action, and their proceedings are only lightly laced with passion. The ropes of precedent bind them tightly and they make their way forward blindfolded, muzzled by the record below, and trapped in the past.

Our court's chambers were then on the third floor of the Capitol and they were a secular temple, the home church of the law. Corinthian columns soared to the high ceilings in the entablature behind the robed justices. Smoky-grained, wooden benches for the assembled penitents marched back in rows to the rear of the room. It was not until years later, after I had appeared before the court many times, that a cynical clerk told me that in reality the pillars supported nothing more than their own weight. And that the magnificent dark walnut was actually only cheap pine with a coat of fake graining.

Storey was not on the bench. But he sat stiffly in the first pew and stared straight at the chief justice, who nodded pleasantly at Street and Haricot as they rehashed the trial court arguments, now tightly reasoned and buttressed with citations.

"Starr's falling asleep," Street whispered to me when he finished. "They've already decided the case." The justices filed out to confer after Haricot completed his rebuttal. It was a silent, solemn processional of the temple priests. They were back in ten minutes and Chief Justice Starr peered down at us from the altar.

"Mr. Haricot, we are not impressed with your position. There has been no showing that a fair and impartial trial cannot be had at this time. We find no abuse of judicial power by the trial judge. And no reason to issue a writ of mandamus. I was personally opposed"—and here he glanced earnestly at his colleagues as they sat with heads bowed and hands clasped—"I was personally opposed to hearing this matter at all. Your motions are denied. A written decision will be issued this afternoon."

With a little help from Storey, Street had turned the Court around and the justices had turned Haricot down. It would take a little time, but we would be back in business in Mason.

═ 24 ═

Deer Camp

February, 1946

Street was waiting for me at our offices the next morning. He
ignored my bloodshot eyes and the tremor in my hand. "Syzmanski's scheduled the jury pick for April Fool's Day," he said,
"so we can think a bit."

He paused and shook a cigarette out of a pack he carried
in his shirt pocket and then looked down at it. "Going to trial
always makes me crave nicotine. Anyway, say the trial takes
a month, until the end of April. What happens then? There's
plenty of folks out there dyin' to know. I don't want to keep them
in suspense."

I shook my head in honest confusion. I had given no thought
to anything that might follow the trial. For me, it was the stuff of
fantasy. Either we would convict Fleming and it would be over,
or we would lose and the truth would begin to seep out. Fleming
and Hennessey were not noted for their short memories or their
benevolence.

Street finally broke the silence. "It's easy. Tell Hennessey
and you tell the whole world. So here's what you tell him," he
said. "Tell him we're going to keep the grand jury going. We're
going to get a shitload of indictments. We're going to keep frog
marching people out of the grand jury room in handcuffs. Tell
him I think that if we indict a stooge a week until June, we might
make the world safe again for Republicans."

I had done at least some of my homework. I knew that June
18th was the day that Michigan law set for the party primaries
for governor.

"We'll run out of stooges by then," I said.

"There's one thing I've learned in this business. The criminal element never rests easy. There's an almost endless supply of coconuts over there in the Capitol with their hands out. They're just looking for a way to fall from grace. It would be almost sacrilegious not to help them along their way. Or at least that's what I want Hennessey to think."

"You want Hennessey to tell Fleming that you're going after more legislators." It was a statement, not a question. Even through the fog of my hangover, I thought I saw where Street was heading.

"Of course. It's not a bluff and who knows where it'll lead. I'm betting Harris Stellinger'll be no different than Leon Storey. He'll indict a ham sandwich if he thinks it'll get him some ink. We need to make sure the judge has a grasp of all the little nuances. We'll all do well if he approaches this in the right frame of mind."

After I passed Street's story to Hennessey in a muttered telephone conversation, Stellinger's secretary called to summon us over to City Hall. On cue, Street and I trudged up the stairs to the judge's quarters. After we chatted patiently with the bailiff, Stellinger's secretary waved us into his chambers as she explained to us that our new one-man grand juror had left for lunch. She expected him, she said brightly, to return at any time.

Street and I made a slow circuit of the office while we waited. All of Storey's memorabilia were gone and in their place were literally hundreds of pictures. The stigmata of politics now lined each wall. Everywhere there were pictures of the great and near great of the Republican party. They were inscribed, sometimes legibly, to everyone's good friend Harris Stellinger.

At the center of the array on the long north wall behind Stellinger's small government issue desk was a grainy black and white photo of three men. They were each dressed in elaborately casual hunting attire and kneeling behind the carcasses of their fresh-killed deer. The inscription at the bottom was handwritten in white ink. "Deer Camp, 1943," it said. Stellinger appeared to be delighted with his buck, as did Governor James McReynolds and State Treasurer Wade Fleming.

"Damned if I understand why a grown man would want to kill a poor dumb animal. And then have his picture taken," Street said as he stood beside me. "What's the sense in memorializing the crime?"

"Killing deer in Michigan isn't a crime. It's a way of life."

Street wasn't listening. He turned back toward the door of the office and walked rapidly across the room, his hand outstretched.

"Harris," he said, "it was good of you to ask us up here."

Stellinger stood in the doorway, his mouth slightly open and his head cocked to the right. He was a small, pale man with rounded shoulders, thinning gray hair, and a permanently puzzled look.

"I thought you were supposed to be here at one o'clock," he said. "My girl said you'd be here at one."

"Crossed wires, Harris. It happens all the time," Street said. "Point of fact, I'm usually running late, not early."

"I like to do things right, Street," Stellinger said. "That's one thing you should know about me. I like to do things right. Well, you're here now. Let's get down to business."

He gestured to the two chairs in front of the desk and then scuttled behind it. As he bent forward, he absently rearranged the neat, rectangular piles of paper in front of him on the desk, his mouth pursed. When we were duly seated, he began again.

"I've been going through the records of the grand jury, such as they are," he said. "They're not in order, not in order at all. How can you be paying all that money to Otto Lammers? Giving him room and board? Buying him liquor? Why, the man's a born liar. No jury will believe him."

"You'll have to trust me, Harris. I'll get a jury that will," Street said.

"They'll believe Wade Fleming sent those men to kill Senator Maynard? That he hired Lammers on the liquor legislation? That he was siphoning money off from the Liquor Control

Commission? Do you believe that?" Stellinger punctuated each question with a quick, irritable jab of his right forefinger.

Street shrugged. "Sure do," he said. "Just like I believe in home, flag, apple pie, mom, and Santa Claus. What the hell difference does it make what I believe? We'll prove those Purple Gang hebes conspired to kill Maynard. And we'll prove that Fleming ordered it."

"I'll thank you to show me some respect, Street. I'm the chief judge now and the one-man grand juror. I'm not going anywhere and you just better get used to it."

Street shrugged again. "How can you be so sure? Boyles and Starr are both gettin' a little long in the tooth. They could keel over any time. The next governor could get two appointments to the Supreme Court in his first term. You could be one of them. If we can work together down here, I'd say you've got a great judicial future ahead of you."

"No, no, I'm not interested in your silliness, Mr. Street. No thank you, no thank you very much."

Stellinger thrust his small hands forward, palms facing Street. "You may think you're the next governor. But you don't have a bit of support in the party. You'll never make it past the primary. I'll have nothing to do with you."

He made a half turn toward the pictures on his walls. "Besides," he said, "Governor McReynolds is a friend of mine. I would never turn on him like that."

Street rose up out of his chair and stood directly in front of Stellinger's desk. "Just because you drank some whiskey and shot up the woods together doesn't make you blood brothers," he said. "You're confusing politics with friendship and that's a big mistake. Fleming's going to prison. McReynolds'll do what's best for himself. You damn well better do the same. He's the past. I'm the future. Whose side are you on?"

Stellinger moved quickly to his left to increase the space between himself and Street. "I don't drink," he said. "And I don't care to be talked to like this. I'm a judge. What makes you think that you can just march in here and threaten me? And try to bribe me? I'll thank you to leave right now or I'll call the bailiff and have you thrown out."

"You may be a judge, but you're a bigger fool. You wouldn't know a bribe if one crawled up and bit you on the ankle."

Street gestured me toward the door. Then he lifted the front of Stellinger's desk upward until it crashed backward amid a cascade of paper. He took a step forward and plucked the framed photo of the deer kill of 1943 from the wall and smashed it twice against the sharp corner of the upended desk. He tossed the broken frame at Stellinger.

"Have your bailiff clean that up," he said. "It'll give him something to do when he's not shinin' your shoes or kissin' your ass."

≈ 25 ≈

Possibilities

February, 1946

John Danto was in our suite at the Olds early the next morning, shuffling his feet and rubbing his hands to take away the chill. After I offered him the obligatory cup of coffee, he reached into his jacket pocket and pulled out a plain envelope. He jabbed it stiffly at Street.

"Judge Stellinger said to give this to you personally," he said.

Street took the envelope and held it carefully between his thumb and forefinger. Then he lifted it to his nose. "It's got a bit of a smell to it," he said. "If you ask me, I think it smells a lot like wet socks and cold feet."

He opened his pocketknife, slit the top of the envelope, removed the single white sheet of paper, and flourished it with theatrical casualness. I knew him to be sensitive about his poor eyesight and when he reached into his vest pocket for his reading glasses, I realized that it was all an elaborate act. He had already guessed what was in Stellinger's letter.

Street nudged Danto in the ribs conspiratorially and said, "Old age is a curse, Johnny. You tell anybody I can't read up close, I'll cut your throat. People see age as a sign of weakness. And we can't have that."

Street peered for a moment at the letter and then carefully refolded it. "You and I will be joining the ranks of the unemployed," he said to me. "Judge Stellinger has decided that once the Fleming trial's over, our services will no longer be required."

"I'm assuming you're not surprised," I said. I was treading water, but I didn't want Street to know it. "You didn't exactly leave him on a high note."

"Well, we'll just see how much good being the governor's best friend will do him. I hear McReynolds is on the verge of making an announcement and it won't have a thing to do with the color of the license plates next year. Discretion being the better part of valor and all."

He turned quickly to Danto, pushing his body up against the court reporter and hooking his arm around the smaller man's neck. "I can count on you to keep what I'm saying between you and me, can't I? You know I buried that business with the transcripts for you when old Ironpants Storey wanted to hang you out to dry?"

Danto nodded vigorously. "Yessir, Mr. Street. You can trust me."

"I know I can. I surely know that. You've got such an honest face. And you're such an accomplished liar. We're just made for each other." He gave Danto a small shake.

"Because you know, Johnny, if I were to find out you were playin' both sides I might be, shall we say, displeased."

"I wouldn't do a thing like that, Mr. Street. You helped me and I kept my job. You can count on me," Danto said. He was so entirely earnest that I almost believed him.

"Of course I can, Johnny," Street said. "Now, tell me what Stellinger's up to. Who's he been talking to, that he's all of a sudden so high and mighty? I don't read him as a gambler. He's not somebody who up and fires his star prosecutor. He must have a hole card of some kind. Any idea what that might be?"

Danto rubbed his temple with his left hand and made a serious attempt to look as if he was concentrating. "He's been sending me over to some senator's office a lot, delivering records and things."

"What kind of records would those be?" Street sounded entirely disinterested, but he tightened his arm around Danto's neck.

"Grand jury stuff. The bills and all that. They've got some kind of special committee they're about to set up. The judge said there was a lot of graft involved in investigating graft. He said the senate was finally getting interested."

Street gave Danto another small, friendly shake. "Who's the senator?"

"Fellow from down in Macomb County, name of Lonergan. Seems like a nice man."

"Oh that he is, John. You tell Judge Stellinger you've delivered the message and there's no hard feelings. Tell him he might want to check in with his friends over there in the governor's office. He might learn something." Street walked Danto across the room and shut the door carefully behind him.

"He's going to tell Stellinger every word," I said.

"Sure as hell. That's just what I want him to do. Stellinger'll shit little green cumquats when he finds out McReynolds is about to call it a career."

"Do you mind if I ask how you know that?"

"I'll tell you this," Street said. "I've known Jim McReynolds for years. He's been around politics for a long time. He's learned the hard way you can't drive a tin lizzy without getting a little oil on your coveralls now and then."

"Everybody says he's going to run again," I said.

"The thing about this everybody guy is, he doesn't know jack shit. Thanks to Hennessey and Fleming, McReynolds is looking at me in his rearview mirror. He knows that once I'm finished with the legislature, he's next. And he's made up his mind that it's not worth it. When I heard he was contemplating an honorable retirement, I sent him a little message. Go quietly, I said, and you've got nothing to fear from me. But he wanted my resignation as special prosecutor. I said I'd go him one better. Get myself fired after the Fleming case is over. Stellinger performed on cue."

"You *wanted* Stellinger to fire you?"

"Hell, I was worried he wouldn't. He's got no balls at all. The poor little bastard's testicles have probably never descended. But now McReynolds'll know I held up my end. I expect we'll soon be seeing an announcement out of the governor's office. Life's full of little surprises like that along the way."

"What about an indictment a week? You can pretty much kiss that goodbye."

"I'm no cardsharp," Street said. "But even I know that you can fill a straight from either end. I wanted Hennessey and Fleming and all those other crooks to think I was going to keep the grand jury going. But I can be a crusader on the courthouse steps as easy as I can inside the courtroom. Easier maybe. It opens up all sorts of possibilities. Politics is changing. It's all about exposure now and I figure I can expose myself as well as anybody. That's why the Fleming case is such a gift. It's practically cosmic."

⇒ 26 ⇐

Standing Down

February, 1946

Governor McReynolds waited until Friday and then notified the political beat reporters that he would be holding a rare weekend news conference the next day. On Street's instructions, I slipped into the basement of the Capitol. Then I walked up the broad stairs to the governor's office on the second floor. I did my level best to fade into the elaborate handcarved woodwork. The reception area was filled with reporters, muttering about working on a Saturday when they could be sleeping off their hangovers. When the press aide opened the double doors to the inner office, I was able to jam my way into the back.

The inner office was a smallish, rectangular room dominated by a huge desk. It stood on a slightly elevated platform, flanked by two carefully furled flags, in front of the curtained window on the south wall. Two small penlights set in the high ceiling painted the flags with a soft glow. They played down on McReynolds as he sat behind the desk, his hands clasped meditatively in front of him. It was a warm day for winter and a ripe, musty smell hovered like a mist over the reporters packed into the room. McReynolds had practiced his trade for some while and he ignored the odor.

"Gentlemen, Miss Loeb," he said. "I have a short statement to make and then I'll take just a few questions."

Our governor had a round, bland face, beetling brows, a straight line of a mouth, pale skin, and a pained expression. He took a shallow little breath as if to gather himself. Then he looked down at the single sheet of paper on his desk and began to read, without emphasis or expression. "I asked you to come over today because I have decided not to seek re-election as governor." he said. "I've been in politics for some time now and I've enjoyed serving the people of this great state."

He paused, looked up, and smiled briefly. "I've had two good terms and I'll miss you all. But it's time for me to take a break and I intend to do so. Fortunately, there's no lack of qualified candidates in both parties. I know I'll be leaving the state in good hands."

He paused again and cleared his throat, a dull whinny. "I think that's all," he said. "Miss Loeb, you have a question?"

"Governor, there are rumors that Hubbell Street is looking into allegations about graft in connection with the branch banking bill and your role in that. Did this have anything to do with your decision not to run?"

McReynolds shifted in his chair and his face reddened. "I don't know what, if anything, Mr. Street was looking into. I do know that once that trial out in Mason is over, he'll no longer be the special prosecutor. Beyond that, I don't have any comment at all."

He turned to his right and pointed to a *Free Press* reporter. "You've made a living covering me and the capital. I'm sure you're just burning to ask one last question?"

"Is this your political swansong, governor?"

"I didn't say I was leaving for good. Who knows, you may have me helping you sell your newspapers some time in the future. And I'm very proud of what we've accomplished for this great state."

McReynolds had caught some of the career politician's natural rhythm and he launched into an extended riff, detailing how under his leadership Michigan had become the arsenal of democracy and won the war. I actually was listening quite intently until Rachel Loeb dug her elbow into my ribs and said in a stage whisper, "You should be getting all this down. Otherwise somebody might charge you with impersonating a reporter."

"Show a little respect. You're witnessing history."

She laughed. "I'm witnessing a funeral. He's just one of the walking dead, with dishwater in his veins. Street should've put him in his grave."

As I walked down Michigan Avenue toward Johnny's, Maloney pulled up beside me in our unmarked police car. He rolled down the window and motioned to me. "Buy you a coffee, Mr. Cahill?" he asked. We stopped at a dingy all-night diner on Michigan Avenue, and after Maloney lit a cigarette and ordered, he glanced around the room. The counterman leaned against the wall, his eyes closed, and a toothpick dancing in his mouth.

Maloney toyed with his spoon. "We got a problem with Hennessey," he said.

I steadied myself. "What's Randy up to now?"

"Just tryin' to keep his job. It's an election year. Case you hadn't noticed. Remember those tipovers he pulled last fall?"

I recalled Hennessey's raids, but only vaguely. Since that day in October, I had been absorbed. Maloney reminded me that the wets had announced a petition drive to put liquor by the glass on the ballot for the city of Lansing. The Temperance League and the Ministerial Alliance promptly pressured Hennessey into a series of midnight forays against the city's saloons and clubs. The raids were reminiscent of the late, great days of Prohibition. To no one's surprise, Hennessey's flying squads found and confiscated over a hundred illegal slot machines. The drys were ecstatic and the prosecutor gloried briefly in the free publicity. Then he buried the cases. Hennessey was not one to upset the natural order of the world.

"Turns out some of the local cops were on the pad, takin' money pretty regular. The do-gooders are pushing Hennessey for some progress. They want some prosecutions," Maloney said.

I waited, but Maloney needed the cadence of question and answer. He looked down at his chipped white china mug, never raising his eyes.

"Al, is it anybody we know?" I asked finally.

"It goes right up to the old Lansing chief. Maybe some guys with the state police." He picked at a sliver of skin on the side of his index finger. "Maybe me," he said. Outside, a police siren wailed away and Maloney's head came up for a moment, reflexively.

"How much?"

"Not that much." He dropped his eyes again to the remains of his coffee and snubbed his cigarette out in the smudged glass ashtray on the countertop. "Maybe a sawbuck a week. They could afford it."

Of that I had no doubt.

⟹ 27 ⟸

Voir Dire

April, 1946

Most jury picks are an agonizingly slow process and this one was no exception. Syzmanski did not allow the attorneys to handle the voir dire, the questioning of potential jurors designed to seek out their prejudices and their fears. When an experienced lawyer conducts the interrogation, it quickly turns from a probing for the truth to a setting of the stage. Syzmanski had obviously decided that he was going to be the director in this particular drama. He required each side to submit written questions that he would then direct to the potential jurors. Both sides objected to the procedure. But Syzmanski was adamant. The fact that his method would focus the initial attention of the press squarely on the man on the bench rather than the men in the arena was certainly not lost upon him.

The selection of the first set of fourteen potential jurors was accomplished through a blind draw. A deputy clerk of the court, chosen because her hand was small enough to fit into the locked lottery box, drew the folded slips of paper upon which the names of the veniremen were subscribed. As she called their names in a lonely, quavering voice, the chosen made their way dutifully forward to the jury box and seated themselves with anxious dignity.

Syzmanski was now in his glory. And he took full advantage of it. He introduced himself, the lawyers, and the court personnel. Then he read the long indictment word for word, exactly as I had written it. The explanation of the plot to kill Senator

Maynard I had woven together was now the official position of the people of the great state of Michigan.

When Syzmanski came to the charging portion, he paused and looked out into the packed courtroom. "Commencing September 1, 1945," he intoned, "and on diverse other days between then and October 10, 1945, the said Defendants Wade A. Fleming, Abraham Lefkowitz, and Isadore Shrieber, and each of them, did unlawfully and feloniously agree, combine, conspire, confederate, and engage, to and among themselves, and to and among each other, and to and among diverse other persons, to kill and murder Harry C. Maynard, then a state senator of the sovereign state of Michigan."

As Syzmanski read, he lingered on the short, flat words of accusation, and his voice became almost a chant. My seat was at the short end of the counsel table so that Fleming was directly in my line of sight. I watched him closely through the reading of the indictment, but his face was expressionless.

Syzmanski then explained the procedure by which we would select the actual jury. It would apply to the candidates who were now in the jury box, and to the rest of the veniremen who squeezed into the worn wooden seats behind the low rail that bisected the courtroom, and separated the elect from those who only watched and waited.

"This is a criminal case. That means a jury of twelve, which we call a petit jury to distinguish it from the grand jury that handed down the indictment," Syzmanski said. Haricot frowned at this and I knew he wished to avoid any mention of the grand jury. Storey was still well respected in the county and the defense did not want his prestige added to the prosecution's arsenal.

"We'll also pick two alternates in case a juror becomes ill or is otherwise unable to serve," Syzmanski continued. "Now, are there any questions before we get started?"

The men and women in the box looked up at him from a great distance. His ruddy face and graying hair, the sober black of his robe, the elevation of his bench and his position set him apart from and above them. Few officials in this country are as intimidating as a trial judge within the confines of his court-room, and this robust, limited man was redolent with power and dignity. The potential jurors were mute and motionless. No one raised a hand. No one said a word.

Syzmanski beamed at them with obvious approval and then launched into the lists of voir dire questions that each side had submitted. He droned away, a dull man speaking to the deaf. When he asked whether any of them had read the *Lansing Reporter* article, eight hands went up. Haricot jumped in immediately.

"The defense challenges each of these veniremen for cause," he said. "That article was prejudicial in the extreme and there is no possible way that we can erase it from the minds of these men and women."

Syzmanski blinked in confusion. Then he summoned the attorneys forward to the inner rail. "Jesus, Mary, and Joseph," he whispered. His kindly face was wrinkled with honest perplexity. "Fellas, how many of these jurors do you think've read that damn thing?"

"Hard to tell, Judge," Haricot said. "If this first flock is any guide, over half. But if they're prejudiced, they can't serve. The law on this kind of pre-trial publicity is quite clear."

Syzmanski now had the serene look of a small boy who was determined to do his duty, however painful. "He's right, Hub," he said to Street. "I'll have to bounce anybody who admits to being even the slightest bit influenced by it."

On our way back to our seats, Street murmured to me, "We just lost half our panel. We've each got forty-five perempts. If we both use 'em all, we won't get a jury. Then Haricot gets his delay and our case gets cold."

He was truly prescient. Of the one hundred and fifty potential jurors, over a hundred admitted to having read the article, and Syzmanski excused eighty for cause after he questioned them. As the jury pool drained out, Street three times declared himself satisfied with the panel. But each time, Haricot used his peremptory challenges to remove a citizen who exhibited a shade too much conviction when answering Syzmanski's questions. As we struggled to see whom they liked and whom they hated, a gentle cloud of boredom settled over the stuffy courtroom.

After two days, each side was down to five peremptory challenges and Street was clearly worried. "Did you see their shoes," he asked. "I want my jurors to have nice tight shoes. Tight shoes mean a tight ass. These people are too damn comfortable."

When Haricot used his last challenge, there were nine men and four women in the jury box, one short of the twelve jurors and two alternates the law required. There was but one venireman remaining. Street slumped in his chair when the clerk read his name from the slip. The candidate was a Lansing jeweler, married, childless, elderly. His eyes were full of questions and full of fear. He was not a comfortable man. But for the prosecutor he was something worse. He was a Jew.

Street had been firm in his determination to keep any of Ingham County's small Jewish population off the jury. "Those hebes are always for the poor defendant. They identify with the underdog no matter what he's done. Hell, a kike'll find something to like about Lefkowitz and Shrieber and that's hard to do," he had said when we picked through the venire list. "If we get a Jew, we'll never get a verdict. All it takes is one to hang a jury," he had said.

Street stared at Herschel Goldberg as he slipped into the last seat in the jury box. After Syzmanski put the questions and Goldberg stated that he had never heard of the *Lansing Reporter*, much less read it, Street leaned forward across the counsel table with his full weight pressing on it. If he used a challenge, the venire would be exhausted. The judge would put the trial over to summer and Haricot would have the time he had fought for so relentlessly. If Otto Lammers was chilled with fear that spring, by July he would be frozen into silence.

Street cleared his throat and said, "Mr. Goldberg is acceptable to the state." We had our jury and the defense had its man to hang it.

⇒ 28 ⇐

Chances for Advancement

April, 1946

After Syzmanski recessed for the week, only Street and I remained in the courtroom. I took a deep breath. I was in uncharted waters and peril circled everywhere around me. "I hate to spring this on you, but there's something I picked up you should know about," I said.

Street looked at me quizzically. "This has been a bitch of a day, Charlie. I don't need any more bad news."

Then he saw my expression. "How bad is it?"

"Bad enough. Maloney tells me that Hennessey's about ready to go after the local cops on those slot machine raids. He won't touch the saloon owners and the police are a good target. They were taking money and the drys are all over him to do something."

"Cops are always takin' money. What's that got to do with me?"

"They weren't the only ones. The state police were in on it. Half our investigators. Maloney himself," I said.

Street sat down heavily. "Now that, that'll just kill us. That fucking senate committee's been waiting for something to get me on. This'll do it. Hennessey's got to listen to reason on this," he said.

"According to Maloney, he's got the bit in his teeth."

"Well then, we'll just have to slow him down. Randall Hennessey doesn't want to be a two-bit county prosecutor all his life. That man's got ambition. It's a common weakness, in case you hadn't noticed," Street said.

We caught Hennessey on his way out of his office at the county building. He did not look at me and I looked over his shoulder, into the middle distance. Every time I saw him, all I could think of was Peter's face. But Hennessey was all Irish charm until Street brought up the slot machine cases.

"Those cases are mine. Stay away from them," he said.

"Of course they're yours," Street said. "As long as they stay local."

"Is that what this is about? You know damn well those state boys had their hands in the honeypot, right up to the elbow. If I want to I can nail them right now. And they know it," Hennessey said.

"What do you mean, they know it?"

Hennessey's face reddened. "I mean they can see it coming. They know I got witnesses who'll say they took payoffs. You understand what I'm saying?"

"I understand perfectly." Street paused and looked up at the ceiling. "The paint's flaking over there in the corner, Randy. You should take better care of this building. It's a public trust."

Street leaned forward suddenly. "I was wondering how Fleming got all those expenditure records. Sure as hell not from little Johnny Danto. You squeezed all that stuff out of those state cops. Then you fed it to Fleming. You've been working for him the whole way. How long's he been payin' you?"

"Bullshit," Hennessey said. "You can't prove a thing."

"I don't have to prove it. All's I've got to do is leak it and it's goodbye Randy. I've got reporters crawlin' out of the woodwork out there in Mason, and they're all lookin' for an angle."

Street blocked out a headline with his hands. "Local prosecutor violates grand jury secrecy. That's a hell of a lead, don't you think?"

"Screw you, Street. You pull that, we're all in the shitter."

"You've got a real way with words there, Mr. Hennessey. You're just a natural born charmer."

Street dropped his voice and upped the ante. "Why don't we see if we can both do some good for ourselves. You know

I'm resigning as special prosecutor after the Fleming trial. To pursue other interests as they say. Suppose I was to recommend you take over the investigation after I leave? A man could make himself a statewide name for himself if he had a mind to. You Democrats are going to get your asses kicked this fall. But '48's a presidential year. You guys always do well when you've got somebody ahead of you on the ticket. Who knows, Truman may turn out to be a hell of a candidate. A real crusader like you could end up attorney general."

Randall Hennessey slouched against the wall with an air of nonchalance. But his eyes betrayed him. Street had seen through the man and into the mirror.

"So, what do you want from me?" he asked.

"Let this slot machine thing go until Fleming's trial is over. After that I don't give a damn. Keep takin' Fleming's money and keep him fat, dumb, and happy until I convict the sonofabitch. Once you're free of him and ridin' the range as special prosecutor, there's no limit to what you can do."

"The drys'll scream to high heaven."

"Let 'em. In a month, Fleming'll be in prison and the drys'll love you. They'll probably endorse you. You'll be a favorite of the anti-sin gang. Hell, I'll endorse you."

"I thought you were a Republican," Hennessey said.

"What I am is a grown-up. Republican, Democrat, that's just how we choose up sides. Once the election's over, it doesn't mean a damn thing."

I stood quietly as the two men struck the deal. Street had played Hennessey like a fiddle and in the process, although he hadn't known it, he had saved me. *Now there will be no more surprises*, I thought. Hennessey was aligned with us, at least for a time. And he had nothing to gain by telling Street what he knew about me. I thought that I could live with that.

≈ 29 ≈

Into the Night

April, 1946

A spring storm had blown in and the night was swollen with heavy, wet snow as I drove Peter's car to Sarah's home. The roads were carpeted with slush and mud and the car lost traction on even the gentlest grade. When I pulled into the driveway, there was a sleek Radio Flyer sled leaning against the house next to the side entrance. Sarah opened the door and I followed her into the warmth of the spacious kitchen. Her mother was seated at the breakfast table with the neat piles of a solitaire game spread before her. An elderly Negro woman sat at the stool by the kitchen counter with her hands folded in her lap, listening to the radio. Two china teacups sat on the table, each with a matching, patterned saucer. There were schoolbooks carefully stacked at the end of the kitchen counter.

Sarah's mother turned a card and smiled brightly at me as I shook the snow from my topcoat. Her back was straight, but she was bowed slightly at the neck. Her head was thrust forward with her chin down.

"It's chilly tonight. Close the door son, before we all catch our death," she said, and she tilted her head stiffly upward. Her voice was soft and low and I caught a trace of Sarah's speech in her inflection. She wore a sober, navy blue knit dress with a single strand of pearls glowing softly at her throat. She was a rich man's wife playing a poor man's card game and she showed no discomfort at the incongruity.

"Mother, this is Charles Cahill," Sarah said. "He's one of the lawyers working on the trial. You remember, I've mentioned him before? Charles, this is my mom Laura St. Clair and Lillian Johnson, her maid." She spoke quite slowly, without emphasis.

"I remember," her mother said. "I remember everything you tell me."

She dealt herself another card and then shook her head in irritation. "I can never win this game. The cards don't favor me." With great precision, she placed the card in the discard pile, turned a black jack, and played it on the queen of clubs. She looked up at me and her eyes were flat and blank, like a coat of fresh black paint on the windows of a deserted house.

I looked away and walked over to the counter, near the radio. In his carefully articulated midwestern voice, the announcer said that Bob Feller was the highest paid player in baseball, making $50,000. I wished him the best.

"Charles, why don't you lay a fire in the living room? The wood's by the fireplace," Sarah said.

She reached in front of her mother and gently moved the jack onto a red queen. "Black on red, Mom. You can't win if you don't follow the rules."

Her mother shook her head again and shot an angled glance at me with those blank eyes. "Lillian's supposed to remind me, not you," she said.

Again I heard the rising inflection, the hint of a question at the end of the phrase. She patted her daughter's hand affectionately. "Let me finish my game in peace, dear."

I turned away from the counter and crossed the shining linoleum floor of the kitchen into the living room. Split cherrywood logs were stacked by the marble fireplace and a small mound of kindling lay between the andirons. I tried to manage one-handed as I knelt to light the paper and twigs. But then Sarah was close beside me, her hand on mine.

"Let me do it," she said. I felt her warmth as she leaned into me. And I smelled the lavender and honey. But I could not respond to her. Not there in what had been Maynard's own house.

"Your mother knows more about the rules than you do," I said. "We can't be alone until it's over. Hennessey knows. Fleming knows. And Hubbell Street's no fool. He may have half guessed. You play these games, he'll guess the rest."

"This isn't a game. There are no rules. Street's just another pol on the make. All dressed up like a lawyer, fit to kill," she said.

"Sarah, if we make just one mistake now, we're dead. Street's made a deal with Hennessey. But the jury's got to convict Fleming before we're safe."

"Oh, there's no mistake," she said, and she slid inside my arm, next to my heart. I was on her then, like a wolf on a doe, my mouth hot on the soft slope of her neck and my right hand up in her chestnut hair. I felt her breath catch and her back begin to arch.

"Stop," she said.

I pulled back immediately. "Damn you," I said. "You started this."

She pointed over my shoulder to the fireplace. "The poker's gone."

She might as well have slapped me. Next to the raised hearth was a wrought-iron rack of implements. A flat scalloped shovel. A wooden bellows. A small, black-bristled brush. Each hung from curved notched holders on the rack. But there was one empty space. The long, hooked poker was missing.

"It was here two weeks ago," she said. "I washed it again with ammonia."

"Maybe your daughter took it."

She looked at me steadily and then said, "Francine wouldn't do that. She knows better."

She stood with a single movement, straightened her dark red skirt, and patted her hair back into place. "Mother may know," she said. Then she stopped in front of the doorway to the kitchen. "We can't confuse her. She's important to us. She's my alibi."

Sarah's mother sat erect in the same chair, her chin dropped to her chest, and her eyes closed. The maid was at the sink, slowly drying the teacups and saucers with a checkered dishtowel. She did not turn around as we came back into the room, but Laura St. Clair's eyes popped open.

"Lillian won't play with me any more," she said. She glanced at me and cocked her head, for a moment a little girl. "Do you play cards, son?"

"Charles is the lawyer, Mother. He's not here to play games," Sarah said. "We can't get a fire going and the poker seems to be gone. Have you seen it somewhere?"

"What do I know about a silly poker? Ask Lillian. She knows everything."

The maid turned away from the sink and spoke gently to Laura St. Clair. "Missus, you do go on. Your girl's funnin' you. She don't need no poker to make a fire."

"Mom, why don't you go get your coat and I'll drive you and Lillian home," Sarah said.

When her mother left the kitchen, Sarah stepped quickly over to the sink and took the last teacup from the maid's hand. "Is there something you should tell me, Lillian?"

"They say I wasn't to tell anybody."

"Who said that?"

"The police. When they came last week. After you left the missus and me here. They say they just want to look around the place. They's only here just a little while."

She nodded vigorously, as if to punctuate the singsong cadence of her speech. Her skin was an ashy mahogany. In the warmth of the kitchen, there was a slight sheen of perspiration at her temples.

"Did they take anything?"

The maid carefully folded the dishtowel over the corner of the sink. "No ma'am. I watched them the whole time. When they's ready to leave, the one he gave me ten dollars and says don't say nothin'. I figure he's the police. He knows what's right. Anyways, it's white folk's business."

"You're sure they didn't take anything. The poker that's gone?"

She looked straight at Sarah and then ducked her head. "I didn't see them take nothin'," she said.

I had to ask. "How did you know they were the police."

"They showed me some badges. I don't need no more troubles with the police." Again, she bobbed her head for emphasis.

Fleming, I thought. He had sent his men to toss the house and tumble us into oblivion. Somehow they took the poker without the maid knowing it. Now we were completely in his hands. Once he gave that poker to the police, the lab techs with their chemicals and their microscopes would know the truth soon enough, despite Sarah's efforts to wash it away.

Laura St. Clair scuttled back into the kitchen. "I do so like my new coat," she said. She twirled in a full circle for us, the foxtail trims glinting in the light, and then swept to the door with a hurried peck at my cheek.

"Good night, Harry," she said to me. "We'll see you next week at our house for dinner. Hurry up, Sarah. I don't want to miss Burns and Allen."

Sarah stared at me without expression. This thin reed was her alibi. Any good cop could break Laura St. Clair in a matter of seconds. He would simply erase all semblance of the story Sarah had so carefully woven into her mother's fragile memory. Without Laura St. Clair to swear that her daughter was at her side that October morning, we were adrift. Fleming and Hennessey already had witnesses putting me at Sarah's house. With the poker, they had independent evidence of the crime.

The wind whispered in the trees as Sarah opened the door for her mother and the maid. There had been the same rustle in the autumn corn stubble when we laid Harry Maynard out in the dust and emptiness. Wait for me, Sarah had said, and the yellow haze was there again, and the smell, and the fear. There was no time to mix a drink and I went straight for the scotch. I found the bottle before I even heard her swing open the wooden garage doors. I poured the first drink straight and neat into the water glass from the sink. It had a fine, smoky taste to it.

The car coughed and stuttered as Sarah jammed down on the starter. But the liquor warmed me inside, the glow spreading slowly upward from my belly into my chest. The car's engine caught, and then turned over, and I tilted my head back, almost under control, as Sarah steered the car down the long, curved driveway. Through the kitchen window, I saw the headlights swing in an arc, dimmed by the blowing snow. As she turned into the night, I took up the bottle again and the fear silently retreated. Perhaps we faced just another problem in a long line of problems.

WHEN SARAH returned from the drive to the St. Clair home, shaking the wet snow from her hair and stamping her feet, the fear had disappeared almost entirely with the warmth of the liquor. But Sarah gave me no peace.

"Lillian's lying," she said.

I reached for the glass, my fingers thick and awkward. "She seems honest enough to me," I said. "Why do you think that?" It was a logical question. I phrased it carefully, hiding behind good diction and remembered manners.

"Because I've known her all my life. She's been stealing from us almost the whole time. When my father catches her, she always puts on the same show. It's yessir and nossir, just a poor old colored lady shuffling along."

"Why do you keep her?"

Sarah took the empty glass from my hand. "She cares for my mother," she said. "Stealing and then lying about it don't count for much against that."

"What about the poker?" The comfortable warmth was damping down just enough for me to sense the yellow light rising again. Why had we not simply thrown the damn thing into a ditch or the river? Why had we been so reckless as to hide it in plain sight? Now we had lost it. And most likely we had lost ourselves.

"Lillian knows where it is," Sarah said. "They didn't buy her for just ten dollars. Her husband Horace is in prison over in Jackson. They probably threatened her. It's happened before. She'll tell me after a while, when we're alone. She always does."

I shook myself and stood up, weaving. I knew that when the heat of the liquor faded, I could not stand the wrenching uncertainty, the changing, shifting vacillations of circumstance. I could scale a cliff, survive a wound, even lay a dead man out in a cornfield, but they were all simple things. I reached across for her and she came to me. Her hair was still damp from the snow, but it smelled of spring.

Suddenly, she was crying. "I want to be with you, Charles," she said. "Just like it was in the hospital, in the sunlight. Not this drunken groping in the dark. I want you to remember me, not the scotch. Charles Cahill, you're not your father." The tears streamed down her face. Finally, when I could stand it no more, she turned away.

"You have to leave. My daughter's upstairs. She can't see this. She's fragile enough as it is. Leave the car here and I'll drive you to your brother's house."

"I'll walk. It's the one thing I do well."

Her head came up, she turned to face me, and her voice sharpened. "Don't expect that if you walk out, you can walk back in tomorrow for another drink and then to bed. If you're drinking, I can't trust you. I had fifteen years of Harry Maynard and his drinking and his excuses. I'm not going through that again, not for anyone."

The anger surged up within me, fueled by alcohol. I measured out my words. My voice was even, though my soul was numbed. I was all Irish now.

"Well, we certainly solved that problem, didn't we? No more excuses from the good senator. Still and dry in the grave he'll be. Now and forever."

I walked toward the door and turned for the fatal last words. "I took care of him for you. Wasn't that enough?"

Her own anger flashed then. "No, it's not nearly enough. Do you care about anything but crawling into a bottle? You said we can't afford mistakes. Well, drunks make mistakes."

I opened the door and walked through it into the darkness and the snow. Over the keening of the wind I heard her slam the door. But I did not look back. Sodden and shivering, I stumbled through the night to Peter's house. Then I made my way to the wide array of brands set out in front of the mirror in his elaborate basement bar. Glass by glass, I drowned all my memories and vanquished all my fears. When I drank myself to the edge of oblivion and the yellow light was gone, I kissed her goodbye. Once again, I had the gift of loss and I wrapped it around my shoulders like a shawl.

Reunion

November, 1996

*M*y *father's voice is softer now and he focuses only on me. But perhaps not. Perhaps it is just the reflex of the consummate advocate, sitting in the jury's lap one last time. He speaks of my mother and his inflection changes and becomes lilting.*

"As long as I live," he says, smiling at me in the faded, drained light of the hospital room, "I'll remember your mother's face when she was happy. She warmed everyone near her. They saw that smile and they couldn't resist her. When she smiled, the heat just radiated from her."

He stops and looks up steadily at the ceiling. "I remember, before she died . . ." I say, and then I halt, appalled.

"It's all right. It was a cruel blow, but we survived." His voice is edged with sadness and longing.

It was more than just a blow, I think. My father went to his office after my mother's funeral and worked the rest of the day. There were those who thought him to be unfeeling, but I did not. That evening and every evening during that long summer he sat upright in his leather chair by the front window of our house, staring at the shadows and running the fingers of his right hand through his hair. I was eighteen then, bound for the university, and I sat with him in the twilight. He bundled up his grief like coal in a bad child's Christmas stocking, and until this evening I had never heard him speak of my mother again.

"Dad," I say, searching for something to divert him. "Dr. Helmsley said if you continue to improve they'll move you from intensive care in a week or so."

"Helmsley's an idiot and you can tell him I said so. I'll die here and we all know it. Tell him I expect full professional courtesy, one shark to another."

By sheer accident, I have diverted him from the darkness. My father's eyes are alight with the pleasure of insulting still another doctor. In the old days, before we went over to the defense side, when he cross-examined a physician he dropped his customary courtesy. He was simple, direct, and brutal, and he went straight for the throat. His clients, ill or injured, got more than their money's worth on those days. When he had a doctor in the dock, he was like a jungle cat circling some poor tethered and frightened goat. His killer instinct, so necessary in a good trial lawyer, was fully engaged. When he was finished, so was the poor doctor.

"Do you know why juries hate doctors?"

Of course, he answers his own question. "It's because they're such obvious liars. The jury can always tell a liar. Particularly one with a medical degree. They're butchers, up to their elbows in blood. You can just hear them whistling gaily and making their little jokes as they leave the slaughterhouse on their way to the bank. Give me an honest crook any day. Or a crooked cop."

"Dad, health care is major money. We can't count on the Bernstein heirs to keep fighting forever. The steadiest income for the firm is from the hospitals and the doctors."

"Then it's time to take my name off the door," he says. But then he laughs. This is a game he and I have played over the years and his response is well practiced. I keep him at it, in the hope that he will turn away from the past and our shared ghosts. There is no need for us to go there now, after all these years.

"Frankie, you're selling your soul and for what? So you can join Helmsley and his gang of ghouls at the country club? Would it break your heart to take a live suffering client someday?"

I play for time. We have plowed this ground before, as the firm's business has changed, and I have learned to keep it light. "Which question would you like me to answer first?" I ask.

"Start at the top and work your way down."

"Big bucks, no, and yes."

"Ah, Frankie, if your mother could hear you now. A money-changer in league with the medicine men. And boasting of it." His mood changes again and he turns his face to the wall.

The room is silent, except for the hum of the machines and the hiss of the wind around the sealed windows, and I think of Julie. Suddenly, she has come back, with her bag of tricks. I saw her on the street. Within an hour we were in bed. At night she brings me to the edge, again and again. But my mind will not let me go over it. Yet, I cannot get enough of her. The hope is there and I chase it like a child. She never mentions the future. I never mention the past. It is as if there is some unspoken truce between us. Could my father possibly understand that? Could he understand anything at all about me?

The nurse comes in to check the monitors and then hustles out. Her shoes make small slapping noises on the hospital floor. When she leaves, my father turns back to me and his face is set. "It won't surprise you that I think a lot about death now," he says. "I think death comes in many different forms. When you're ill, death comes as a woman, soft and slow and seductive. We think the grim reaper's a man with a sickle ready to harvest you like so much wheat in the field, but that's not right. When you're alone in a hospital and dying by inches, she's a woman and she's dark and quiet and she sits at your side. And then one night she asks you to slip away with her, just for that night, just for a visit. You know what she's asking and when you go with her, then it's over."

My father clenches and unclenches the fingers of his right hand and then he says, "Forgive me, I'm just tired and I'm rambling on. Come back tomorrow night. I'll tell you everything I know about conspiracies and convicts."

The next evening I keep my appointment and he keeps his word. The gulf is the difference between his world and mine. I realize that I cannot dissuade him from telling his story. It is his truth and I can only let him pour it out as he remembers it. Even as the cold seeps into my mind and my heart. Even as it freezes me into silence and solitude.

Openings

April, 1946

On the first day of the trial, Street stood before the jury box with a large legal pad in his hands. The jurors could not see it. I had and I knew it was entirely blank.

"The jury's my tabula rasa, Charlie. I just use the pad as a prop. Makes 'em think I've done a little preparation," he had explained earlier. Now he began to tell his story and he told it large.

"Ladies and gentlemen, there's a beautiful cemetery over in Lansing, south of downtown, out at Mt. Hope. Perhaps some of you have been there. Some of you may have relatives or friends who sleep there now. You may visit them on a Sunday afternoon after church now that the weather's good, to pay your respects or lay out a sprig of flowers. I know I do. I get some comfort from praying with my father. Even though I can't hear his voice."

Street paused and his eyes glistened. He cleared his throat and began again. "Beautiful is a funny word to describe a cemetery, isn't it? But if you were to go out there today, I'm sure you'd find it beautiful and peaceful. With the buds on the trees just coming out, and the wind soft and gentle and the spring peepers starting to sing."

He paused a second time. Then he raised his hand in a warning. "But I wouldn't want any of you to visit that cemetery right now. You've got a case to hear and a decision to make. Suppose, though, you were to go out there, early of a spring morning. What would you see, over in the east section?" Street stopped and looked down at the floor and jammed his hands into his pockets, letting the question linger in the jurors' minds.

"Why you'd see the new graves, the earth still sort of fresh-dug and unsettled. And in front of one of those graves, you might see a brand new headstone. It's just arrived because it took some time to carve the words into that hard granite. That headstone says, 'With honesty he lived, for honesty he was taken.'" Street stepped around in front of the jury and placed his hands on the low wall of the jury box and his voice was almost a whisper.

"Senator Harry Maynard spends his mornings, noons, and nights in that coffin. Below that headstone. That coffin, it's air-tight and waterproof. So his eternal night is airless, dry, and endlessly still. He didn't die of some terrible disease. His death was no random accident. He is entombed there forever because someone bashed his skull in. And then shot him twice in the face. Although we can't prove it today and we won't try, we think we know who did it. The reason we won't try is because we know who *planned*"—Street raised his voice to a near shout as he came down on the last word—"we know who *planned* it. And that we will prove to you beyond a reasonable doubt."

Street stepped back from the jury box and turned toward the courtroom audience. "Now I just said that if you went out to the cemetery, early of a morning, you might find it peaceful. But it's not very peaceful for that woman over there, the one dressed in black. She's Sarah Maynard. She's the senator's widow. She visits his grave every morning. She talks to him, but he does not answer. Sometimes she recites a little poem for him, but he does not hear. Mostly, though, she cries for the man she's lost, the man we've all lost."

I watched Sarah's face carefully out of the corner of my eye as she raised her gloved hand to her eyes. It was just as Street had asked her to do. Her face was calm, though, and she did not produce the tears that he had asked her to summon up for the man she'd lost. She could not bring herself to do that one thing, that final, meaningless thing. *God, how she hated him,* I thought. *And God, how he deserved it.*

Street turned back to the jury and now his words came faster. "Let me make it simple. This case is about deceit and murder and corruption and conspiracy. Those aren't pretty words. And this isn't a pretty case. We will prove to you that one man"—he turned and he now was Jeremiah, his arm outstretched in accusation and in judgment—"that man, Wade Fleming, is the boss of one of our political parties. We will show you how he was not satisfied with his great wealth. We will show you how he sought to profit from his high position. We will prove to you that he paid bribes to secure the passage of legislation that was beneficial to his private interests."

Street paced before the jury box. Every step was slow and measured, every word distinct and damning. He had left his legal pad behind and as he spun out his web he gestured expansively, like a conductor in the pit with his orchestra. I watched the jurors move their heads with his hands.

"The state will show you that he made his plans known to Senator Maynard," Street said. "We will show you that when he discovered that the senator had come forward to do his duty, he entered into a vicious conspiracy to have the senator killed. The state will prove to you that he sent two of his creatures"— he stretched his arm out again—"those men, Lefkowitz and Shrieber, once members of the infamous Purple Gang, to Lansing to arrange Senator Maynard's death. The state will prove to you that he boasted of his plan. We will prove to you that he said he would have that good man taken for a ride."

Street dropped his voice. There is a dark beauty in violence and he meant to let the jury members have their guilty pleasures. "Do you know, ladies and gentlemen, that's exactly what happened. Harry Maynard was taken for a ride in his own car. He was brutally beaten. Then he was taken out to a cornfield and shot twice in the head. He was butchered out there. All alone and without pity."

I had lowered my head as Street swung the axe and I jumped when Haricot slapped his hand down on the counsel table. "Your honor, please," Haricot said. "This is highly prejudicial. These men are not on trial for murder. We've not been at this five minutes and there's already grounds for a mistrial."

"Mr. Street, please confine yourself to the elements of the offense that's been charged," Syzmanski said. "This is a conspiracy case. Let's keep it to that." His words were stern, but his face was placid. He made no effort whatsoever to put the cat back in the bag.

Street made a good act of contrition. "Yes, your honor," he said, and his shaggy head fell forward until his chin touched the knot in his tie. He brooded in front of the jury for a moment, long enough for them to see he yearned to tell them more of the end of Harry Maynard's life. Long enough for them to curse Haricot and Syzmanski for silencing him. Long enough for them to luxuriate in the details of violent death. Then, with a snap of his head, he plunged forward into the technical details of our case. He explained the elements of conspiracy. He identified our witnesses and previewed their testimony. He spoke for over an hour and it was a colloquy in which there was but one voice.

When he reached the end, he stood by our counsel table and again lowered his voice and the jury leaned forward to hear him. "Our witnesses are not all angels," he said. "We didn't find them at a prayer meeting. But when this trial is over, you will know that the defendants plotted the death of Senator Maynard. Lefkowitz and Shrieber stalked him like a rabbit. They did it because Fleming told them the senator's voice had to be stilled. And why? Because he told a grand jury of graft and corruption."

Before Haricot could object, Street raised his hand to the jury. Now it was a gesture of benediction. "That is all there is to this case. And that is enough," he whispered. He slumped into his chair and the jury members leaned back against their seats.

A defense lawyer has the option of making the opening statement at the beginning of the trial or of waiting until the prosecution has put in its case. Some lawyers prefer to hold back. They feel this gives them the opportunity to attack the prosecution's proofs while they are still fresh in the jury's mind, and to set up their own case only moments before it begins to go in. But Joel Haricot was unrelentingly aggressive and he chose to respond immediately. His strategy was clear from the outset. He meant to try the prosecution. If he could he could plant enough suspicion of us in the minds of the jury, he could then lead them into the shadowland of reasonable doubt.

"I hope you noticed that Mr. Street didn't talk much about the facts," Haricot began. "But I'm going to. The first fact is that this is not a prosecution at all. Mr. Street and Mr. Fleming are old political enemies. When he became special prosecutor, Mr. Street saw a chance to get even. He took that chance and this trial is the result."

I looked at Street and mouthed the word: object? He shook his head.

"The second fact is that there's a conspiracy all right. It's a conspiracy between those two men"—Haricot whirled his wheelchair around in a quick half-circle and pointed directly at Street and me—"Hubbell Street and Charles Cahill, to get Wade Fleming. To get him for their own ends. These men are the conspirators. Not Wade Fleming. Not Abraham Lefkowitz. Not Isadore Shrieber."

What has Fleming told him of me? I thought and I looked at Street, but again he shook his head.

"The third fact is that the fulcrum of this case will be the testimony of two men, out of all those Mr. Street has identified," Haricot said. "Oh, we'll have witnesses galore. But it is these two men who will count. These men, Nathan Vanik and Otto Lammers, they have immunity. As I am sure the judge will instruct you, if you believe from the evidence that they were induced to testify by the granting of immunity, you must take that fact into consideration when determining the weight you give to their testimony."

Syzmanski frowned at this and I knew Haricot had taken an unnecessary risk. Although the judge had ordered both sides to prepare jury instructions, we had not yet submitted them. When Syzmanski tilted, he tilted toward the prosecution. He might well refuse to give the instruction Haricot had just outlined.

Haricot then turned to our case, to destroy the web we had woven. If Street painted his picture with broad, flamboyant strokes, Haricot was surgically neat. If we sought certainty, he sowed doubt. If we sought answers, he offered only questions. He ended where all good defense lawyers end, with the presumption of innocence. In theory, it is the strong shield of the defense. In practice, it is a fiction. Jurors have only the most general understanding of the law and the workings of the police system.

But juries have one shared bond and that is great good sense. They know if a case is brought, someone is guilty. And they know the defendants are usually a very good bet. In a prosecution such as ours, guilt was everywhere. The jury would vote to convict unless they were convinced that Fleming, Lefkowitz, and Shrieber were innocent. Not only of this particular crime, but of crime itself. When our jury members entered the box, they had almost certainly turned the presumption on its head. If we could parade all the defendants' gangland sins around that quiet rural courtroom, that might be enough. *Enough to rid us of Fleming*, I thought.

Joel Haricot knew this from a hundred verdicts. Now he sought to right the world. "Ladies and gentlemen," he said. "I want you to remember that when my clients walked into the court this morning, they were innocent. Innocent not just in my eyes, but in the eyes of the law itself. Take that one fact home with you tonight and sleep with it. These men are innocent."

With that, Syzmanski gave us an hour for lunch. As we worked our way through our sandwiches, I complimented Street on his opening. "I didn't know your father was buried in Lansing," I said.

"Hell, I have no idea where he's buried. He lit out after my sister was born and we never saw him again. I hope he's plenty warm. He couldn't stand the winters here. I hope the sonofabitch is somewhere down below getting his chestnuts roasted for all eternity."

≡ 31 ≡

Courtroom Dancing

April, 1946

That afternoon, the trial began in earnest. Good lawyers always start at the foundation, like a mason building up a wall brick by brick. We opened our case with the testimony of Harold Detering and he was at the very bottom of our wall. Like my brother, he was a distiller's representative. Like my brother, he paid Wade Fleming a kickback on every sale he made to the Liquor Control Commission, the state's liquor monopoly. Like my brother, he was once Fleming's man. But now he was ours and Street had made him my witness. "Let's have the jury see one of Lansing's wounded heroes in action," he had said. I had said nothing.

As I stood to begin my direct examination, my hand was shaking a little. I had not taken a drink since I walked out into the night, away from Sarah. But Street appeared not to have noticed. I regarded myself with some amusement. *Charlie Cahill, the teetotaler,* I thought.

Haricot almost saved Detering from becoming a turncoat. "Your honor," he said, "I'd like an offer of proof with respect to this witness."

Syzmanski peered down from the bench. "Approach, gentlemen," he said. When we had clustered before him at the inner rail, out of the jury's hearing, he turned to me. "What's this guy going to say?"

"He's a foundation witness," I said. "He'll testify that Fleming got him his job. He'll say he paid Fleming a piece of every order he got from the Liquor Control Commission. Then we'll work our way up."

"That's absolutely ridiculous," Haricot said. "Even such a young lawyer as Mr. Cahill here should know that kind of testimony's totally irrelevant. The defendants aren't on trial here for extortion, if that's what he's trying to show. What does this have to do with Harry Maynard?"

Street cut in immediately. "It goes to the reason for the conspiracy. It's why they had to get rid of Maynard. He knew what was goin' on. And he was startin' to talk about it. We'll pull it all together at the end," he said.

Syzmanski studied the ceiling and I held my breath. Finally he said, "I'm going to let it in, for what it's worth. You'd better be able to make the connection. Or I'll have to strike it all."

Haricot wheeled his chair with a look of disgust. But as he rolled back to his position on the defense side he allowed himself a small smile. He was already planning his appeal. Street and I had argued endlessly before the trial began about this kind of collateral evidence. I thought it went beyond risk. It virtually guaranteed a reversal.

"This stuff's all irrelevant," I had said to him. "If Syzmanski lets it in, the Supreme Court will kick it and us along with it."

Street had listened silently and leaned back in his leather chair. It had been a cold April night and the radiator in the corner made a soft hiss with the effort of heating the room. When he stirred, Street ran his square farmer's hands through his hair and then looked up at me.

"Let's take a walk," he said. "The night air clears the mind."

We walked down the stairs, through the deserted first floor of the hotel, and then out across the street to the great square that surrounds the Capitol. There was a fog rising from the bare ground and its gauzy curtain soon cut us off from the cheerful lights of the hotel. Austin Blair, the Civil War governor of Michigan, stood astride his perpetual pedestal, frozen in bronze. The pigeon droppings formed an irregular halo on his high forehead.

Street slapped his gloved hands together with a sharp crack. "You remember what Storey said? That he had but one chance and he was going to take it? This is my one chance at Fleming. McReynolds isn't going to run again. With Fleming out of the way, I can ride this thing as far as I want. Governor and then who knows what? You think I give a damn if it's reversed a year from now?"

"What if Lammers doesn't testify? Fleming will get a directed verdict. Jeopardy will attach. We'll never be able to try him again on this charge," I said. *We've got to make it stick or I'll be looking over my shoulder for the rest of my life,* I thought.

When Street spoke, his voice was scratched with fatigue. "I've got to get Fleming now. Not a year from now. I'll take my chances with Lammers."

And so Harold Detering was the first brick in our wall. He was a hunched, sallow man with a face as worn and creased as an old map. But when he answered my questions, his voice had the rasp of authenticity.

"When did you first meet Wade Fleming?" I asked, after I had him sworn in.

"In '44, right after the election. I was between jobs and they told me to go see the man in Lansing, name of Fleming. They said he might be able to put me onto somethin'."

The juror in the first chair of the jury box was a retired grain elevator manager. He never looked at Detering, even when the witness spoke. But there was a gleam of animosity in the man's eyes and I thought we had lost him with our first witness.

"And this man was Wade Fleming, the defendant here?" I asked.

I watched the second juror, a pretty young housewife, and she watched only her hands. I could not read her at all. It was a common failing of mine with women.

"Objection, counsel's leading the witness," Haricot interjected.

There was a flash of irritation on the face of the third juror. He worked for the county welfare department and he dealt with the impoverished and the disabled. He didn't like Haricot because he was crippled. And he probably didn't like me for the same reason.

I walked away from Haricot's objection. "Let me rephrase that. Can you identify this man? This man in Lansing they sent you to?"

Detering pointed silently at Fleming. Fleming rose to his feet in response to a slight gesture from Haricot. It was a good tactic. To the jury, Fleming actually looked forthcoming.

"Let the record reflect that the witness has identified the defendant, Wade Fleming," I said. "Now, just what did you and Mr. Fleming discuss?"

Juror number four actually bobbed his head and I could see the line of his farmer's tan, faded over the winter.

"He said he could get me a job with one of the distillers. With Mohawk. But he said it would cost me. Twenty-five percent of my commission on every case I sold."

I looked over at the fifth juror to gauge her reaction. She was a small wren of a woman whose husband once worked at the Highway Department. She would be shocked by the testimony. Perhaps shocked enough to convict.

"Did you accept that?" I asked.

Herschel Goldberg was in the sixth chair. He was impassive, but his eyes darted from the witness to Fleming to Haricot. He would be the one to hang us.

"Not right away I didn't. It was pretty steep. But he said he'd make sure I got lots of orders. So's it really wouldn't cost me nothin' in the long run."

Juror number seven was a local clothier and he was clearly enjoying himself. He watched Detering expectantly.

"And did you get a lot of orders from the Commission?"

"Yeah, Fleming made sure of that."

The juror in the eighth chair was another farmer and his eyes were already half closed. The easily bored are always a problem.

"Objection," Haricot snapped. "Conclusionary. I ask that it be stricken."

Syzmanski bobbed his head solemnly. "The jury will disregard the witness's last statement."

The bailiff walked around to the back of the bench, up on the riser, and whispered in Syzmanski's ear. He probably had a hot tip on a horse.

"So, did you pay Mr. Fleming his twenty-five percent?" I asked Detering.

The bailiff shuffled back to his seat and the jurors watched him. Perhaps they were seeking some meaning in his slow progress. There was none that I could discern.

"Every month. At least until you guys found me and started askin' about bribes and all that. Made the last payment just before Christmas."

The ninth juror was a stocky ex-marine. He stared at Fleming. Perhaps he had little sympathy for a man who built his fortune while other men died in the sand.

"And a nice present it was, I'm sure," I said. "Your witness."

Haricot was brief and destructive. He rolled his chair forward until he was directly between Detering and me. "How did you make these payments, Mr. Detering?" he asked.

"Here in Lansing. In an envelope."

Juror ten was a tall, slender bus driver. The world trooped through the doors of his vehicle every day and he looked at Detering with a wary cynicism.

"These payments, they were in cash?" Haricot asked, with the smallest smile.

"That's the way Fleming wanted it. I went with whatever he said. If he'd of wanted it in gold coins, that's what I'd of given him." Detering leaned to the right in the witness chair and craned his neck so that he could see me.

"I'm sorry," Haricot said. "Am I in your way? I wouldn't want you not to be able to see Mr. Cahill. He's pulling the strings, after all."

"Objection," I shouted, and Syzmanski banged his gavel.

"The jury will disregard Mr. Haricot's last comment. Let's get on with it, counsel." One of the spectators in the back of the courtroom was seized with a fit of coughing and Syzmanski frowned at the interruption.

"Sorry, your honor," Haricot said. "Now who did you give these envelopes to?" he asked Detering. He was grinning openly at the witness.

"To Fleming. At his office." Detering said.

Juror eleven smiled back at Haricot. He looked a little like my father and he knew what was coming.

"Anybody else around?"

"Nope. Just him and me. And the money."

The woman in the twelfth chair was a plump schoolteacher. Her dark hair was shot with white, like snow on black ice. She had asked to be excused so that she could return to her fifth graders, but Syzmanski had refused. Teachers live with the easy lies and the thoughtless transgressions of the young. As she eyed Detering, I hoped that she would see the boy within and not the man he had become.

Haricot chuckled along with the jury. "That's very clever. Did you think that up or did Mr. Cahill here?" He lifted his hand. "Don't answer, I just couldn't resist." As his hand fell, his voice sharpened.

"So, all we have is your word that you paid Mr. Fleming this cash money, with no one else present?"

"It ain't the sort of thing you'd mouth around to lots of people."

James Sixtas was the first alternate juror. Somehow, Haricot had missed him. He was ours if only we could get him on the panel in place of one of the chosen twelve.

"I'm sure it isn't. Tell me, Mr. Detering, how is it that you've come to know so much about the liquor business?" Haricot's voice was now light and cheerful.

"Well, I been at it since the twenties. One way or another."

The second alternate, seated at the far end of the jury box, was also a housewife and she looked at Detering without expression. She was on the fence.

"Indeed," Haricot said. He picked up a stack of papers from the counsel table. "Mr. Detering, I'm going to ask you to review these. I believe you'll find them to be copies of your criminal record."

Detering fumbled through the documents. "Good Christ," he said. "These all mine?"

There was a mutter of laughter from the left side of the courtroom and Syzmanski glared at the press section.

"All yours," Haricot said. "You've spent a good deal of time on the wrong side of *People v. Detering.* Now that you've refreshed your memory, can you tell the jury how many crimes you've been charged with in federal and state courts?"

"It looks like four felonies. But the misdemeanors, I can't count 'em all. There's a lot."

"And most of these convictions relate to violations of the liquor laws, do they not?"

"Most of 'em. Not all. Here's one for assault," Detering said. He held up one of the sheets with the look of a slow student doing his best to impress the teacher.

Again Haricot smiled for the jury members. This time they smiled back at him. "Now, really, what you are is a bootlegger. Isn't that right?"

Detering shook his head slowly. "Not no more."

A wave of laughter rolled through the courtroom. Syzmanski banged his gavel until the noise subsided. "Do you have anything more for this witness," he asked Haricot.

"No, I think Mr. Detering is through."

In the faces of the jury members, I saw a flicker of agreement.

Turncoat

April, 1946

"Charlie, I want you to do something, not that you'll like it. I want you to feed Hennessey some more shit. He's just aching to doublecross me and I want to give him the chance," Street said. Syzmanski was not one for long hours. He had recessed immediately after Detering's testimony. With the afternoon off, Street and I were the only customers seated at the long bar at Johnny's. He did not appear to notice that I was drinking only coffee and I saw no need to explain. It was just as well, as he was uncharacteristically preoccupied, almost nervous. When he spoke to me, he fidgeted on his bar stool and looked over my shoulder or down at his hands.

"I need to know what that senate committee has got and what they're going to do with it," Street said, finally. "They've passed some damn resolution, complete with subpoena power. Worse yet, they've hired some local yokel as their lawyer. Name of Frank Reno. You know him?"

"He and I were in the prosecutor's office together, before the war."

"Ain't that just a coincidence. Call our good friend Hennessey. Tell him you're fed up with all the funny business over here. Tell him you want to have a little conversation with Reno. Hennessey'll want to be there, to earn his pay from Fleming. But you need to be a little coy. Tell him you're not going to spill your guts unless Reno can convince you he's really got enough to get me booted off the Fleming case."

"He'll want me to give him something up front. Reno's a pretty good lawyer and Hennessey's no fool."

"Open up the kimono a little. Show Hennessey something Fleming'll be interested in. Tell him there's a lot of money going to Lammers to get him to testify."

"Is there?"

"Of course there is," Street said. "And it's coming right out of my own damn pocket. But don't tell him that. Tell him I'm running a slush fund of some kind. That should get his attention. Maybe it'll get Fleming to make a move."

Once again, he was right. With uncommon haste, Hennessey arranged a meeting that night at Reno's home on Lansing's west side. It was a modest frame bungalow with a small neatly trimmed lawn, beginning to green up from the early spring rains and glistening in the darkening light of evening. When I knocked on the door, Reno motioned me in after a quick glance up and down the street. He was a short, stocky man with square shoulders and close-cropped black hair. I remembered that his wife had died young of cancer and that he had become something of a religious recluse. After attending Mass each morning, he would walk over to the prosecutor's office to engage in decidedly more secular pursuits. Then he would slip quietly away after work. When we shook hands, his skin was moist with perspiration.

"We can't start until Randy's here," he said. "Want some coffee?"

I nodded. As we walked toward the small kitchen, I saw the glittering brass crucifix hanging over the doorway to what appeared to be a hallway to the bedrooms. Now that Street had cast me as Judas, I thought it perfectly appropriate.

We made small talk, seated around the red linoleum-topped counter that filled most of the space in the kitchen, until Hennessey arrived. "Gimme a drink," he said immediately. "It's been one fucking thing after another all day." His voice was unnaturally loud in Reno's silent, monastic little home.

"There's no liquor in this house," Reno said. "Hasn't been any for years."

"Before you got religion, you sure weren't such a goddamn saint. You got a bottle, Charlie? You were always good for a drink. You and your dud of a brother."

"I'm out of the family business," I said. I kept my tone even. Hennessey would not provoke me. Not now and not here.

"I'm surrounded by assholes," Hennessey said. "Let's make it quick. What've you got for us?"

I smiled patiently at him and spun out my tale of woe. Street was no better than the grafters and thugs we prosecuted, I told them. We were paying Lammers a small stipend out of state police funds. But Street had other sources of cash and the money was flowing freely to our star witness. Lammers was ready to testify and he would name Fleming as the chief conspirator.

Reno jumped in quickly. "Where does the money come from?"

I looked at him and then at Hennessey. "Wait just a minute," I said. "I told you I wasn't going to get into specifics. Not until I know what you've got on Street. I need to be damn sure you can get him out of Lansing for good. If he goes back home, then maybe I can settle down here to a normal life."

"You and Sarah Maynard. Nothing normal about that," Hennessey said.

I stood up slowly. Street had said that I would have to bluff, and there could be no better time. I turned to Reno, drawing it out.

"Frank, I remember you were always careful," I said. "I need to hear from you, not from Hennessey here. He's a politician, looking for an angle. You're the counsel to a senate investigating committee. I'm sick to death of the corruption and the lying and the cheating. But I've got to be able to trust you. I can't begin to do that until you tell me what you've got on Street." *Too smooth,* I thought. *Too rehearsed.*

I stepped over to the stove and poured myself another cup of coffee. Stand up, Street had said. Stand up, but don't walk out. Reno leaned forward, his hands clasped in front of him. Then he decided to believe me and it came flowing out. Stellinger had given the senate committee everything. They knew of every move we had made. Every corner we had cut. They knew about the stipend to Lammers and that we kept him supplied with liquor and women. They knew Street paid himself $100 a day plus expenses, seven days a week. They knew he often had dinner for two brought up to his room at the Olds, though his wife was back home in Grand Rapids. And they knew one more thing. It was the one thing I didn't know. They knew Street paid a weekly consulting fee to one Daniel Spann.

When Reno finished, I sipped my coffee, all cautious deliberation. Street had coached me on the close very carefully.

"You've got some things," I said, finally. "But they don't amount to much. I can give you a list of every dollar that's come in to pay Lammers and where it came from. Street keeps records and I can get at them. That'll get you the headlines you're looking for."

It was a complete lie. Street's records, to the extent they existed at all, were entirely in his head. But he had been confident that Hennessey would take the bait. I had doubted it. I had thought the man venal, not stupid. But Hennessey proved me wrong. He could change sides as easily as he changed his socks.

"Shit, Cahill, we need those records now. Tonight," he said.

I turned to face him and he lurched quickly to his feet. "I don't give a damn what you need," I said. "I'm tired of politicians and what they need. You'll get the records as soon as I find out where Street's hidden them."

He reached for my arm, but I brushed him aside and walked toward the living room, past the hallway door. I noticed that the door was now open about an inch. No wonder Hennessey was blustering so loudly. He'd probably hidden a stenographer in one of those bedrooms to take down every word.

When I reached the front door, Hennessey called out to me from the kitchen. He could not mention his witnesses who put me at Sarah's house the morning of the murder. Not in front of

Reno. Not with someone else listening. So he went for the next best thing.

"Bet that gets to you about Spann, don't it, Cahill? Seein' as how he beat the piss out of your brother for bein' such a smartass," he said.

"No skin off my nose," I said. "He deserved it and I'm not going to waste my time crying about it." Street had schooled me well.

≈ 33 ≈

Codes and Snares

April, 1946

Street wasted no time at all the next morning. Jonas Hine was in stark contrast to Harold Detering. If Detering was a bootlegger, Hine was a bureaucrat. But they were both in the same business. Hine's face was open, his hair slicked back and parted, his cheeks apple red as he took the oath and recited his name. He was Street's witness and the special prosecutor took him through the opening jumps in a hurry.

"By whom are you employed?" he asked.

"I work for the State of Michigan, at the Liquor Control Commission."

Street circled in front of the counsel table and fixed Hine directly in his sights. "What is your position with the Commission? What do you do?"

"I'm the Commission's Secretary. I keep the books of account. Place the orders with the distillers. Organize the Commission's agenda for the monthly meetings. That kind of thing."

"Are you a good Republican, Mr. Hine?" Street asked.

The judge and every member of the jury jumped as Haricot slammed his hand down on the counsel table next to his wheelchair. "Your honor, that's an outrageous question. The constitution prohibits any kind of partisan politics in the civil service. Mr. Hine's political affiliation is his own affair and no business of the special prosecutor."

"Now your honor, I'm sure we're all real interested in my brother from New York's views on Michigan's constitution. I'm just sure he stayed up late at night studyin' that at Columbia." Street grinned broadly at Haricot. Then raised his hands in a gesture of mock supplication.

"Let's save some time, here," he said to Hine. "Just tell the jury how you came to be Secretary of the Liquor Control Commission."

"Well, when Governor McReynolds was elected in '44, I'd supported him. When the job at the Commission opened up, they thought I'd be a good man for it."

"Be a little more specific for us, if you can. Who exactly got you the job? Anyone in this room?"

"Why, that man there. Wade Fleming," Hine said.

Haricot's hand came down again, but this time no one jumped. "I demand an offer of proof," he said. "What this has got to do with a conspiracy is beyond me. And I'm sure it's beyond the jury."

Judge Syzmanski sighed and waved us forward to the bench. "Hub, it's no crime to be a Republican," he said. "If it was, half the state'd be in jail. Have you got anything at all in mind here?"

"Sure I do. This guy is Fleming's man on the Commission. The orders came through him and he took care of Fleming's friends. Remember what Detering said. For every order he placed, Fleming got a kickback. Senator Maynard knew that. Fleming found out Maynard was spilling the beans. And he just naturally wanted him out of the way."

"Keep your voice down, Hub, they can hear you in the next county," Syzmanski said. I turned back to look at Sarah, but the judge had exaggerated. None of the spectators gave any indication that they had heard the whispered arguments.

"I presume you don't agree, Mr. Haricot," Syzmanski said.

"Of course I don't agree," Haricot said with an edge of sarcasm in his voice. I knew instantly that he had made a mistake. Syzmanski might be dull, but he could be exceedingly vindictive when challenged. Haricot realized his slip and tried to make amends.

"What I mean is, your honor, even if everything Street says is true, my clients are not on trial here for bribery or corruption. They're on trial for conspiracy to murder. So far as I know there's not one thing that ties them to the senator's death." His voice was controlled. But his face was tight with anger.

"Oh bullshit, Joel," Street said, and Haricot flushed at his crudity. "You've seen our witness list. You know we've got Vanik and Lammers waiting in line. You know how they're going to testify. I'll say it again, Judge. I'll tie this thing up in a pretty package for the jury in the end. Then we'll all sleep better at night."

Syzmanski looked expectantly at Haricot. The defense lawyer paused for a second and then said, "You're all motor and no brake, Street. We'll see how it plays out." He spun his wheelchair away from the bench with a sudden jerk of his hands.

"Places, gentlemen," Syzmanski said. When we were at the counsel tables, he rapped his gavel once to quiet the conversation behind us in the courtroom, and Street began to turn the screws down on his witness.

"How often did you talk with Wade Fleming after you became Secretary of the Commission?" he asked. Hine hesitated. When we rehearsed his testimony, Street had been his best friend. Now he was on the attack and Hine could only recoil backward into the witness chair.

"I don't really recall," he said. "Maybe once or twice a month."

"Let's get to it," Street said. Now, he let the jury hear the hostility in his voice. "Isn't it true that you had a private phone installed in your office? Isn't it true that phone was just for Fleming's calls? Isn't it true that Fleming called you every week to give you the orders?"

"Objection," Haricot snapped. "If counsel is going to lead all his witnesses like this, maybe we should just put him on the stand so I can cross examine. It sure would save a lot of time."

"Time's the last thing Mr. Haricot wants to save. It's the defendants' skins he's worried about," Street said. Syzmanski reached for his gavel but Street bulled ahead. "Let's be honest.

We all know these witnesses are testifying under a grant of immunity. If this civil serpent"—he rolled the phrase out with obvious pleasure—"can't be more forthright, then I move that he be declared a hostile witness."

"Counsel's statements in front of the jury, these statements alone are grounds for a mistrial and I ask your honor to so rule," Haricot shouted.

The judge finally found his gavel and banged it down. "I won't have this in my courtroom. I just won't have it," he said. His voice was a righteous roar and his face was crimson above his tight collar, startling against the black of his robes. "You're each right on the thin edge of contempt. Both motions are denied. Now get on with it. Try the case."

Street took a deep breath. Then he bobbed his head obediently. "Yessir," he said. As he circled back around the counsel table, his back to the judge and the jury, I saw him smile for Rachel Loeb in the press box. Only then did I realize that it was all an act, all counterfeit rage and careful planning. Haricot had raised the immunity issue in his opening statement and Street wanted to get it in front of the jury on his own terms. He had baited Haricot from the beginning just to set him up for a failed mistrial motion. Haricot hadn't seen the trap. Now any challenge to the immunized testimony of Vanik and Lammers would be blunted. Haricot's vanity, his sense of his own affronted dignity, had become Street's weapon.

With that in his pocket, Street was all courtesy. "Mr. Hine, let's try again. Tell us about your talks with Wade Fleming. Just take your time," he said.

"He'd call me every Monday on the private line. Just four companies had the inside track, Walker, Mohawk, Arrow, and Schenley's. The others, they were all Democrats. He had a code. Arrow was Red Arrow and Mohawk was the Indian. He'd say that Red Arrow was a good line to travel with, to see what I could do for them. Or to take care of the Indian. I knew what he meant. They'd get the orders that week. That's how I got my job. Fleming said if I couldn't do it, I wouldn't have my job very long."

"Objection, irrelevant," Haricot said wearily. "Your honor, sometimes I feel like I've wandered into the wrong trial. This has nothing to do with the charges against the defendants."

"Denied. I've ruled on this before, counselor." Syzmanski was ours now. From the look on his face, Haricot knew it.

Street then took an enormous chance. "One last question. Who first contacted you about testifying in this case?"

Hine pointed at me and said, "Mr. Cahill. He came and talked to me out at the Commission's offices."

"And what did Mr. Cahill say to you?"

Hine grinned at me. "Oh, we talked a long time. At first I was scared and I couldn't think very well. Couldn't remember much. Then he explained how immunity worked. It was real clear how he explained it."

Street turned to Haricot. "Your witness, counselor," he said, and I was stiff with disbelief.

Haricot rushed in and his eagerness betrayed him. "What else did Mr. Cahill tell you?" he demanded.

"He just said to tell the truth and that everything would be fine," Hine said.

It was all false. I had never interviewed him alone. I had never been to the Liquor Control Commission's offices. I had never spoken the words Hine so blithely attributed to me. Street had set another trap. Somehow he had primed Hine for this precise sequence of questions. Now Haricot was caught in a mistake that a second-year law student would be embarrassed to make. He knew it and he hammered away grimly at Hine for the rest of the day, but he could not shake the man's testimony.

After the adjournment, I leaned over the counsel table to Street. "Suborning perjury will get your license lifted," I said.

He leaned back comfortably and pulled the gold watch from his vest pocket. "Three o'clock," he said. "According to Grandpa John's watch, Stainless is keeping bankers' hours." He snapped the cover of the watch shut with lazy amusement. "It's exactly what you would have told him. I just rearranged the speaking parts. I've done worse and so will you."

Over my shoulder, I heard the measured creak of Haricot's wheelchair. He stopped squarely in front of Street. "A good day for you, Hubbell," he said. "I don't usually make that many mistakes with just one witness." He ran his hand along his jaw line, a small gesture of resignation. "But I wouldn't count too much on Lammers if I were you. These guys play by a different set of rules."

"Joel, I learned long ago it's better to shun the bait than to struggle in the snare. I think that's from the Bible, somewhere. Anyway, Lammers'll be here," Street said. "He's got nowhere else to go."

⇒ 34 ⇐

Committee Work

April, 1946

The phone rang early the next morning, and I lunged out of a
fitful doze to answer it before the insistent jangling raised the
dead. It was Street. He had no time and few words.

"Maloney's on his way over there for you," he said. "Get out
to the courthouse. Get to Syzmanski before Haricot and his
army show up. We've got to have an adjournment, at least for
the rest of the week. That goddamn senate committee's scheduled a hearing for this afternoon. They know we're in trial and
they're hopin' for some free publicity."

I wiped the sleep away from my eyes and shook the tatters
of my dream away. "Grounds," he said. "We need some grounds
for delay or Syzmanski will kick me out of his office. We've
pushed this trial hard from the beginning."

"For chrissake, I know that. Syzmanski owes me. Use your
imagination. Tell him Ike Wolfe's risen from the dead and he's
got pictures."

The phone clicked off and I was left only with my dim recol-
lection of the life and times of Isaac Wolfe. Late at night at the
Olds, Street had often regaled me with stories of his cases. His
representation of Wolfe was one of his favorites, told with great
relish over too many drinks.

Wolfe was a Detroit numbers runner until he fell on hard
times and into disfavor with the Sicilians who controlled that
business on the east side. Their legbreakers left him with a
lasting limp and a serious grudge. When the corruption case

against Detroit's mayor went before the Ferguson grand jury, Wolfe approached Street with a simple proposition. Trade my testimony, Wolfe had said, in return for immunity and safe passage to California.

"I didn't have a piece of any of those trials and I wasn't too happy about it. I wanted some of the action," Street had said. "I thought I'd take a flyer with Wolfe. So I went down to see old man Ferguson. He jumped at it and overnight that little shit was a star. He wasn't worth a damn as a runner. But he kept good books and he had the kind of memory lawyers love. He was, how shall I say it, open to suggestion. Too bad he couldn't pay my fees."

"Why did you do it if you didn't get paid?" I asked.

"Hell, I was just stirrin' the pot, hopin' to get lucky. Wolfe ran a string of whores on the side and I could always take it out in trade."

Street had laughed at the memory. "At least it got me in good with Syzmanski. St. Stainless sure liked a walk on the wild side."

"What happened to Wolfe?"

"Oh, he made it to California all right. Or at least most of him did," Street said. "I think he left a few of his soft parts behind. Those dagos have a real fixation with manhood. And they don't favor squealers. They figured if they circumcised Ike again, it'd shut him up. When they finished carving him up, they put a couple bullets in the back of his head and shipped him out west in a barrel. I heard they sent his balls and pecker to his brother as a Christmas present. But that's probably just a rumor."

I had discounted Street's story as another lawyer's tale, spun out on a winter's night from equal parts of bravado and bourbon. Syzmanski, fresh from morning mass, did not.

"Wolfe's long dead," he said. He sat down suddenly behind the plain wooden desk allotted for his chambers. He folded his hands in front of him and leaned his chin on the platform they made. He was the picture of nervous rectitude.

"What's Hub trotting him out for now?" he asked.

I didn't know enough to be clever. "Judge, we need a favor," I said. "Something serious has come up and we need some time to deal with it. Street said you'd understand. He said you'd remember how he helped you in the Wolfe matter."

Syzmanski cleared his throat. "Hub's an honorable man. If he needs some time, I'll give it to him. I'll tell Haricot and the others I've had a death in the family. We'll give the jury the rest of the week off. God knows they deserve it after that circus yesterday."

He handled it with great authority, announcing with a slight catch in his voice that he was needed in Detroit to make the funeral arrangements for his favorite aunt, newly dead. The jury filed out gratefully, freed for a time from the pounding monotony of the law.

Syzmanski lumbered down from the bench and the courtroom emptied. But Wade Fleming did not move. He stood at the defendants' table. Polished. Compact. Every part in place. He gestured to me and I walked stiffly over to him.

"Life's just full of unexpected developments, isn't it?" He smiled at me then. The same even, perfect smile. "How's your little family?" he asked.

I slid in behind him and swung the empty left sleeve of my suit coat around his throat and pulled it tight with my right hand. Haricot's young associate hammered at my shoulder and I shifted my weight and swept his knee outward, foot to fulcrum as the Rangers had taught me. He cried out and fell away. Fleming began to gag as I cinched the noose tighter around his neck.

"You filthy shit, I've got you," I whispered to him, my mouth an inch from his ear. I was constricted by rage. Caught in it. And narrowed by it. Only two minutes and it would be over. Fleming clawed frantically at the noose and made a cawing noise like a captured crow. That trivial thing slowed me and saved him. *No more death*, I thought. Then Shrieber slammed into me from my left side and Fleming was free.

He saw only weakness in my hesitation. "You've got nothing, Cahill," he shouted. His voice was a rasp and his hands fluttered at his neck. "You've got nothing and you are nothing." I stared at him, panting.

"Get out of here, son," Haricot said to me from his chair. His voice was composed and tired. "You have no idea what you're doing. Go downtown. See for yourself."

I spun away from Shrieber, but Fleming had the last word, the same word. "Nothing," he screamed at me, "nothing at all."

I MET Street in the Capitol, outside one of the ornate committee rooms on the Senate side. The hallway was jammed with reporters bustling about importantly, photographers with their cameras in hand, local lawyers come to see the show, and political functionaries with nothing better to do. Street walked down the hallway, with Maloney and a slender balding man that I did not recognize at his side. The reporters descended on him immediately, shouting questions, but he waved them off.

"No questions now, boys," he said. "But don't leave until the show's over. There's a little surprise ending." He was always the showman.

When I reached his side, he threw his arm around my shoulder and whispered in my ear. "All I need you to do is sit down with me at the witness table. When we get through with the formalities, Lonergan's going to try to clear the room. Then all hell's going to break loose. That's when I want you beside me. One arm and all."

There was no chance to respond and I had no notion of what Street intended to do. The door to the committee room opened and we swept in and seated ourselves at the witness table. I turned my head to watch the crowd push and shove for seats in the folding chairs arrayed in neat rows behind us. Three senators filed in from the door at the rear and sat behind a long cloth-covered table. They were trying, without much success, to look at ease amid the tumult. Senator Michael Lonergan sat in the middle and Frank Reno took a place at a side table. His face flushed every time he looked at me.

Lonergan pounded his gavel. "Quiet," he said. "I'll have quiet in this room so we can start." He was a red-faced man, with a triple chin and a potbelly that strained the buttons on his vest. When the noise subsided, he looked once, then again, at the balding man to Street's right. *He knows that man from somewhere,* I thought.

Lonergan cleared his throat and began to read from the sheet of paper on the table in front of him. "Let me welcome you all to this session of this special committee to investigate the Ingham County one-man grand jury," he said.

He cleared his throat again, turned his head, and coughed loudly. "We've talked to Justice Storey. We've talked to Judge Stellinger. Now we want to talk with you, Mr. Street. We're happy to see you could make time in your busy schedule. But before we commence, I must tell those of you from the press and the public that we want to preserve the secrecy of the grand jury proceedings. So after we administer the oath to Mr. Street, we'll go into closed session to take his testimony."

Street was on his feet immediately. "Mr. Chairman, I most strongly object. I'll answer every question you have. But not in some star chamber. What are you afraid of, Senator?"

Lonergan slammed the gavel down. "Forego the theatrics, Street. We know a lot about you. You can't deny you paid Otto Lammers more than $10,000 from state police funds and he was an admitted briber. You can't deny you paid him under a false account. You can't deny you paid Daniel Spann, a man known as Nightshirt Danny, through another false account. If you can't deny these charges, we must take it that you admit them."

Street laughed at him. "Here's what I admit. I admit I convicted the grafters. I admit I put the criminals behind bars. I admit I hired people like Charles Cahill here, decorated for gallantry in the war. Wounded when people like you hid behind your exemptions. Beyond that, I admit nothing."

Lonergan banged the gavel again. "Will you go under oath, Mr. Street?"

"Absolutely. Just as soon as you do, Senator. Just as soon as you raise your right hand and admit to the bribes you took from those bawdy houses and gambling joints you frequent." Street stopped as the flashbulbs cracked away. Then he stepped out from behind the witness table and pulled a folded piece of paper from his coat pocket.

"There's one more thing, Senator," he said. "I know you recognize Sheriff Langford here. He's the Macomb County sheriff. He swore me in this morning as a special deputy, and we're here to serve you with this warrant for your arrest, for taking those bribes."

Street strode forward and slammed the folded paper down on the cloth-covered table. "Sergeant Maloney, arrest this man," he called out. The room erupted into chaos. And that was the end of the special committee to investigate the one-man grand jury. But it was not the end of Fleming or Hennessey.

≡ 35 ≡

Otto's Turn

April, 1946

When I reached the hotel the next morning, the lobby bustled with life, but our offices upstairs were deserted. I walked down the hallway to the room into which we had moved Otto Lammers for safekeeping. One of our investigators leaned against the closed door. His arms were crossed and he had a short unlit cigar jammed in his mouth.

"Hope you got a strong stomach," he said as he shoved the door open for me.

Hubbell Street was slouched in the brocade armchair next to the unmade bed. "I assume you brought hell with you," he said. "No? Well, see it for yourself. Fleming's been a busy boy."

He jerked his heavy head toward the open bathroom doorway. Otto Lammers was in the white porcelain tub, his oiled black hair plastered back in disarray, his head back, and his mouth half-open. His eyes were finally still. His right arm dangled outward across the rim of the tub. His palm was up and his fingers were streaked with blood, and drops of it fell slowly to the tile floor. The slash across his wrist was open, raw, and red.

The tub had overflowed, the floor was puddled with water, and the bathroom rug was sodden with it. His left arm lay across his chest, slashed open almost to the bone. The blood was congealed there, on the mat of his body hair. The water in the tub was a thick brownish red. As he died, his bowels had opened and there was a pervasive stench. A straight razor lay on the glass shelf over the sink, coated with blood.

"Death with dignity," Street said from behind me. "Don't touch anything. The lab boys always want everything pristine pure."

"When did you call them?"

"Twenty minutes ago. I've just been sitting here. Contemplating morality and watching Otto drain."

"How could you be sure he was dead?"

"Hell, you don't need a doctor to find a pulse. When I got here, Otto was gone. Gone in the gray light of dawn." His voice was singsong and he grimaced at his little rhyme and then was still again. He lit a cigarette and leaned back against the chair, watching the ash burn. There was a heavy hotel ashtray on the floor by his feet, with a half dozen snubbed-out cigarette butts in it. Finally, he swung his head once, a curious rocking motion that shook the flesh in his jowls.

"There's a note over there on the nightstand," he said.

I scanned Otto's last testament quickly. He had written it on the hotel stationery in the same script he used to tote up the obligations in his little black book. The style was stilted, confessional, and funereal. He regretted his sins. Mourned his ill-spent life. Appointed his brother the executor of his worldly estate. Told his estranged wife he loved her. And bid farewell to life. He also completely exonerated Wade Fleming from any complicity in Senator Maynard's death. It was sensible, even touching. It was also entirely fake.

"Otto didn't write this," I said to Street.

"You're learning. Of course he didn't. Otto was no Roman. He couldn't write a letter like that, even on the point of dying. Sober reflection and repentance were not exactly his strong suit. Now, why don't you just put that letter in your pocket before the state boys get here."

"Somebody dictated the letter to him?"

"Damned right they did. Probably even helped him open up the veins. He sure as hell didn't have the stomach to cut *both* his wrists."

"Fleming," I said.

"Go to the head of the class. He and his boys must've paid Otto a little visit early this morning, when nobody else was around. Knowing Fleming, they probably took their time."

"I had him. I had him in my hand," I said, and I told Street how I had stopped just short of murder.

Street was quiet for a moment, his eyes hooded as he looked up at me from the embrace of the chair. I had finally managed to shock him. He gave a short, barking laugh. "No killing in the courtroom," he said. "It's not allowed."

The state police lab techs arrived and began to measure out the last details of the life of Otto Lammers. Street gestured to me and I walked over to his chair. Then, in a quiet voice, he launched into one of his stories. "When I was a kid," he said, "I was swimming out in the big lake. It was rough that day. Big chop and a hell of an undertow. I was cold, just coming out. Then I heard this woman screaming out there, way over her head. I was a pretty good swimmer and I got out to her. But I was dog tired. The truth is, I was just about to let her go. If it was her or me, it was going to be me. But then I hit a sandbar. And we both lived."

He had not moved from the chair. His head was down, his voice still low. I sensed that, for once, this was not a story he had polished beforehand.

"To this day, I don't know whether I'm a coward or a hero," he said. "Probably some of both."

I leaned over and whispered into his ear. "What about the letter?"

"Tear it up and throw it in the Grand River. No need to polish up Wade Fleming's good name."

"Without Lammers testifying, Fleming will walk," I said.

"You've got a genius for the obvious," he said. "I should've known Fleming would come after Lammers. And he did, just like Pavlov's dog. Now it's nothing but spilt milk and me who spilled it. But with Vanik's testimony, I can still tag Lefkowitz and Shrieber. It's enough to run with. You've got to make sure that little puke Vanik comes through for us. Make sure there's a guard on him over at the jail."

"What about him?" I gestured toward Otto. He was pale and quiet and his skin was beginning to pucker in the filthy water.

Street raised his voice as he heaved himself out of his chair. "Otto Lammers killed himself. That's the end of it. Right, boys?"

The state police lab techs were quick to assent. As I left the hotel room, they were lifting Lammers' body out of the tub. Over my shoulder, I watched them roll him over into a gray hotel blanket. Now, truly, he had nowhere else to go.

= 36 =

All the World's a Stage

April, 1946

We took our seats in the courtroom the next day when Syzmanski banged his gavel. He paused, preening for a moment in the silence. Then he said, "I'm afraid I have some bad news. Mrs. Goldberg called me this morning. Her husband's had a heart attack. I've talked to the doctors and there's no possibility he'll be able to finish this trial."

He paused again to contemplate the inconvenience of Herschel Goldberg's illness. Street stared straight ahead. The judge turned to James Sixtas, seated at the end of the jury box. "Mr. Sixtas, you're the first alternate. You'll be taking Mr. Goldberg's place in the jury room."

I had an unobstructed view of the side door of the courtroom. A tall, rawboned man leaned against the wall, next to the door. When Syzmanski finished, he turned and left quietly, nodding at the state troopers at the door. I glanced at Street. But he had not moved.

Syzmanski banged his gavel again. He was all business and judicial economy now. His heartfelt sympathy for Herschel Goldberg was no more than a passing glance.

"Gentlemen, let's proceed. Who's got the next witness?"

"I do, your honor," I said. "We call Nathan Vanik."

Vanik shuffled forward to the stand. The state police trooper had removed the man's handcuffs before we brought him into the courtroom. But Vanik was still a prisoner. His dull brown hair was shorn high around the temples in the jailer's white sidewall haircut. The cheap suit we bought for him hung loosely on his thin shoulders.

I handled him with care. Just as Street had instructed. "Mr. Vanik, I want you to talk right to the jury. Speak right to the lady there on the end. Can you do that for me?"

Vanik nodded. He was without words. "I know this is new for you. You have to speak out. The court reporter can't get it down if you just nod."

"I understand." His voice was small, just a whisper. The reporters in the press box strained forward to hear him and I heard the crowd behind us fidgeting uncomfortably.

"What's your occupation? What do you do for a living?"

"I'm a driver. I take people around."

I looked at my legal pad and the silence stretched out. I was alone with him, perched on a high ledge at stage left. It was down to shorteyes Nathan Vanik now. Down to what he feared the most. There was a large encased clock on the rear wall of the courtroom and I heard it ticking as I hesitated on the edge.

The jailhouse network, the web of whispered conversation and scribbled notes, had known immediately of the death of Otto Lammers. And Vanik knew of it as well. When Maloney and I had picked him up earlier that morning at the city jail, he had immediately begun to plead with me.

"They'll kill me if I name them. Please. Please don't make me," he had said.

On cue, Maloney pulled the car to the edge of the road and slammed the gearshift into neutral. He leaned back over the seat and thrust one hand between Vanik's legs and jerked upward. Vanik screamed and Maloney jerked again.

"Used that on those little boys, didn't you, Nate," he said.

Vanik clawed at Maloney's arm with both his hands, but Maloney merely grinned at him. "Hurts don't it, shithead? It'll hurt worse down in the Detroit House of Corrections. You're gonna love bein' the prom queen. They'll pass you around, Nate. Every night someone new. And those boys, Nate. Those boys're mean as snakes. They like to make it hurt. When they're done with you, they'll stuff your head down a toilet. Drownin' in shit's a bad way to go. At least with us, you got some chance."

He jerked Vanik upright and held him for a moment so that the pain suspended him. Then Maloney released him. Vanik fell forward and he cradled himself silently as we drove to the courthouse. I had not looked at him again, but now he was mine alone. And I had to have him. All of him.

"Now, in the fall of 1945, who were you driving around? Anyone you see here today?" I asked. I stood in front of him, as the clock measured out the seconds.

Vanik came up out of his chair and pointed at the defendants' table. "Those two men, Lefkowitz and Shrieber," he said. "I drove them over to Lansing. They said it was to case a job. They said it was to set up a hit on some lousy politician." The words tumbled out into the record.

"Tell me what a hit is, Mr. Vanik." He was in the confessional now and I helped him along with the words.

"A killing. They're killers. They kill people." Haricot shouted his objection and Syzmanski ordered the jury to disregard Vanik's outburst. But it was already in the minds of the jurors.

"Who was the politician?" I asked after Syzmanski gaveled the courtroom into silence.

"It was Harry Maynard. I seen him. I seen him with his wife and his kid. They was all on the porch when we drove by. Izzy pointed at him. He said the boss wanted him dead."

Haricot shot forward in his wheelchair and exploded into the hearsay objection. On the law, he was right and again Syzmanski excluded the testimony. For the jury and the press, though, the law was only a means. I began to think that even without Lammers we might bring an end to Wade Fleming as well as his henchmen. *Put Fleming in the center of it*, I thought. Then Sarah and I could go our separate ways.

"Who was this boss? Who did you all work for?"

Vanik hesitated and Haricot cut him off. "There's no foundation for this testimony. He's established no relationship at all," he said.

Syzmanski temporized. "He's right, Mr. Cahill. Lay a few bricks and maybe I'll let him in."

With the doorway open, I plunged forward. I took Vanik through his history as a wheelman for the Purple Gang. I established that he drove Bernstein, Millburg, and the Keywell brothers to the Collingwood killings. I traced the transition from rum-running to numbers and prostitution, and the political intrigue that followed Prohibition. And every step of the way, I kept Wade Fleming on stage. But only at the end did I put him in the spotlight.

"Now, who was the paymaster for all of this? Who wrote the checks?"

Syzmanski overruled Haricot's shouted objection and Vanik answered. "That man there, Wade Fleming. But he didn't use no checks. He always paid cash."

I sat down and Haricot wheeled forward to play his part. "Where are you staying these days, Mr. Vanik?" he asked.

Vanik's head dropped forward. "I'm down at the city jail."

"Speak up, the jury wants to hear you. Why are you staying in a jail?"

"For some things down in Detroit."

"What things? What things are you under arrest for?" Haricot had moved his wheelchair forward and now he was between Vanik and the jury. They looked squarely at Vanik's face as he answered.

Vanik tried to twist away. "Stuff with some kids down there."

"In fact, you're under arrest for sodomy with minor children, are you not? Here, let me read you some of the particulars."

Haricot reached into the pocket of his suit coat for a folded charging warrant. I jabbed at him with the relevance objection, but Syzmanski waved me off with a flip of his hand. Haricot then slowly read into the record the dull prose of Nathan Vanik's pederasty. When he was finished, Vanik was freshly branded. Haricot spun his chair away from the jury in righteous disgust and then paused for his last lines.

"Who's in the cell with you? Down there in the jail?" he asked quietly.

"Lupton. Bobbie Lupton."

"And what are goyem, Mr. Vanik?" Again Haricot was quiet, studious.

"People who aren't Jewish."

Haricot wheeled back before the jury and spat out the words. "Suppose I were to tell you that Robert Lupton's outside this courtroom? Suppose he's ready to testify you told him you were going to put on a show for the goyem today. Just like you put one on for him last night. What would you say to that?"

"Bobbie'd never say that. Bobbie loves me," Vanik cried.

I was on my feet shouting futile objections as Syzmanski pounded his gavel and our case collapsed. Haricot had played out the jailhouse informant gambit perfectly, and I had no idea what we could do to counter his performance.

⪼ 37 ⪻

Sacrifices

April, 1946

"You know, it's real hard to get drunk on beer," Street said. The legislature was in recess and the bar at the Olds was quiet and forlorn. My postmortems were just as tired, the dreary review of a case that had evaporated in front of us. It had been our ritual from the first day of trial and Street forced me through it again. Although he drank steadily, he was distant and reserved. I did not dwell on my failure to protect Vanik from Haricot's assault. Perhaps there was no protecting him. Perhaps he was doomed from the start.

Street read my mind. "Our little faggot sure didn't play very well there at the end, did he? Joel did a nice job," he said. "But he's in for a little surprise when he finds out Lupton's disappeared into the night."

I pressed him for some explanation, but he merely changed the subject. "For a moment there at the beginning, I thought Vanik wasn't going to come across at all. You and Maloney have a talk with him?"

"You said we had to have him. Maloney did the talking."

"Well, I told the jury the first day we didn't find our witnesses in church. It's a shame we're stuck with two-way perverts like Vanik and crooked bureaucrats like Hine. But it's how the world works."

He stopped and grinned. "The beer in this bar tastes like warm spit and it's turning me moral all of a sudden. This job is steady indoor work. No heavy lifting and the pay's good. What more could a man want?"

I had no answer. He knew it and he shifted again. "Hell," he said, "I need a real drink. Then I need to have a little talk with brother Haricot. There's a bottle of Jack Daniels upstairs. Otto's last gift. Haricot's going for a directed verdict tomorrow and I think better with a hangover."

It was a shiny blue morning, all warm sun and fair wind, as Street and Maloney and I drove out to Mason the next day for the curtain to fall. Street rested his head against the car seat. His eyes were closed and his face was still. There was not an empty chair in the courtroom, and a line of spectators coiled away from the door and around the rail of the rotunda, patiently waiting for a seat to open. Reporters circled the defendants' table, but they quickly came our way when Street slammed his briefcase down and settled back into his chair. Syzmanski made his usual grand entrance and we were swept back into the battle.

"Anything further, Mr. Street?" the judge asked.

"The people rest their case." Street underplayed it, his voice flat and resigned.

"I have a motion, your honor," Haricot said. After the jury filed out, he launched into his attack. Over the course of the trial, the judge had ordered that a second shift of court reporters be employed to produce daily transcripts. The full record, every slip, every evasion, every admission was available to Haricot, stacked in neat piles of blue bound volumes, and he was soon up to his elbows in the typewritten minutia of our case.

Haricot was a good butcher, with a taste for blood. He spared nothing as he ground away. But I noticed that he did not say a word about Lefkowitz and Shrieber. He ended where he began, with our failure to join Fleming in a conspiracy to kill. When we had Otto Lammers, we had Fleming. Now we had neither.

Haricot made it explicit. "When this case began, there were promises of insider testimony, damning testimony," he said. "Mr. Street told us we'd hear all the lurid details. But all we have is rumor and gossip. Your honor cannot submit a case to the jury where a verdict would be based only upon conjecture. I ask this court to end this travesty and to direct a verdict of not guilty as to Wade Fleming."

I could not comprehend it. "He's letting us take Lefkowitz and Shrieber to the jury," I whispered to Street.

"Believe it, Charlie. Two pawns for a rook."

He stood quickly and faced the judge to play his part. With our case against Fleming gone, Street had nothing left but the practiced, measured flow of his words. When he neared the end, he addressed the judge. But he talked to the press box. Again he underplayed it, for the effect.

"Before your honor rules, consider this one thing," he said. "The people are watching us here today. They will note well what we do. They have seen what's been going on here in Lansing. And they are disgusted by it. Men fought for this country"—he looked at me and I looked away—"men suffered for this country while Wade Fleming turned the Capitol into a bazaar, with everything for sale at a price. This case should go to the jury. Let them judge the guilty. Let them stand surrogate for the outrage of our citizens. Let them do what needs to be done."

The courtroom was silent, breathless. Syzmanski leaned forward and toyed absently with the papers on the bench in front of him. *He's a better actor than he is a judge*, I thought. Then, on cue, he ended our case against Wade Fleming. "I grant your motion as to the defendant Fleming, Mr. Haricot," he said.

The courtroom exploded. Reporters swarmed forward to the defense table and flashbulbs cracked like chain lightning through the clouds of a summer night. Syzmanski banged away rhythmically with his gavel and gradually the storm subsided.

"I'll empty this court if there's another outburst of any sort," he said. He cleared his throat and then set out the basis for his opinion, reciting like a schoolboy from the notes in front of him. When he finished, the courtroom was calm with boredom again.

"We'll break for the day and start at nine o'clock sharp tomorrow morning. I'll expect everyone to be on their good behavior, especially the ladies and gentlemen of the press." As he left the bench, he stopped at the door to his chambers and posed patiently for the photographers, presenting his good side for their cameras.

Outside the courthouse, I watched as Fleming read out his statement, braced against the west wind. He looked down at the papers he held in front of him, squinting down in the white glare of the sun. The words were precise, the cadence stilted and stiff, and the slur now quite pronounced. His conclusion was as dull as his voice.

"I will go home now to my family in Grand Rapids," he said. "I hope that Mr. Lefkowitz and Mr. Shrieber will join me soon."

Maloney was beside me and he laughed aloud. "Fat chance," he said. "Those hebes are going home to Jacktown." *But Fleming will be free,* I thought. *Free to use what he knew against me and Sarah.*

⇒ 38 ⇐

Nightshirt Danny

April, 1946

The next morning it was Haricot who started Lefkowitz and Shrieber on their way. When Syzmanski banged his gavel and turned expectantly to the defense table, Haricot said slowly, "The defense will call no witnesses. We are ready to take this case to the jury."

Street had anticipated it, but Syzmanski had not and for once he was speechless. He stared at Haricot, his mouth open, his nostrils flared. His soft hands fluttered at the sleeves of his robe and he stuttered in confusion.

"Do I understand correctly that the defense rests its case?"

He was an actor without a stage. From the beginning, he had relished the attention, the press, and the deference. He was looking forward to another week in the limelight. Now Haricot had robbed him of that.

"We have no need for further testimony," Haricot said. "The prosecution's brought us nothing but felons and perjurers. We're confident the jury will see them for what they are."

Street was on his feet. "Move to strike," he said. "Brother Haricot should save his fine words for closing arguments. Not that it'll do him any good. The jury can weigh our witnesses' words against the defendants' silence."

Haricot wheeled his chair. "That's grounds for a mistrial right there, your honor. He knows full well these men need not testify. Yet he makes a statement like that in front of the jury."

He wheeled his chair forward until he directly faced our table, his back to the judge. His words broke over us, like water on sand. "Is there nothing you won't say? Nothing you won't do?"

Syzmanski was pounding his gavel, roaring for order. But Street only smiled. He leaned forward, across the table. His voice was as soft as the night wind in the pine forest. So soft that only Haricot and I could hear. "Nothing," he said. "Nothing at all."

THE JUDGE gave us the rest of the day to prepare for closing arguments, but Street waved away my offers of help that night at the hotel. "Finish up our instructions," he said. "The judge wants them by noon and we don't need to be late. He's pissed off enough with his little show comin' to such a premature end. Put in something profound for him to say on self-incrimination. The more Syzmanski says on that, the more the jury'll remember Lefkowitz and Shrieber sittin' there, still as stones."

I had been polishing our jury instructions for weeks, as if I could bring some structure to the case by carpentering the jumble of fact, conjecture, artifice, and impression into one of the measured cubicles of the law. There were the facts the jury had heard. And then there were the facts as I knew them. The two versions of reality were so at odds that it was hopeless, and I trudged back to my small office with my mind a blank.

Out of Street's sight, I propped my feet up on the steel desk. I poured a water glass full of scotch and set it on the corner of the desk, well within reach. It was a cool spring night and the radiator hissed and coughed in an effort to bring a modicum of heat into the drafty room. I looked at the glass, my old friend. I reached for it once. But then I dropped my hand. It would be so easy. So familiar. So recognizably a part of the pattern of my days. My father beckoned to me, across the years. Have a drink, he said, and I heard him well.

I raised my hand again, but then Street's voice rang out from the next room. "Goddamnit, what the hell do I pay you for? What do you mean the jury's split?"

The other voice was as low as Street's was loud and I strained to hear above the sputtering radiator. "Don't blaspheme at me, lawyer. I ain't your nigger and don't you forget it."

I swung my feet down and walked as softly as I could to my half-open office door. Street still sat at his mahogany desk. From my vantage point behind him, I saw his ears redden with anger. The tall man I had seen in the courtroom when Syzmanski called Sixtas to the jury box leaned back against the wall, both hands in his pockets. He was angular and rawboned and one shoulder was higher than the other. His shiny black suit fit him oddly as a result. He wore a soiled and wrinkled white shirt buttoned tight at the throat in the style of a country preacher. His hands were huge and square, like coal shovels, and they dangled halfway to his knees.

He saw me in the doorway. "You want your messenger boy to hear this?" he said to Street.

Street swung around in his chair. "Come on in," he said to me. "Meet the right honorable Daniel Spann. Most people call Mr. Spann here by his proper name. He's old Nightshirt Danny. On account of the fact he spends most of his time parading around in a sheet and burning crosses on colored folk's lawns. Mr. Nightshirt here was just going to explain to me why he's so proficient at scaring coons, but can't do a man's job when it's set out for him."

"You lay your tongue on me again, you'll be talkin' to thin air," Spann said. His voice was as sharp as a straight razor. "I got Goldberg off the jury for you. You won't be seein' that jewboy again. I'll keep the rest of them in line."

Street's laughter rippled through the room. "I'm so sorry. We can't afford to offend the grand klaxon, now can we?"

He stood abruptly, still smiling. He motioned Spann around the desk and draped his left arm over the man's shoulder. He gave Spann a small shake, much like an annoyed parent with an offending child. Then he turned to me, his right hand thrown out in a parody of the orator's flourish.

"Nightshirt here, he just doesn't seem to understand the nuances of jury interaction. He thinks he can just scare them to death," he said. "Now, what's a man to do with thinking like that?"

He shook Spann again. Then he whirled and drove his heavy farmer's fist into the man's stomach. Spann fell forward, gagging. With his left hand, Street wrenched open the top drawer of his desk and pulled out a state police issue revolver. Then he whipped the kneeling man twice across the face, forward and back. Blood sprayed from Spann's mouth and spattered against the flowered wallpaper on the wall next to Street's desk.

"You'd best kill me, you sonofabitch," Spann mumbled, and he spat an upper denture out onto the faded hotel carpet. Blood dripped slowly out of both sides of his mouth, down his chin and neck, onto his white shirt.

Street dropped to his knees next to Spann and looked up at me. "Good old Nightshirt still doesn't understand." He ran the fingers of his left hand up Spann's neck, into his hair, almost in a caress. Then he pulled the man's head upright.

"Now you listen to me, you jerkwater piece of shit," he said, and he jammed the barrel of the revolver into Spann's open mouth, splintering his lower teeth. "You stay away from my jury. I'll handle them from now on. You get your ass back down to Indiana. If I need you, I'll call you. Can you handle that? Or should I just blow your brains out here and now?"

Spann bobbed his head, his eyes closed. His right cheekbone was almost concave. When Street pulled the pistol barrel from his mouth, Spann touched the fracture with his fingers. He moaned once, but I felt nothing for him. *Let him bleed*, I thought. *Let him bleed as Peter had bled.*

Street tossed the pistol to me butt first and I fielded it clumsily. The barrel was shiny with saliva and blood. Street rose with one motion, pulling Spann forward toward the door. Quite deliberately, he ground the denture down into the carpet with his heel.

"You won't be needin' that," he said to Spann. "You'll be takin' your meals with a straw and glad of it."

Spann staggered through the door into the hotel hallway, and Street sprawled back into his desk chair, flicking absently at the spots of blood on his white shirt. "You can put the gun down now. It's not loaded," he said.

"Is that nightcrawler really working for you?"

"Well, he's sort of a volunteer. His personal views don't get in the way of business and I like that in a man. I always did have an eye for natural talent. Of course, he's crazy as a loon. That's part of his charm."

"Were you paying him? Frank Reno said you were paying him."

"Sure I was. I hired him away from Fleming. Right after he had that little run-in with your brother. What difference does it make?"

My eyes were wet as I turned away. "Peter can't walk without a cane. Damn you. You hired the man who did that to him and Peter can't even walk."

Street scuffed his foot at the blood that stained the carpet. "Think the Olds can clean that up? Probably a common problem around here," he said. He looked at me for a long moment.

"What's done is done and there's no undoing it. Spann'll be down in Indiana for a while, gumming his food like a baby. I don't see how your brother's got any complaints in the revenge department."

"What about Fleming? He's off scot-free. He'll be back to haunt us."

"Fleming's not going to be a problem to anybody. Let me worry about him. You go on home. I've got to take a drive over to Jackson, fix up a little showstopper for tomorrow."

He started toward the door, but then he wheeled back to face me. "You know what that Shrieber's nickname is, Charlie? Izzy the rabbi. Isn't that something? Those kikes, they've got a lot of class. Maybe Nightshirt Danny's a necessary evil."

⇒ 39 ⇐

Snapshot

April, 1946

As Street stood in the well of the court for his closing argument the next morning, he was all crusader. He began, of course, at the end.

"Ladies and gentlemen, there is only one verdict you can return in this case," he said. "That verdict is guilty. Guilty on all counts. Guilty as charged. These creatures"—he flipped his right hand scornfully toward Lefkowitz and Shrieber—"these creatures are killers for hire. They come to us out of the night, out of Detroit. They stalk our elected representatives. They conspire together about a murder for money."

He paused and took a sip of water from the glass perched on the edge of the prosecution's table. The courtroom was still and the jury was bright-eyed with attention, suspended in air. As Street played out his theme of search and redemption, the welfare worker and the young housewife glanced at each other. From my angle I saw him pat her hand, once, lightly. They were ours. All they wanted to do was get it over and find a quiet hotel room.

"Never forget," Street said, "that the grand jury is the people's tool. It's there to protect our democracy against corruption. Against wickedness. Against sin."

James Sixtas grinned slightly. He knew all about sin. Next to him, the little widow was perched on the edge of her seat. I could see her in the jury room, pecking away like a wren through the evidence, finding guilt in some small seed of testimony.

Street walked them carefully through the work of the grand jury, the cases we brought, the guilty pleas, the payoffs and the paybacks. But he veered away from the mercantile references. I had watched him long enough now that I could almost read his thoughts. Don't dwell overly long on the political bazaar, he had concluded. Some on the jury might view it as just another form of commerce. The clothier, the elevator manager, the two farmers were at ease in a world where everything was for sale at a price. No need to upset their sunny composure. Let them see Lefkowitz and Shrieber as strangers from a wholly different universe.

Street then turned to our biggest weakness and sought to make it a strength. "I told you at the onset that the state did not bring its witnesses in from a prayer meeting. When you're down in this other world, the underworld, you take your witnesses where you find them. Sometimes that means you take them from the streets, like Harold Detering. Sometimes you take them out from behind a desk, like Jonas Hine."

He walked forward to the jury rail and placed both fists on it and leaned forward, close to the jurors. "And yes," he said, "sometimes you even take them from jail, like Nathan Vanik. Yes, we gave them immunity for their testimony. I don't apologize for a minute. That's how we got them to come in out of the shadows. That's how crimes like this one get solved. Even a sorry little sodomite like Vanik, even he can speak the truth. And when he does, we ignore it at our peril."

The plump, grandmotherly schoolteacher blinked rapidly at Street. I didn't know whether she was shocked or simply intent. But I was sure we had the bus driver and the young ex-marine. They had seen the world, one in the fury of battle and the other in the tedium of a menial job. They knew all about human frailty.

Street methodically recited the testimony of our tarnished angels. When he came to the end, he paused again. The last juror, the one who looked like my father, sat upright in stiff discomfort. I wondered if he wanted a whiskey as badly as I did.

I poured myself another glass of water and drained it in three rapid gulps. I was adrift without the certainty that I could take a drink when this was over.

Street reached for the climax. If he couldn't use Danny Spann to frighten the jurors into a guilty verdict, he meant to do it himself.

"Now, I know what Mr. Haricot will say. He will say that Lefkowitz and Shrieber must be presumed innocent. Let him stand in front of you with a straight face and say that. Let him say they should walk out the front door of this courthouse as free men. Let him say they should mingle with us in our streets, our shops, and our diners."

Street was shouting now in righteous anger, slicing his right hand downward, his face contorted. "Why they might even want to come into our churches, to read the Holy Scripture in Hebrew," he said. "Should they be allowed in our homes as well, with our children? These men who planned to gun down Senator Maynard in front of his wife and daughter? They are nothing more than beasts, these men. They must be separated from us. They must be locked away so that they can never bring their evil schemes to fruition."

He walked away from the jury and sat down at our table, his face red, his eyes wild. Suddenly the courtroom was awash in applause. I turned, astonished, and the sound broke over me as those in the audience came up from their chairs and shouted and cheered. All but Rachel Loeb. She rose from her seat, and walked quickly up the middle corridor and out of the court-room. Her head was up, her back was straight, and the muscles in her calves clenched with every step. Street watched her leave and then leaned over to me. His smile was as bland as a carved Halloween pumpkin.

"I could never keep my women in line," he said. "Nothing wrong with a spell of rabble-rousing. If anybody knows that, it sure as shit ought to be that little twit. But she's nothing to me now. You only walk out on me once." He spaced his words out like a chant and grinned again as I turned away.

After the noon recess, Haricot waited until the courtroom was entirely still before swinging his wheelchair directly out in front of the jury, into the ring. He hammered away like a good welterweight. But his timing was just a beat off. He circled us, never coming straight in. He scored his points. But there was none of the fire and venom that typified his defense of Fleming. Then he was all attack. Today he was counter-punching. I watched the jurors, but they were expressionless. If Street had tried to frighten them into action, Haricot was content to leave them with questions.

"What does Mr. Street want you to do?" he asked, after he plodded methodically through our case. "He wants you to forget that there is no credible evidence of a conspiracy. He wants you to guess these men into Jackson State Penitentiary. He wants you to do the easy and popular thing. The thoughtless will approve of his vile demagoguery. The bigots and the haters will applaud. But I ask you to rise above that. I ask for your understanding, for your charity, for your kindness. Above all, I ask that you remember that now, this very moment, the law presumes these men innocent. I ask you to remember that as you go to the jury room. That's all I ask and that should be enough."

It was almost three and Syzmanski reached for his gavel. But Street was on his feet immediately. "I don't need a recess," he said. "Here's my rebuttal, straight and quick."

He was in front of the jury box in three steps, and again he put both fists on the rail and hunched forward. "It's an old rule among lawyers on the defense side that you never let the defendant be tried. You try someone else. Maybe you try the police. Maybe you try the victim. If all else fails, maybe you try the prosecutor. But you never try the defendant."

He walked to the end of the jury box, directly in front of James Sixtas. "Now Mr. Haricot here, he's tried all three," he said. "He's tried and he's tried, but even he can't hide the truth. Look at them. You know who they are and what they are. They're Detroit hoods. They used to work for the Purple Gang. You can see it in their faces. They tell you everything you need to know."

Lefkowitz shifted in his chair and dropped his head, but Shrieber stared back at Street. Then he turned to the jury and smiled, slowly and softly. Street picked up on it immediately.

"Look at him. He's laughing at you. He thinks you don't have the courage to find him guilty. Him and his buddy with their silk suits and their smart street talk."

Shrieber turned back toward Street and nodded, once, at the prosecutor. He lifted his right hand with his first finger pointed at Street, his thumb straight up. And then he mimed the firing of a single shot.

"You're dead," he said. "You just don't know it yet."

Syzmanski slammed his gavel down and came up out of his seat and over the bench. There were angry fingers of red reaching up across his cheeks and toward his silver temples.

"Bailiff, restrain that man. Cuff him to that chair," he shouted. The bailiff stood hesitantly and motioned to the two uniformed state troopers by the door. They walked carefully down the center aisle, the leather of their high black boots creaking in the silence. The taller one reached down for the low wooden gate of the bar of the court and held it open for his partner. They moved silently and in tandem in behind the defendants' table.

Shrieber shrugged, shook himself, and placed his hands behind the chair back, close to the lower rung. The smaller trooper threaded his handcuffs through the rung and snapped them on Shrieber's wrists. Shrieber settled back in the chair. He was still smiling.

Syzmanski waved us forward to the bench. Haricot began to speak, but the judge cut him off. "I've never had something like that in my courtroom, before a jury. Never," he whispered. His face was a dark crimson and his breathing was short and staccato. He was like an exhausted swimmer fighting against the tide.

"Hell, don't worry so much, S.T.," Street said. "That little shit's just showing off. There's no harm done."

"No harm? Why it's prejudicial. It's grounds for a mistrial," Syzmanski said, gulping for air.

"Now just take it easy, judge," Street said, and then he threw Syzmanski a life ring, the precious buoy of precedent. "There's a hundred cases that say that a defendant's words, freely spoken, can't be prejudicial. Our own Supreme Court ruled on it just a year ago in the *Mahaffy* case.

I closed my eyes for I knew that Sebastian Mahaffy was a defendant who had waived the privilege, taken the stand, and then blurted out a confession. It was a first in Michigan jurisprudence. Shrieber's pointed finger, his silent shot, and his spoken words were worlds away from the case Street cited so confidently.

Syzmanski looked down at Haricot, and the defense lawyer picked at an invisible piece of lint on his precisely folded trousers. I listened to Syzmanski's breath whistle as Haricot flicked his hand twice at the sharp vertical creases that bisected the blue cloth on his thighs, down to his knees.

"*Mahaffy*'s good precedent, your honor," Haricot said. "If you order a mistrial, you'll be reversed. We'll be right back here next year. Let's get this case to the jury. Then we can all go home."

Street sighed, a muted groan of pleasure, and Syzmanski brought his hand down softly on the bench in front of him. "Right you are," he said. "Places gentlemen and I'll read out the jury instructions." A flashbulb popped behind us and he smiled dimly. He was only a second too late and a lifetime too slow.

40

Shadowland

April, 1946

Syzmanski droned his way through the instructions, reading both ours and the defendants' verbatim in the same dull monotone. When he finished, the jury members filed out silently. I wondered if they were aware that the power had passed into their collective hands. Street and I walked back to the lawyers' library, next to the judge's chambers. It was a rectangular room with a small window that looked out over the courthouse square. A narrow table was jammed against the left wall. A pile of law books was scattered on it.

Street walked across the room and lowered himself carefully into a straight-backed chair next to the window. He tilted back against the wall and folded his hands comfortably in his lap. Over his right shoulder, down through the window and through the steady spring rain, I saw the large clock over the jewelry store across the main street. It was next to a bar I knew all too well. The clock said it was exactly four o'clock.

"Rest yourself. This shouldn't take too long," Street said.

"It sure shouldn't. Not with Haricot throwing the case. What the hell's going on?" I whispered to him.

"I told you, two pawns for a rook. If there was any trouble with the jury before, we don't have it now. Not after Izzy the rabbi put on his show."

His line of sight shifted and he raised his voice and pointed his finger to mime a shot toward the door. "There's some symmetry to that, don't you think? An act within an act?"

"No, I don't," Haricot said from behind me, before I could speak. "Did I startle you, young Mr. Cahill?" he asked, for I had shied like a nervous racehorse at the sound of his voice. With a wave of his hand, he dismissed the lawyer pushing his wheelchair.

"Close the door behind you and keep everybody else out," he said. "I need some privacy with Mr. Street and his second."

Street rocked forward in his chair. "The only thing private in this life is the grave," he said. "You of all people should know that."

"Here's what I know," Haricot said. "You're going to run for governor and you need a win. What I don't know is why Fleming told me to offer it. And I sure don't know why Shrieber put on his little act."

Street rocked back and shifted his weight until he was comfortable. "Joel, I know something about Wade Fleming. Something you don't know. Something nobody knows."

He stopped and cleared his throat. "Fleming's got the same thing as Lou Gehrig. Some kind of sclerosis. In a year, he won't be able to change his underwear."

Haricot shook his head in disbelief, but Street ignored him. He looked directly at me. "Fleming's no threat to anyone now," he said. "Besides, do you really think Fleming could've gotten Shrieber to put his dick on the block? I needed Lev Bernstein to do that. He's the one pulling the strings."

I looked at him without the slightest degree of comprehension. "Bernstein's in prison," I said. "In Jackson prison."

"Of course he's in goddamn prison. It's the safest place in the world for him to be."

"Why is he involved in this? What's in it for him?"

"Bernstein stays with his friends," Street said. "He's propped Fleming up for all these years. Used him. The least he could do was keep Fleming out of jail. Let him die in comfort. There's a certain honor among thieves. Even murderers."

"You're so full of shit your eyes are brown," Haricot said. "I represented Lev Bernstein in the Collingwood appeal. He'd drop Fleming over the side before breakfast if he had to. There's something else. Fleming never said a word about Bernstein. He just told me to make a deal with you to trade his ass for Lefkowitz and Shrieber."

"Fleming's got his pride. He wasn't about to tell you he was just middle management all these years, taking orders like everybody else. But you can rest easy. You played your part. Like you said, I'm gonna get my win. Now Fleming can crawl back in his hole and die by inches, yelling things that nobody can understand. And may God rest his miserable soul."

"What about the killing?" I sought a mooring, something to which I could tie my hopes for a future.

Street gave me more than I wanted. "Everybody is this room knows Lefkowitz and Shrieber didn't kill the good senator. They're professional hitmen. They don't go around shooting a man in the middle of a goddamn cornfield after he's already dead."

He looked straight at me again. "No, somebody else got to Maynard before Lefkowitz and Shrieber. A real amateur."

He paused, and I heard the water dripping from the eaves outside the window. "Right now, I don't give a good goddamn," he said. "I've got other things on my mind."

Haricot rolled his wheelchair forward, along the side of the narrow table. The axle of the chair jarred one of the table legs and the stack of books cascaded down onto the floor in a dusty jumble. But Haricot never looked away from Street.

"Did Bernstein say that? I'll tell you this, Street, one hired gun to another. If you're making deals with Lev Bernstein, Shrieber was right. You're a dead man and you don't even know it," he said.

Street stood suddenly as the door opened and his laughter exploded through the room, like a rolling thunderclap. "Here's the bailiff," he said, "come to tell us we've got a verdict."

He spun Haricot's wheelchair around and ran it through the pile of law books. "To hell with Bernstein. And to hell with you, you sawed-off shit. The only thing that can stop me now is that damned jury. And sure as God made little green grasshoppers, they haven't had time to work that out."

I looked down at my watch. It was four-thirty.

THE NEWS that the jury was returning had flashed through the courthouse, and the courtroom was jammed when we took our places. The press box held at least fifteen reporters. Every other seat in the courtroom was filled and the aisles were packed with standing spectators, crowded in together like cattle in a pen at feeding time.

"Christ, look at them," Street said. "If Stainless had a brain bigger'n a road apple, he'd be selling tickets. It sure beats the hell out of honest graft."

On cue, the judge banged his gavel until there was a murmuring silence. "The bailiff will bring the jury into the courtroom," he said.

In single file, the jurors trudged in to their seats. Our little widow was the first, tiptoeing on her bird legs, solemn and shy. The merchants and farmers were in a group, and they had the satisfied look of men who had done their duty and done it in a hurry. The schoolteacher followed, shaking her head slightly. She was resigned, but to what? The welfare worker and the pretty housewife were next. The look on her face was one of simple fear. She needn't have worried. The contemplation of adultery is usually worse than the consummation of it. The bus driver and the marine were expressionless, but my father's double was stooped and red-eyed. I wondered if he had found a bottle somewhere along the way. The last man into the jury box was James Sixtas, wearing his dignity like a suit of armor.

When they were all seated, Syzmanski cracked his gavel and asked, "Have you selected a foreman?" Sixtas rose slowly to his feet. *It's over*, I thought. We had convicted two men of a conspiracy to murder Harry Maynard. Never mind that their conspiracy never came to fruition. Never mind what really happened at Maynard's house that morning. Never mind how we had cast Maynard as the blameless victim when all he had deserved was to die. *It was over,* I thought. *And Sarah and I were free.*

THAT NIGHT, after Sixtas spoke his lines and Syzmanski walked away from center stage for the last time, Street stood at the top of the courthouse steps. It had stopped raining, and a light fog rose slowly from the wet ground and floated on the wind, its tendrils reaching gently up into the trees that surrounded the courthouse. The wooden doors framed Street in the night, and the glow from within backlit him perfectly so that his shadow stretched out in front of him. The reporters and photographers crowded up to the steps, and he clasped his hands over his head in the traditional victory pose while the flashbulbs popped and flared. Before him, the curious and the committed stood jammed together on the cement walkway and out onto the soft ground. They stamped their feet and clapped as he moved toward them, the sound curiously muffled in the fog.

We had borrowed a lectern from the local funeral parlor. It was the only establishment in town with a working reading light attached to a podium. When Street grasped that lectern, the applause died. He waited until it was entirely quiet. In the stillness, they were his. We were all his. And he wooed us openly, with simple words and great relish.

"Guilty," Street shouted. "Lefkowitz and Shrieber are guilty." He held the jury slip aloft. "That's what it says. That's what the foreman wrote right here on behalf of his fellow jurors. Guilty on all counts. Guilty as charged."

The side street that paralleled the courthouse square was set aside for police vehicles, and in the first car I saw the shadowed head of one of the troopers from our detail. He pounded the horn steadily in short bursts and the crowd caught up the cadence, stamping and clapping, as Street reached for the climax.

"There is only one way to beat Wade Fleming and men like him, and that is to take back control of our state. That is why I stand before you tonight to announce that I am running"—he raised his right hand and pumped it to the sky, urging us upward into the mist—"running for governor of Michigan."

He dropped his hand, bowed his head, and then plunged forward into the crowd in front of him, into the barbed wire of a political campaign. At the edge of the square, our handmade signs blossomed in the night, red on black. Street for Governor.

As Street feasted on his moment, Maloney tugged at my coat and at my heart. "That sheeny bastard Shrieber said to give this to you. He said it was from the big boss. From Bernstein."

He handed me a sealed envelope. I opened it awkwardly, my fingers stiff and slow. The plain white sheet of paper inside contained just three sentences, in a broad, slanted script. *I saw what you did,* it said. *I own you now,* it said. *But I don't know what I'm going to do about her yet,* it said. Lev Bernstein finally had said hello. It wasn't over.

41

The Big Lake

May, 1946

Lake Michigan was flat and quiet in the early morning, and the water shifted and sparkled in the slanting light. Along the shore, there was a narrow curving strand of pebbles and small polished stones that glistened against the sand. The beach grass grew in tufts up into the dunes, small islands of pale green. Where the grass was the thickest it swayed with the breeze. The trees crowning the ridges of the dunes were leafed out in the rains of spring and their leaves were shiny in the sun. The wind and the rain had scoured the beach clean and marked the sand with sculpted ripples and hillocks, motionless silicon waves that lapped silently away to the south, parallel with the dunes.

There was a haze in the middle distance and it hung like blue-gray gauze over the sand spits that reached out into the lake. The season did not begin until after Decoration Day and there was almost no one along the lakefront except the locals. The only footprints on the beach were my own, silently following me. I walked with no particular purpose. It was enough to feel the grainy sand under my feet and listen to the gentle murmuring of the waves as they lapped up against the shore.

After the trial, Street had offered me the cottage he owned near South Haven. I found it curious that he went to such trouble to get me out of the way, but I raised no objection. I needed the time and I needed the solitude.

The cottage had only two cramped bedrooms, a sparsely furnished living room, and a rudimentary kitchen. When the wind came up, it whistled through the clapboard siding and the sand filtered in. Enough sand that I swept the floors each morning. It was cool at night and on rainy days. When the wind came up, I often made a fire in the small brick fireplace that Street had laid in against the south wall. There was an upright radio sputtering with static, but no phone. The cottage had a long open porch fronting on the lake, and in the clear evenings I watched the glowing sun slip into the water, my feet propped up on a white wicker chair in the slowly dying light.

I spent my mornings walking the empty beach. Often the wind whipped up the water, and the waves, topped with white foam, chopped at the shore. But on this day the lake was still, with only the windrunners dappling the surface calm. When I turned to retrace my steps, I saw that a flock of gulls had landed behind me. Their heads bobbed when they pecked rhythmically at the sand.

As I walked back up the beach, the sun warmed the air and the haze lifted. There was someone coming toward me on the water's edge on the other side of the gulls. Perhaps a local out for a morning stroll. The breeze came up for a moment, ruffling the gray and white feathers of the birds and rippling the lake. The person walking toward me reached upward and then her hair tumbled down. It was bright chestnut in the morning sunlight, startling against her pale sweater.

I saw the white streak and I knew it was Sarah. My mind turned over and I started toward her. The sudden motion frightened the gulls and they exploded into the sky, wheeling and cawing out over the lake. When I reached her, she smiled at me.

"You mustn't scare the wildlife, Charles," she said.

"You just happened to be in the neighborhood and thought you'd stop by?"

"Of course not. Your brother said you were taking some time off. He said you might like some company."

The gulls fluttered down behind us and their high-pitched shrieks began to die. They watched us, their eyes alert. When they decided we posed no immediate threat, they resumed their foraging, scuttling forward and back, hopping primly from one webbed foot to the other. The breeze faded and the beach was quiet again. The only sound was the slow slosh of the water against the shore.

She reached out her hand. "Walk with me, Charles, back up to your little house. I don't walk enough these days. Mother can't go out and I won't leave her alone."

"Is she all right?"

"She's dying. Dad's with her now. But he can't stand it for more than a few days at a time."

I took her hand and we walked quietly up the beach. "I know I shouldn't. But I pray for it to be over," she said when we reached the foot of the weathered wooden stairs to the cottage. "There's no one there, inside her. She stares at me and her eyes are frantic and she says things, but I can't understand a word. When she dies I won't feel anything more, because she's already left."

"She's your alibi."

She looked at me steadily, her head cocked slightly to the right. "I know," she said. "Who else knows?"

"Street probably knows what happened, or most of it. He knows that you and I were seeing each other. He knows that Lefkowitz and Shrieber didn't kill your husband. He may even know about that damn poker."

"Do you think he knows who killed Harry?"

"I doubt he knows for sure. But it's not him I'm worried about. It's Bernstein," I said, and I told her about the letter.

Nothing showed in her face, but again she cocked her head. "It isn't going to be enough," she said. "I did what I had to do. But it isn't going to be enough. Not with a man like Lev Bernstein."

I put my arm around her waist, above the swell of her hip. We climbed the stairs and she leaned into me. The wind came up again and she shivered. When we reached the porch, I opened the screen door for her and tried to make a joke.

"The army taught me all sorts of survival skills," I said. "I can boil water. I can build a fire. I can turn on the oven. I can even make you a drink, if you want one."

She pulled away. "Peter said you weren't drinking. If you're drinking, I don't want to be around you. I can't trust you if you're drinking."

"Sarah, there's a bottle of whiskey in the kitchen cupboard. I don't drink from it. I just look at it every morning when I get up, like an old friend. Then I look at it again every night before I go to sleep. I'm building up my character. Someday I may be a normal human being."

She looked at me, a level unblinking stare. Then she arched her back and slowly, very slowly, pulled the ribbed sweater up over her head. She wore nothing underneath and I felt the desire rise within me. She smiled that dazzling sunburst of a smile as she walked toward me. She was stunning, white teeth and auburn hair and sparkling eyes. And the grace of a dancer.

"I don't think we'll need the fire, Charles," she said. "Perhaps some blankets. That wicker looks awfully sharp."

She was right about the wicker, but wrong about the fire. The couch on the porch was barely able to support one person, let alone two. It was supremely uncomfortable to boot. We moved inside the cottage and, in a comic frenzy, wrestled a mattress from one of the bedrooms into the space in front of the fireplace. She insisted on clean sheets, pillows, and a down comforter, and laughed aloud at my impatience. But she was as ready for me as I was for her. And it was like the spring itself, long and slow and sweet.

The wind came up later in the morning and it blew storm clouds in from the north. When the slanting rain began to spatter against the windows, it became suddenly colder and I kindled as large a fire as the little fireplace could accommodate. She slept then, and I listened to the rain and to the wind whispering and whistling through the old cottage. *I don't know what I'm going to do about her yet*, Bernstein had said. They would do nothing to her. I would not let them harm her.

We spent that day idling in the spring rain. I had Peter's car, since he no longer could use it, and I drove into town to get a paper. She found my fascination with the comics laughable, and so I read *Terry and the Pirates* and *Dick Tracy* and *Smilin' Jack* aloud with our coffee. Over the static of the antiquated radio, we listened to Tex Beneke conduct the Glenn Miller Orchestra. She insisted that we dance to "String of Pearls," and she put her arms around my shoulders and did not laugh at all at my clumsy foxtrot.

When the weather cleared, we hiked barefoot along the beach, rolling up our pant legs and dashing in and out of the water like children. The lake was still cold from the ice sheets of winter. But it did not matter. I watched her that night as she bathed in the claw-foot cast-iron tub in the tiny bathroom, wet and shiny and complete. It was beyond voyeurism, beyond lust, beyond thought itself. When she finished, she washed and combed my hair, just as she had done at the hospital. In front of the fire, she ran her hands lightly over my scars and murmured of love and we were lost in it.

I KNEW it could not last. It was bright and crisp the next morning when Maloney pulled up behind the cottage in his battered state police sedan. He wasted no time. "All hell's breaking loose in Lansing," he said. "Frank Reno's dead and the cops've got his nigger girlfriend. She says she wants to talk with you, Mr. Cahill."

"What's that got to do with me? I'm out of it now."

Maloney ducked his head. "I can't stand here and argue with you about it. Street says he needs you right now. He's the boss. It's a long drive so you'd best get going."

I was ready to refuse, but Sarah would have none of it. "You have to go back," she said. "But there's something you should know."

I turned to Maloney. "Give us a minute, will you, Al?"

He ducked his head again. "Mrs. Maynard, good to see you."

When he was out of earshot, I turned to Sarah. Like Maloney, she wasted no time. "You remember Lillian, mother's housekeeper? Her daughter came to see me. She must be the one the police have arrested. She was at Frank Reno's house when you met with Hennessey and she heard every word."

I was dumbfounded. "What was she doing at his house?"

"She's been living with the man ever since his wife died. It's white on black and everybody in Lansing knows about it except you."

She stopped and looked at me, and then she looked over my shoulder, at the lake. "And Street doesn't just think you killed Harry. He's sure of it. But he doesn't care. He's not the prosecutor any more. The last thing he wants to hear about is the murder. He's got his verdict. He thinks he's going to be the next governor."

"How do you know what he cares about?" It was an obvious question, a lawyer's question. Had I thought about it, I would have said nothing. But I did not think and I had to ask. And then, the answer. Oh, the answer.

She looked down and then her head came up and her voice was just a whisper, like the wind. "I told you I've done what I had to do. I've been sleeping with him. After the night you got drunk at my house."

"For God's sake, why?"

"God's got nothing to do with it. You were drinking. I couldn't count on you. I had to protect myself. I had to protect my daughter. Men will tell you anything in bed and they'll do anything to get you there. Harry did. You did. And so did Street. It's not as if it means much of anything. It's just anatomy. You told me that once, a million years ago."

Then she walked away from me, toward the beach and the emptiness of the lake. She said something over her shoulder, into the wind. But I could not hear her.

⇒ 42 ⇐

Grace

May, 1946

Street and I were early for Frank Reno's funeral. The faithful were praying the rosary as we made our way down the center aisle. Street was immediately uncomfortable. After I made the ritual genuflection and knelt to pray for Mary, full of grace, to be with me, he fidgeted beside me, straightening his tie, adjusting his belt, tying and then retying his shoelaces. He had not wanted to come, complaining that he disliked churches and hated funerals. But I persuaded him. I thought he could do me less harm in public, with people listening.

"Word will get out that you were there," I had said. "Everybody knows that Frank was on the other side. They'll think you're a big man to come and pay your respects. Besides, you might learn something." I had said nothing at all about Sarah. There was nothing to say. And I no longer trusted him with anything.

"What could I learn? I already know who killed Reno. His damn lady friend. I've got no time for some fallen choirboy. There's a primary coming up in June, in case you hadn't noticed," he said. "What I really want you to do is go see Grace Johnson. Find out what she knows. Who she's talked to. What's the point of screwing around at some half-assed funeral?"

But he finally agreed and now he was having second thoughts. He twisted in his seat and I saw that, as the cathedral filled up, he was counting the crowd.

"The mayor, the congressman, Randy Hennessey. All the usual ghouls come to rally 'round the casket," he whispered when the rosary was ended. "How long is this going to last?"

"One hour, no more and no less."

He was not at all assuaged and as the priest led the procession down the center aisle, I realized that he was actually nervous. Perhaps he saw in the death of another an intimation of his own mortality. Or maybe he thought I knew about him and Sarah. Or perhaps he was concerned over what Grace Johnson might tell me.

Street laced his hands across his midriff and stared straight ahead. His face was a mask of studied indifference. But his eyes betrayed him. *Just as Sarah had betrayed me*, I thought. I shook myself and became lost in the liturgical rhythms that I had breathed in like air in the Catholic churches of my childhood. Before I knew of betrayals. The priest hurried through the homily, skirting the grim facts of Reno's death. After the faithful had inhaled the incense and taken communion at the rail, the cathedral emptied quickly. Street walked off toward the Capitol, without a word or a backward glance.

"The priest said go with God. Looks like your man took it literally." Hennessey was standing behind me and I started at his words.

"But he's got nothing on you," he said. "I hear that nigger roundheel who killed Frank Reno is asking for you. And here you are at your old buddy's funeral, cryin' crocodile tears. You've got a set of brass balls on you, no doubt of that."

"She's got a right to a lawyer," I said.

Hennessey jabbed his forefinger into my chest. "She's got no goddamn rights at all. She's just a nigger whore who killed a white man. She's lucky we don't have the death penalty in this state or she'd be ridin' old Sparky by New Year's Day. I'd flip the switch myself, sure as hell. Don't tell me about her goddamn rights."

The funeral home functionaries were forming up the cars for the procession to the cemetery, and the mourners were quietly waiting in front of the church for Frank Reno's last journey.

Several of them turned toward us, startled by the ferocity in Hennessey's voice. I realized I didn't care at all and I smashed my heel down on his instep. He gasped and stumbled backward, almost falling. I wrapped my good arm around his shoulders, just one lawyer helping another. Then I whispered into his ear.

"You'll let me see her this afternoon," I said, "unless you want this all over the papers tomorrow. The NAACP may not mean much to you, but they can get a reporter's attention and so can I. And one other thing. I don't ever want to hear from you again about the Maynard murder. You doublecrossed Fleming. Then you doublecrossed Street. I'm sure the Purples would love to hear all about it. Now smile pretty and shake my hand or I'll break your jaw." Perhaps it was the combination of pain and political calculation, but he nodded his agreement and there was no more violence on the church steps.

THE POLICE brought Grace Johnson to a holding cell in the old city jail when I arrived after the graveside service. She was younger than I had anticipated, perhaps in her late twenties. When the turnkey unlocked the door and let me in, she was sitting quietly on the long planked bench that ran along the back wall. There was only one window and a single shaft of light angled down into the choked, fetid silence of the cell.

I sat down next to her, awkwardly. There were no Negroes at all in my small rural schools, few at the University of Michigan, and the armed forces were strictly segregated during my war. I had no idea of how to address her. There was no shared experience that I might call upon to bridge the gap between us.

She sensed it immediately. "I'll bet this is the first time you've ever been alone with a woman with a black skin," she said. Her voice was clear and modulated and there was no hint of the patois that characterized her mother's speech.

"Don't worry." she said. "Frank was the same way when I first met him. It took him a year before he could even admit he was embarrassed. But he got over it. How was the funeral?"

I gave her the particulars as best I could, omitting any mention of my exchange with Hennessey.

"In my church it would have taken all afternoon," she said. "That's the one thing you can say for us. We know how to bury our dead. We've had plenty of practice. Well, Frank's with the Lord now and here I am."

"Have they hurt you?"

"Oh, they called me a coon and a whore. They kept me awake three nights running. They fed me stale bread and warm water. The matron wants to get her hand up my skirt. But I wouldn't say they've actually hurt me."

"What have you told them?"

She stood up from the bench and walked across the cell into the shaft of light. She raised her arms above her head, toward the light, and turned slowly toward me. "It's so dirty in here," she said. "I feel dirty all the time. But I can wash myself in the sunlight."

She dropped her arms and looked at me steadily from across the cell. The light accentuated her high cheekbones and the darkness of her hair. "My daddy's doing his second term in Jackson prison," she said. "The police found me with Frank's body. In my profession, I have to know something about the police. I know enough not to tell them anything. But I'll tell you. Don't you want to know what happened?"

I hesitated. Before I volunteered for the Rangers, I had defended court-martials in the Army, and I had learned from bitter experience that with crimes of violence it was sometimes best not to know the exact circumstances of the offense this early. Grace Johnson had just told me that the police had found her with the body of a murder victim. Perhaps she was alone with Frank Reno when he died. Perhaps she killed him in anger over some domestic slight.

Again she read my thoughts. "You think we're all just naturally violent, don't you? I didn't kill Frank. But I know who did. That's why I asked for you. You know them too. Or at least two of them."

I started to answer, but she raised her hand. She walked back over to the bench and sat beside me. Then she leaned toward me and spoke softly and slowly. Street's performance before the Senate investigating committee had humiliated Frank Reno, she said. "I thought I could help him. Bernstein pays my dad to run errands for him. Daddy told me Bernstein was having him deliver packets of money to your friend Hubbell Street at the Olds Hotel. Daddy said he made the run every month, since the first of the year."

"But how did your father get out of prison?"

She dropped her voice lower still and spoke more rapidly. "Convicts come and go from that prison all the time. It's a regular beehive. The last time my daddy was in town was two weeks ago. He came over to our house and told Frank that Bernstein wanted to see him. Frank was really excited. He thought if he could get Bernstein to admit he was paying Street, he would have enough for an indictment."

I circled back. "Are you sure your father said Street was taking money from the Purples?"

"I'm sure. And so was Frank. He said that if it took a crook to catch a crook, it was fine with him. But I was scared of Bernstein. I told Frank that Bernstein was a killer hiding out in plain sight in jail. But Frank wanted my daddy to set up a meeting with Bernstein at our house."

"When was that?"

"Daddy showed up last Friday, with Bernstein, Lefkowitz, and Shrieber. He was proud as a peacock that he could get the big boss to Lansing. Frank told me to stay in the bedroom. But I left the door open far enough that I could see into the kitchen. They all sat around the kitchen table. When Frank went over to the stove to get some coffee, Bernstein walked up behind him. And then he cut Frank's throat. Just like the mailman, delivering the mail."

"Did they know you were there?"

"I came out of the bedroom to help Frank. He was coughing and gurgling and the blood was gushing out of his throat all over me and I couldn't stop it. When his legs stopped kicking and he was quiet, I went after Bernstein with my nails. But Lefkowitz grabbed me. Bernstein wiped Frank's blood off his knife on my dress. Then he dropped the knife on the floor."

"You were lucky he didn't kill you too."

"Why should he? There's a white man dead and me soaked with blood and the murder weapon right there on the kitchen floor. Everybody knows coloreds like to use a knife. They made me call the police, and Lefkowitz and Shrieber laughed about it the whole time we were waiting. But Bernstein was a perfect gentleman. When the police finally came, he paid them all off. It was a hundred dollars apiece and here I am. Besides, they have perfect alibis."

"What do you mean?"

"Check for yourself. Bernstein and Lefkowitz and Shrieber were there in Jackson on Friday. They were on the count at both the morning and evening roll call. They couldn't have killed Frank. They were all in prison at the time. My daddy does the same thing, when they want him to run their little errands. Most of the time, the warden loans him his own car."

I was swimming in disbelief. "How did you meet Frank?" I asked, finally, banally. It was the only thing I could think of to say. I was the rarest thing in the world, a lawyer without words.

Her gaze remained level. "I teach high school civics. Frank's nephew was in one of my classes. I met him when he came with his brother to a PTA meeting. I thought he was nice."

I sat silently, considering what she had told me. Street had cast himself as a crusader, but from the day we indicted Fleming he had been taking money from the Purple Gang. I had been Street's front man at the trial, the wounded local hero, sent out to impress the judge and the jury. It had been the price from the beginning and I had known it and had paid it for my own reasons. But I had also been part of a larger conspiracy. Of that I had known nothing. Just as I had known nothing of Sarah's affair with Street.

I had been a naïve fool, I told myself, and now I had no idea of what to do or of where to turn. One by one, Street had cleared the board. He had used Hennessey's ambition to put him on the sidelines. Altman and McReynolds would not run again. Lonergan had resigned in disgrace. Lefkowitz and Shrieber were in prison. Fleming was dying by inches. Reno was dead. According to the papers, the Democrats were in disarray. Street was favored to win the Republican primary and then the general election. With any luck, he would be governor.

⇒ 43 ⇐

Bargains

June–December, 1946

The day after he won the primary, Street called me. "I was lucky," he said. "And only a fool counts on luck. Get down here. You and I need to come to terms." I thought of refusing him, but I could not. Not with what he might know. Not with what Sarah might have told him.

Volunteers jammed Street's headquarters at the Olds. Red and black posters covered the walls and they contained only three words: Street for Michigan. A teletype in one corner chattered away mindlessly, while a steady stream of visitors flowed through Street's corner office. The phones rang constantly, but one of the staffers told me the calls were mainly the stuff of practical politics, jobseekers wanting positions in a Street administration, local officeholders hurrying to align themselves with the frontrunner, rumormongers with the latest inside information on the rival Democratic campaign, radio stations with time for sale, chronic complainers with their endless stories of governmental waste or persecution, and the occasional ordinary citizen who simply wanted to speak to the man who would be governor.

Street dismissed it all. "This place gives me a headache," he said, after he motioned me into his office and sat down behind his huge desk. "Everybody wants a job and I don't know who half these people are. And I damned near lost to a nobody."

"You could close it down tomorrow morning," I said. "Of course, then you won't be governor."

Street turned to me, his eyes flat and glittering. "Oh, I'll be governor all right," he said. "And you'll be helpin' me. You're a quick study and you know how to organize things. You're what I need right now."

I saw no reason to hold back and so I pushed at him. "Grace Johnson says the Purples killed Frank Reno. She says they're putting up the money for your whole campaign and Frank found out about it."

His smile was practiced and easy. "Of course that's what she'd say. The cops've got her with the knife practically in her hand and blood all over her. She's a smart one. She knows she needs somebody to blame. Who better than a bunch of kike gangsters?"

"If Hennessey takes her to trial, I'll put her on the stand. The part about the money will come out. Maybe you won't be governor after all."

"There's two reasons you won't do that," Street said. "First, there won't be a trial. Grace Johnson doesn't have to do a damn thing and neither do you. Tell her to sit tight. Snuggle up to the matron a little. Some night after the election's over, the turnkey'll forget to make his rounds and then she walks out. Free as a little bird and no hard feelings. It's a big country and she can get lost in a hurry."

"She's a schoolteacher. It'll ruin her life."

"Good God, Charlie, how dumb are you? Do you really think they'd let her teach white kids? She may draw a paycheck to make the school board look good to the NAACP. But she sure as hell wasn't teachin' school. She was probably sleeping in the infirmary. Grace Johnson works the night shift at Jimmy Six's cathouse down on Turner and that takes real stamina. That's where your choirboy Frank Reno met her. He was a regular. Jimmy says he liked his women hot and black. Just like that damn coffee he was always drinking."

It had the ring of truth, down to the last detail. I should not have gone further, but I did so anyway. Better to know than to wonder.

"What's the other reason?"

"It's simple. You killed Harry Maynard."

There it was. Sarah had betrayed me. After all this time and all my convoluted efforts, there it was. I could not deny it. But neither would I admit it. So I sought to keep him at bay.

"You're saying I'm a murderer?"

"Hell, if anybody deserved killing, Maynard did. He was a liar and a squealer and a pervert. I don't give a rat's ass. But the fact of the matter is, you bashed his head in and then you hauled him out to some godforsaken cornfield and shot him twice in the face to cover it up."

"And you're taking money from Lev Bernstein. Looks like a stalemate to me," I said.

Street leaned back and laughed. "Welcome to the real world," he said. "Now here's the deal. You don't piss on my boots and I don't piss on yours. It's the American way."

I said nothing and we both listened to the phones ring for a very long minute. Then I reached across his desk and shook his hand.

THERE WAS a true Michigan blizzard two days before Street's inaugural, and as Lansing dug itself out, we gave serious consideration to postponing the event. But Street would have none of it. He regarded the heavy snow and the icy, whistling winds with some amusement. "It's a good omen," he said as we went over the plans for the inaugural. "There's been a godawful odor to the Capitol for years. Come New Year's Day, I'll tell them we'll blow that musty smell out of here, once and for all. Maybe I should put that in my speech."

I did not respond. Street had won by a landslide. He had even carried Detroit, a first in recent memory for a Republican. It was mainly a matter of money. If Robert Straddard, the Democratic candidate, drove to a junior chamber of commerce breakfast in Battle Creek, we chartered a small plane. If his campaign headquarters were storefronts or decaying warehouses, we took over entire floors at local hotels. If all he could offer to a prospective campaign worker was the possibility of a job in the next administration, we could pay our help the going rate each week.

There were no polls then, but each party had its regulars, organized county by county. The word that came pulsing back to us over the summer through the Republican network was that labor was sitting on its hands, that Straddard was pulling small crowds, that their money was short, and that their local candidates were quietly separating themselves from the statewide organization.

With the money flowing, I had pressed our advantage. We bought ads in the newspapers. We bought time on the radio. We bought flyers and we dropped them by the planeload over Briggs Stadium when the Tigers played at home. When summer turned to fall, our Street posters were plastered everywhere. And on a gray and ugly November day, Street crushed Robert Straddard. When he raised his right hand on the Capitol steps on New Year's Day, he would become the fortieth governor of Michigan. *And Lev Bernstein and the Purple Gang will own him*, I thought.

It was one of my rare moments of introspection. During the campaign, the days had become virtually indistinguishable. Each one had melded into the next, until they became a seamless whole, a whirl of motion and sound. They were supremely boring and then suddenly thrilling, sandwiches on the run and coffee gulped from a thermos. The days were long and hot and the nights short and restless. All I knew was dull fatigue without time for reflection or regret. It was battle without gunfire. I loved it and I hated it.

Now I was determined to stay in the present. There was no past older than yesterday's headline, no future beyond today. I had run Street's campaign, written his press releases, spent the money, arranged the events, and even carried his bags one-handed. But I had remained apart from him and not once did I raise his affair with Sarah. *She did what she had to do*, I had thought. That was the end of it. I did not need to hear any explanations. As she had said, it was just anatomy.

When we finished plodding through the fine dust of the ceremony, the twenty-one-gun salute and the National Guard flyover, the arrangement of the dignitaries on the inaugural platform and the procession of bands down Michigan Avenue, the banquet at the Olds and the ball at the Masonic temple, I drove east to Peter's house. I was still using his car, as I had from the beginning. The snow had finally stopped, and the air was cold and crystalline as I drove the deserted streets. There was no wind and the steam from the manholes spiraled upward at regular two-block intervals, small wispy sentinels in the frozen air. When I wheeled into Peter's driveway, I stopped the car and set the brake. I reached across to the driver's side door with my right hand and struggled with the chrome handle to open the door. Then Sarah stepped out from between the garage and the house and slipped into the back seat, directly behind me. She must have known I would come home eventually and so she waited there, alone in the cold.

"Just listen," she said. "Just listen."

I leaned back against the seat and exhaled slowly. The vapor from my breath hung in the air briefly and then floated away. I reached across my body to pull the door shut and turned around so that I could see her face. The words formed in my mind, but I could not speak them. The best that I could manage was a nod.

"Lillian Johnson came to see me," she said. There was no recrimination in her voice, no anger, no regret. But she would not look at me. I wanted to raise my hand to her, to touch her face, to feel her hair, but I could not do it.

"Her husband's in town and he's drunk and mean," she said.

I found my voice. "How did he get out of prison this time?"

"He paid off the guards," she said. "But Lillian says it's not like always. Her husband's talking about Bernstein and how they've got a surprise for New Year's. Lillian says that Horace has always been one to brag. But something's different this time."

"You're freezing," I said. "Come inside."

"I can't do that. My car's around the corner and I have to go home. I don't want to leave my daughter alone. But you have to know two things. I didn't tell Street anything about you and the murder. And Lillian says Bernstein's got the poker."

I was frozen into silence. Sarah looked directly into my eyes. "Now we know for sure," she said. "Bernstein's got the poker and he's the key to it. Can you do it?"

"What do you mean?"

"You know exactly what I mean. Street won't do anything now, I've seen to that. But Bernstein might. If it comes to it, can you stop him?" She put her gloved hand up to my cheek and leaned forward and kissed me lightly, and I tasted the salt on her lips, from her tears. "If not for me and my daughter, for yourself? Can you do it?"

She didn't need to say anything more. Even then, I couldn't refuse her.

⇒ 44 ⇐

New Year's

January, 1947

The sunlight glanced and sparkled off the snow the next day, sharp and dry as the ice itself. The wind had come up again and the trees surrounding the Capitol shivered in the cold, but there was a sizable crowd gathered around the front steps for the Inaugural. Seated on a phalanx of folded chairs, their cheeks red and raw from the wind, they dutifully whistled and applauded as Street worked his way through his speech.

For all of the strength of his delivery and his air of authority, it was curiously mundane, almost dull. He talked slowly, solemnly promising to carry out the wishes of the thousands of people with whom he had spoken during the campaign, and the party faithful responded on cue. He envisioned a state in which the ordinary citizen's voice would always be heeded, and the assembled reporters stamped their feet against the cold and looked at their watches. He pledged to justify the voters' confidence, secure in the knowledge that with their support he could not fail, and Maloney slouched against the side steps and squinted into the frozen sun with his blank, careful eyes.

When Street finally reached the end, the crowd rose appreciatively and began to chant his name. He gave them the prize-fighter's symbolic salute, hands clasped above his head, and we trudged up the steps into the Capitol itself, and then up another flight of stairs to the governor's office, now officially his. McReynolds had removed every stick of furniture except the huge desk. The carpet was rolled up against the north wall and the air in the room was stale and still.

Street breathed it in and then pushed at the desk with one hand. "Damn thing's too big to get out the door," he said. "They must've built it by hand inside this room. Typical of Jim McReynolds. No sense of proportion."

He sat down on the corner of the desk, lit a cigarette, pulled open the right hand drawer, and idly rummaged about in it. "Empty," he said. "He left it flat empty for me. Just like I left them with that speech."

"What more could you have said?"

"It's the end of a long road. But I couldn't very well say that. And I sure as hell couldn't tell them the truth. My friends, let's talk about how I let a guilty man walk. How I took money from gangsters. How I did every damn thing I could to be governor. But now that I've got it, folks, it smells sort of old and musty. They'd have just loved *that* speech."

He looked at me with hooded eyes. "But to date I haven't killed anybody," he said.

"Before we go over to the banquet, there's something you should know about," I said. I had carefully planned how to work Sarah's warning into our conversation. My first thought was to put Street on the defensive. "Remember Grace Johnson? She came to see me last week. She says she walked out of the jail. Seems the door to her cell was unlocked and the turnkey was having a cigarette. She's on her way south. Oh, and I talked to Sixtas. He says he's never heard of her."

"I'm sure he's never heard of her," Street said. "What the hell would he know about a schoolteacher?"

"You said she was one of his whores."

"I said a lot of things over the past year and most of them were true. That one wasn't. You were talking about putting her on the stand and I had to head you off. It seemed like a good idea at the time and damned if it didn't work. The wind's blown that little problem away and nobody's the wiser."

"It doesn't bother you that you ruined her life? That your thugs killed a good man in the process?" I had not thought to go so far. But now I was into it and I could not stop.

"There's one thing I know for sure," Street said. "If you're going to get anywhere, somebody's always going to have to die on the beach. Now can we get over to the damn banquet? We can't keep the good people waiting."

Before I could mention Horace Johnson, Maloney hurried into the room through the side door. "No time for banquets," he said. "Bernstein's taken over the warden's mansion at Jackson prison. Says he's going to start shootin' people unless you get down there."

I KNEW something of Jackson prison. I had been there once before the war, on a routine visit to corroborate the testimony of a convict whom we had convinced to implicate his accomplice. I knew that before there had been a capitol in Lansing, there had been a prison at Jackson, crouched over the horizon to the southeast. Its five-story red brick walls dominate the rolling, pastoral landscape and enclose over fifty acres of yard, ostensibly devoted to inmate recreation. Inside, the cellblocks are stacked one on top of another in glazed brick and steel layers, joined to the walls but facing inward. On every level, rows of cells extend with mechanical repetition down the long corridors, with metal walkways in front and cramped catwalks in the back through which the guards can prowl to observe their charges. Answering the roll call every morning and every evening back then were the flotsam and jetsam of the Michigan underworld. And after the Collingwood killings in 1931, that roll call included Lev Bernstein, late of the Purple Gang.

"Does the press know Bernstein's got the warden?" Street asked, after we slipped quietly down the rear steps of the Capitol and hurried to the unmarked car Maloney had parked on a deserted side street.

"Not yet," Maloney said. "The state bulls've got the mansion surrounded and the main road is blocked off. On account of an accident that ain't actually happened yet. We'll stop at the state police post and then use an ambulance from there. The screws think it's only Bernstein and Lefkowitz and Shrieber inside the mansion, along with the warden and his family. And maybe some nigger."

"Not exactly how I wanted to start my administration," Street said. "How the hell did they get out in the first place?"

Maloney looked back over his shoulder and laughed aloud. "Boss, you've been there. You know they can get out any time they want. You've seen them up there in aristocrats' row on the top floor of 15 Block, with their cell doors wide open. Slip the block captain some green and it's out the south gate. Hell, during the season Bernstein and the rest of the Purples go over to Detroit and take in the Tigers' games. Anyways, it's not much of a walk from 15 Block to the warden's place. Or maybe the warden invited them over for a friendly dinner on New Year's Day. He's a boozer. And they've got plenty of good whiskey. I did a tour of duty over there and I used to get my share."

Street lapsed quickly into silence and stared out of the car's side window. We all knew that the prison walls could neither keep the convicts in nor the outside world out. After one particularly spectacular escape, the McReynolds administration had scrambled to cut its losses. In short order, McReynolds fired the warden outright and installed Ralph Swinton in his place. In his rush, McReynolds ignored the fact that Swinton was a chronic alcoholic. Now the Purples had him, and with him they apparently thought they had a way out.

After we arrived at the state police post, we made the transfer to the ambulance quickly, Street with Maloney's slouch hat rolled down over his forehead and the collar of his chesterfield pulled up around his ears. There was a circular driveway, carefully shoveled clean of snow, in front of the warden's mansion. As we pulled in through the darkness, I picked out at least ten state troopers crouched in the snow around the structure. Several of them had rifles slung over their shoulders military style.

When Maloney opened the back doors of the ambulance, Street heaved himself to his feet. I took a long breath and then I stopped him.

I have to be the one to get to Bernstein, I thought. "You can't go in there," I said. "Right now all they've got is a warden nobody knows, along with his wife and kids. With you, they've got a governor. If you go in there, they're holding the whole state for ransom."

"Don't be a hero, Charlie. It doesn't become you. Bernstein wants this face to face. We might as well get it over with."

I put my hand on his arm. "Maloney and I'll go in. They don't even know you're out here. It gives us a chance to size up the situation and buy some time. The worst they can do is send us back."

"The worst they can do is kill you out of hand. Bernstein may have sanded off some of his rough edges, but he'll cut your throat in a New York second if he thinks it's to his advantage."

"He gains nothing by killing me. He'll recognize a messenger boy when he sees one," I said. Street hesitated, and I listened to the wind sift through the stand of pines by the mansion's entrance and watched their branches shift and flutter. *If I can get to Bernstein, I can end it,* I thought.

"All right," Street said. "See what the bastard wants and then get back out here. Tell him you need to get in touch with me by phone from the state police post."

"He'll want me to use the phone in there."

"Not if the cops've cut the phone wires. Which is what Maloney will tell them to do right now. We sure as hell don't want those jailbirds makin' any calls to the local paper. Isn't that right, sergeant?"

"Right you are, boss," Maloney said.

≈ 45 ≈

The Spider in His Web

January, 1947

The cement steps up to the massive wooden door to the warden's mansion were steep and icy. I slipped once and almost fell, but Maloney grabbed my arm. My chest was tight and I was shaking in the breathless cold. When we reached the narrow porch, I saw a face through the stained-glass window to the right. Maloney nudged me in the side, but I was so numbed that I scarcely felt it. *Can't stop*, I thought. *I've got to keep going.*

Maloney looked at me for a moment and then pounded on the door with his gloved hand. "Best get on with it, Mr. Cahill," he said. Then the door opened and it was Bernstein, silhouetted in a nimbus of golden light.

"Why, if it isn't two paddies on my doorstep, bright as new pennies," he said. "Come in. I've been waiting for you."

He was grayer than when I had seen him in the market with my father, all those years ago. Extending from his left eyebrow to his jaw line was a curved scar, shiny and purple against the pasty white of his skin. His cheeks were round and puffy, and he wore spectacles that accentuated the pouches under his eyes. He had grown stout on prison food and his shoulders were hunched forward. When he put his hand out to me, I shook it, unthinkingly, absurdly. His skin was dry and papery, as if he were running a fever.

"I've been looking forward to meeting you," he said. He had a pleasant baritone voice. Comfortable. Conventional. Even grandfatherly. But his eyes were dark and cold, and there were narrow yellow flecks at the corners that glinted when he turned his head.

He turned to Maloney and repeated the ritual. "And it's always good to see you, Aloysius," he said. He opened the door wide and, with an elaborate show of courtesy, motioned us into the foyer. Abraham Lefkowitz and Isadore Shrieber stood on the top of the landing, up the wide staircase. Bernstein coughed into a wadded white handkerchief that he carried in his left hand, and then gestured to them.

"You know my associates," he said. "They're taking care of Mrs. Swinton and the children upstairs." Shrieber smiled and pointed his forefinger at me and snapped his thumb back. I stamped my feet to clear off the snow and leaned against the curved railing of the stairway to steady myself. *Don't show them anything,* I thought. *If they see fear, they'll kill us.*

There was a spacious living room with upholstered chairs and sofas to our right, through a set of double doors. Polished oak trim framed the windows, and matching baseboards offset the richness of the dark red carpet. Shaded lamps were scattered throughout the room and the lighting was soft and subdued. It was a grand room in a grand building. A graceful country manor less than a hundred yards from the main gate of the largest walled prison in the world. There was an enormous fire blazing away in the brick fireplace and heat radiated from it. A circular wood coffee table sat next to the fireplace. There were only two objects on that table. The first was a long-barreled Colt. The second was the iron poker from Sarah Maynard's fireplace. The yellow light clouded my eyes then and I could barely see across the room. I shook my head, but it had little effect. *I'm on the beach again,* I thought. *All that's ahead are the dying and the dead.*

Bernstein patted me down for weapons and then turned to Maloney. "I know you're heeled," he said. "Put your piece on the table there, alongside mine." Maloney removed his snub-nosed revolver from his shoulder holster and placed it on the coffee table.

"All our weapons are out in the open," Bernstein said, and he turned back to the double doors. "Horace, you can bring the warden in now."

Swinton shuffled into the room, his head down. There was an angry bruise under one eye, and specks of blood at the corners of his nose, and his lips were cracked and swollen. He had leg irons on both his ankles, connected with a steel chain. His hands were handcuffed together in front of him. Behind him was a tall, broad-shouldered Negro carrying a sawed-off shotgun. He walked unsteadily and I knew he had to be Horace Johnson, fighting a hangover with more liquor.

Bernstein walked over to the warden and ruffled his hair lightly, as if he were a small child, and then led him by the arm to one of the chairs. "It's been quite a New Year's for the warden," he said. "He was under the impression that he was actually in charge. We had to subdue him a bit. I think he deserves a drink now that he's seen the error of his ways. Bring the bottle from the bar, will you, Horace? Then we can talk a little business."

Bernstein smiled at me. But his eyes were blank, black holes against the prison pallor of his skin. *There's no laughter in those eyes*, I thought. *He's like a patient old spider watching his prey.*

"Warden Swinton is a very knowledgeable man about business," Bernstein said. "Tell our guest about our meeting with the new governor, will you, Ralph?"

Swinton answered immediately, willingly. "I figured Street was going to be governor," he said. "He called me and said he wanted to come over for a meeting with Bernstein. I set it up. We made the deal right here. It was $50,000 in cash for him every month, with $1,000 off the top for me. Bernstein would count it out in the morning and in the afternoon I'd give it to Johnson. Then he'd take my car and deliver the money to Street in Lansing."

Swinton glanced at me, over at Maloney, and then back down to the cuffs on his hands. "What else could I do? Once Street took over, all it would take was one word and I'd be gone. I've got kids."

Bernstein tousled the man's hair again and coughed into his handkerchief. "I thought it would be good business to buy myself a governor," he said to me. "And Street, he's a smart boy. Once Ralph took the money from me, Street owned him."

I began to sweat and the bile rose in my throat. I didn't know how long I could keep the fear at bay. But I knew we had to come to terms.

"What is it you want?" I asked.

"Patience, Charles, always patience. Come over here with me, so we can talk a bit among ourselves, in front of the fire like gentlemen." His voice was low and there was a strangled sound to it, as if he were straining to catch his breath. It didn't stop him from talking, though. In fact, he appeared to relish it. But there remained a stillness about him, an economy of motion, so that at his core he was anchored and unmoving even as he spoke. When we reached the fireplace, out of earshot of the others, he turned to me.

"There's a proper way to conduct these affairs and we must all play by the rules," he said. "Your governor, now, I knew he'd send someone here on his behalf. In my business, we use go-betweens all the time. I would've done exactly the same thing."

Bernstein walked over to the coffee table and picked up the poker. The heat from the fireplace closed in on me. "As you can see," he said, "I thought it would be you."

"You've got the gun too?"

"We saw you drop it in the river. But we couldn't fish it out."

It made no difference. Bernstein had the murder weapon, and with it he had Sarah and me. "What are you going to do?" I asked. For a man in the corner, I was asking too many questions, but the habit was engrained. After all, what is a lawyer without words, without questions? So I turned to words.

Bernstein was happy to engage me. And why not, he was the one in command. "For the moment, nothing at all," he said. "It's been a long day for the people's choice out there. No doubt he's exhausted. We'll let him sit for a while in the cold."

He rubbed his hands before the fire, but the heat had no visible effect on him. "It's just a tactic, Charles. One of the things prison teaches you is that anxiety increases with the passage of time."

He gestured at the tall grandfather clock on the far side of the room. Its hands showed that it was ten-thirty. "Our governor, he's a creature of impulse," he said. "Just as I was when I came here to be corrected. He acts without regard for consequences and it's in all our interests to protect him from that. If we wait a while, perhaps his judgment will be impaired enough that we can put our deal back together. Do you have those drinks yet, Horace?"

Maloney was leaning silently against one of the double doors, and Johnson brushed by him into the room without a glance. Maloney only smiled and watched Johnson with hooded eyes as he carried an ornate serving tray, with stacked crystal highball glasses, a large silver bucket filled with ice, and two unopened bottles of Seagram's blended Canadian whiskey across the room. Johnson placed the tray down on the coffee table and began to fill one of the glasses with ice.

"I don't think you've met Horace, have you?" Bernstein asked. "But you know his wife. And his daughter was briefly your client?"

Johnson nodded once at me. Then he broke the seal on one of the bottles, poured a long slug of whiskey into the glass, and pushed it toward the warden who was still slumped in his chair, his handcuffs resting on his knees. Swinton wet his lips, but then he shook his head. Johnson set the glass down and backhanded the warden squarely across the face. As Swinton's head snapped back, Johnson picked up the bottle and poured the whiskey down into the man's open, bloody mouth. Swinton bucked and gagged, but Johnson would not relent, and the whiskey cascaded down onto the chair and then to the floor, staining the red of the carpet.

"Drink it," Johnson said. His voice was loud and rough. But he glanced sideways at Bernstein for approval. "Head screw, he just like a little child. Got no manners," he said.

Bernstein walked across the room and placed his hand on Johnson's shoulder. "Give our host his drink," he said. "I'm sure he'll be quite appreciative now." Johnson pushed the glass forward again, and this time the warden raised his manacled hands from his knees and took it. He gulped the whiskey down noisily and turned to Bernstein.

"Tell your houseboy to pour me another," he said. Johnson drove his fist into the warden's face and I heard the crack of the cartilage in his nose. The chair went over backwards and Johnson leapt forward, cursing, but Bernstein stopped him.

"That's enough," he said, and Johnson was immediately still.

Bernstein turned to me. "I trust you're sufficiently impressed with our capacity for violence. No doubt you're thinking we can do the same to you." *And to Sarah and the girl*, I thought.

Bernstein leaned over the chair and grasped Swinton by the shirtfront with both hands and pulled him onto his feet. "Take the warden back into the kitchen and clean him up," he said to Johnson. "Then put him in the dining room and cuff him to one of the chairs by the window. Sit there with that shotgun so the state bulls can see you and him and the gun. Be careful. Don't let them get a clear shot at you. I'll be needing you later."

Bernstein walked back to the fireplace and pulled two of the heavy chairs close to the coffee table, grunting with the effort. "Come sit with me," he said. "I get a little out of breath and a short one always takes the edge off. It's good medicine." I sat down slowly and tried to ignore the heat and the nausea.

Bernstein gestured expansively toward the fireplace. "Cocktails at the country club, just like Grosse Pointe. But much more stable. A prison is the most law-abiding place in the world. If you violate the rules, the punishment is always quick and painful. And we make the rules. I think the warden may have begun to realize that now."

I put my right hand on my knee, in plain sight. If I could get between him and the weapons, I might be able to stop him long enough for Maloney to get to his gun and then we would have him. I shook my head again, to clear it. *Be fast*, I thought. *He won't give you much time.*

Bernstein raised his hand. "I wouldn't," he said. "I may be old and wheezy, but sudden violence is still my specialty. You get near me, I'll kill you." I didn't interpret it as a threat, just a statement. He pulled a heavy clasp knife from his pants pocket and thumbed the hooked blade open. "How many dead men have you seen, Charles?"

"Probably more than you."

"Maybe. But in my business you see them up close. It's something of a matter of honor. I always made a point of looking them in the eye when they died. So I would remember them. Someone had to."

I sat back slowly as he placed the knife on the end table next to the serving tray and poured himself a whiskey, straight up. He rested his head against the chair and the silence stretched out. Finally, he looked over at me and said, "It was smart of you to send the Maynard woman to be with Street. Now you've got a hold on him."

I fumbled in astonishment. "I have no idea what you're talking about," I said. I saw his yellowed eyes flare with amusement behind his spectacles. Maloney was still leaning against the doorway and I glanced over at him, but he only stared back at me.

"You think I'm just an ignorant thug," Bernstein said. "Maybe I was. But there's nothing but time in prison. Time matures a man. Broadens the mind."

He leaned forward and took a sip of his drink. "With all that time on my hands, I've read almost every book in the prison library. Dickens, now. His London's like my Detroit. When you think about it, what's the difference between this prison and your government? Someone's at the top giving the orders. Someone's at the bottom doing the rough stuff. It's a tale of two cities alright, but they're both the same."

"What do you know about Sarah Maynard and Hubbell Street?"

He ignored me. "My father used to say the Cossacks hunted us *zhids* for sport in the old country. Like rabbits, he'd say. But it was different in Detroit. We had the guns then, my brothers and me. We paid the cops and they were happy to take our money. My parents could never understand that. They died thinking we were still rabbits."

He poured another shot of whiskey into his glass and twirled the liquid slowly. "Why shouldn't I know of your governor's little affair with Mrs. Maynard? Do you actually think that J. Edgar Hoover is the only one who can tap a telephone or put a bug in a room?"

I stared at him in disbelief and his amusement grew. "Street's showing very poor judgment." he said. "It'll catch up to him in time. And if he loses in '48, all my investment's just money down a rat hole. I need to do some hedging."

"Is that why you staged this whole business, to doublecross Hubbell Street?"

"But it's Street that's the doublecrosser," he said. "Not a word since the election. And me his old friend the moneyman. It causes me no end of grief. I gave him everything he needed. Now he's about to walk away or let out a contract on me? I think it's time I put paid to his account."

He looked straight up at me. I saw the malice then, in the golden flecks in his eyes. *He means to kill Street this night*, I thought. *Unless I put an end to it.*

"I'll say it again. What is it you want?"

"Jackson's a very dangerous place for me now. I've had the run of the yard for a long time. I've made my share of enemies." With his left hand he traced the scar down the side of his face. "I need to get out."

"You can't think Street is just going to let you walk free."

"Street's no idiot. I'll probably die in prison, bored stiff. But not yet. Not quite yet."

Bernstein swirled the liquor in his glass again and took another small sip. "What I want is a transfer back to Marquette," he said. "It's maximum security up there. I won't end up face down in the yard, eating gravel with a shank in my ribs. It's cold in the winter and it's almost always winter. But business is business. It's a longer string, but I think the puppets will still dance the same."

He looked up at the clock. "It's time for you to go relieve our new governor's anxiety. Tell him that's my proposal. His first day in office and he can put down a jailbreak. Tell him to come in here out of the dark and we can shake hands like gentlemen. Then we go our separate ways."

I lurched to my feet and I felt the weakness, down to my bones. It was such a simple proposition and I was absolutely convinced that he was lying. With all his contacts inside and outside the prison, Bernstein could have arranged a move up to Marquette with one phone call. No, what he really wanted was to get Street inside.

As Maloney and I walked to the door, Bernstein put his hand on my shoulder. "There's one more thing," he said, "but it's nothing to do with Street. All my brothers are in the family business. But little Lennie, he wants out. I think he's crazy, but he wants to be legitimate. Who ever heard of a Jewish oilman? But he wants it and he'll need a good lawyer with political contacts to keep the law off him. Once Street's gone, take care of Lennie. You'll make some money and I'll owe you a favor."

My anger flared and I spoke without thinking. "I'll never work for any of you. My father's dead because of you and my brother's crippled."

"Forget your brother. He was trying to con his way into a better deal. We don't negotiate with the hired help."

He paused and rubbed the scar again. "It's embarrassing," he said after a moment. "Until now, I never put either one of you together with Sam Cahill. I remember him. He was that puller who got shot up on the river and drowned. I remember he drank too much to be in our line of work."

"What the hell was it to you?"

"Not a thing. He was just unlucky. That was the year we decided to get rid of the independents. They were cutting into our take, so we put the word out on the Canadian side. The

Canadians knew where they made their money. It wasn't from small change like your father."

I turned away. He had all the weapons and there was nothing I could do to him. At least not yet. But he was not finished.

"And you can stop worrying about the always available Mr. Hennessey. He disappeared this morning. Left a note about the pressures of the job. It irritated me the way he kept switching sides. He never realized there is really only one side." He paused, thinking about his turn of phrase, relishing it. Then he said, "Remember, the past exists only in the mind. Stay in the present. You're the go-between for Street and me. Tell him what I said, and don't let what's already been done get in the way of business."

"I'll have to drive over to the state police post to call him."

"Of course you will. That's why you had the telephone wires cut and why that ambulance is out front. It's good to keep up appearances. Don't worry." He put his hand on Maloney's arm. "Aloysius and I will be here. Waiting."

⟫ 46 ⟪

In the Wire

January, 1947

When I went out the door and down the steps to the parking area where the ambulance was waiting, there was a pale half moon directly overhead, shimmering in the night sky. The stillness was absolute and when I inhaled the frozen air, it seared my lungs and cleared my head. I clambered my way up through the two back doors of the ambulance. The heater was laboring away at full blast to counter the cold, and the heat was just short of suffocating. The light on the roof of the ambulance flickered uncertainly as Street and I faced each other, hunkered down on the stretcher slabs by the back doors. Cigarette butts were scattered at Street's feet, and the flat, stale smell of smoke hung in the air.

"Give us some privacy, will you," Street said to the state police driver. After the trooper swung down from the front seat of the ambulance and closed the door, Street turned back to me. "I'm dyin' out here in this sweatbox while you and Bernstein jerk off," he said. "What the hell's going on?" There was a sheen of perspiration on his forehead as he leaned toward me.

At first, I told him only a little. "Bernstein wants out of Jackson. He wants a transfer to Marquette."

"Bullshit," Street said. "That's not what this is about. What game is he playing now?"

"He says if you give him your word on it, then the warden and his family are home free."

Street rejected it out of hand. "It'll never work," he said. "One of these cops'll get drunk and shoot his mouth off. Or some con'll get wind of it and pass the word. We're here to put down a jailbreak. It's nothing more than that and damn sure nothing less."

"He wants you to come back with me. To seal the deal."

I paused for effect and took a long breath. *Finish it,* I thought. *To be free, I had to have a hold over him.* "But that's not what he's got in mind at all," I said. "He wants to get you in there to kill you. He knows there's no death penalty in Michigan. He'll be sent to Marquette, out of harm's way. And you'll be dead on your first day in office. Maybe he sees it as poetic justice."

Street looked at me and cocked his head to the right. "You're finally wising up," he said. "I'll have to watch my ass with you from now on. Now here's what we do. You go back in there. Tell him there's no deal. Tell him somebody's got to die. And that somebody's the warden. Tell him to shoot that asshole and we're all settled up. He'll be off to Marquette and he can live out his life like the filth he is."

He had managed to surprise me yet again and I took another breath, to steady myself. "The warden's wife and children are in there," I said. "Swinton's a crook. But he's done nothing to you."

"Christ, do you really think I'm a murderer? No different from Bernstein? Go in there and tell him what I just said. And then get him close to a window. One of those troopers'll put a bullet in his brain and that'll be the end of it."

"And if that doesn't work?"

Street opened the back doors of the ambulance and yelled for the state police driver to come around to the back of the vehicle. "Give me your piece," he said.

The trooper gave his service revolver to Street and he thrust it at me. "He won't think to search you. He thinks he's got you halfway on his side," he said. "Walk in there, brass balls and all. If we can't get a shot from outside, then blast him. You've done it before. It's not like you need the practice."

Street motioned the trooper away, leaned forward, and whispered in my ear. "He's the one who told me how Maynard died. If you kill him, who's to know? Just Sarah and you and me. I guarantee you, Sarah won't mind. Do what needs to be done, and then we keep everything quiet. Then it's business as usual."

Can you do it? she had asked me. Street was asking the same thing. His eyes glistened in the uncertain light, and I knew that there was no answering him. I left him there in the ambulance and walked slowly back up the steps. *I'm in the wire*, I thought. *There's only one way out.*

Bernstein did not challenge my bona fides and I was in, with the revolver tucked into my trousers in back on my right side, behind my belt. Maloney took up his post by the doorway, and when we were seated in front of the yellow of the fire, Bernstein listened to me attentively and without interruption.

"Fleming I could deal with," he said when I finished. His voice had a raspy edge and he measured out the words. "We both spoke the same language. Smart boy out there, he speaks a different language. Words mean one thing to him on Wednesday and another thing on Thursday. That's why you can't make a deal with him. His terms change from day to day."

He walked slowly over to the floor lamp in the corner of the room and flicked off the switch. "I can see your shooters from here," he said, "but they can't see me. No rabbits shot dead in the moonlight tonight."

He stepped over to the chair furthest from the window and sat down in it with a small sigh, his legs extended toward me. "I'm getting outdated. In my time, when a politician set a price and you paid it, he stayed bought. Street's right, though. We need to settle our accounts here and be on our way."

Then he too surprised me. "You're a Catholic, aren't you?"

"A bad one. I don't go to Mass very often." I put my hand behind me and curled my fingers around the butt of the revolver. I was shaking slightly. But Bernstein did not appear to notice.

"Do you take communion?"

"Sometimes," I said. I loosened the gun and eased the hammer back.

"Moran told me it emptied his mind. He considered it almost blasphemous, but he told me when he took communion he had a sensation of pure release."

"One of your imports?" I was dragging it out on purpose. I could not be sure that I could pull the trigger. Not with the haze rising all around me and the smell of cordite and burned flesh floating in the air.

Bernstein looked over his spectacles at me and there was the same flash of amusement in his eyes. "No one imported George Clarence Moran"—he mimicked a drawling Irish brogue—"he was pure North Side Chicago. And my, but he was a dandy. I never saw him in anything but a three-piece suit, and as friendly and courteous a man as any I ever met. But he was a mick like you and he had that Irish wildness to him. Sometimes he did things without thinking, crazy things. That's why Capone hired us to kill him."

"Moran was your friend?" I was close enough that the shots would be fatal. All I had to do was raise the gun and pull the trigger and it would be over. Perhaps there would be a moment of release in the yellow fog.

Bernstein laughed. "There're no friends in my line of work. Just momentary allies. We sold whiskey to the Irish mob in Chicago for years. We all made a very tidy profit. But Moran irritated Capone. And Alphonse was not a man to irritate. He finally hired us to put an end to George Clarence Moran"—again the drawling brogue—"but we missed him."

He paused, and methodically polished his spectacles with a white napkin from the serving tray. "We didn't miss the others, though," he said. "It was a cold St. Valentine's Day when we lined them up in that garage, and a dark and bloody business. Six thugs and one little *zhid* for good measure. The Cossacks must've been smiling. It's funny, I only remember the Jew. The rest are just shadows on the wall."

I eased back on the trigger.

"Perhaps the act of killing is like communion," he said. "Perhaps it empties the mind for that moment." He looked at me steadily. "When you go to church, do you pray?"

I hesitated. "I pray for the gift of forgetting," I said, finally.

"But not of forgiveness? That's an interesting answer, Charles. Perhaps you're deeper than I thought."

He leaned forward suddenly and began to cough, his head and his shoulders hunched forward. When he finished, he wiped his mouth with the napkin and looked at me again. "Smart boy out there thinks you killed Maynard," he said. His voice was so soft and ragged that I could hardly hear him.

"He's right." I said it immediately, without thinking.

"No, he's a fool. I told him that and he believed it. But it was Sarah Maynard who killed him. I saw you running up the driveway of their house that day and no one runs *to* a killing."

"You were there?"

"We were way ahead of you," he said. "Fleming wanted us to kill Maynard and his wife and daughter. But we don't kill civilians. Except for that one little *zhid* in Chicago. And that was a mistake. I finally made a deal with Fleming for Maynard himself. Then the warden gave us his car."

"But why?" I asked. "What did you gain?"

"We were making good money off Fleming, until he got sick and crazy. We drove over to Lansing in the morning. After the roll call. We were ready to send your senator on his way. But then you showed up. We watched you and Sarah Maynard carry his body out. We followed you out into the country and watched you shoot a dead man in the face. It was all a string of coincidences. Just like me buying Street. Just like tonight."

He looked up at the clock and came up out of his chair. "Almost the witching hour. Horace," he called out, "let's have the warden in here. Time to give Street his due."

Johnson brought Swinton into the room, jamming the shotgun into his back as the warden stumbled forward. Maloney walked behind them, fumbling in his shirt pocket for a cigarette. "Stand him up over here by the fire," Bernstein said. "But not too close to the windows. We don't want some trigger-happy cop to muddy up the waters."

He turned to the coffee table and picked up Maloney's snub-nose and tossed it to him. "Arrest me when this is over Aloysius. Then Street can transfer me to Marquette, according to plan."

He leaned over and picked up his knife. Swinton tried to break free, but Johnson smashed the butt of the shotgun into his stomach and the warden fell to his knees. Johnson leaned back, relaxed and easy. He was grinning, his face alight with anticipation. He was waiting to see the warden die.

I stood up from the chair and slowly lifted the revolver from my side and pointed it at Bernstein. He was close enough that I could not miss. I curled my forefinger around the trigger. Sarah's fate and mine hung in the balance. But I could not do it.

I dropped the gun to my side. The yellow fog was gone and the fear had slipped away, out into the darkness. Let them do their worst. I was not a murderer. Not that night or any night.

Bernstein smiled at me and shrugged his shoulders. His face was calm, but the purple scar was inflamed. His eyes were alive and hungry and he no longer looked quite so old.

"Let's make an end to it," he said.

He walked toward the warden and Johnson with his knife dangling loosely from his right hand. He lifted the knife up and snapped the blade back into the handle.

"Horace, it's time to go," he said to Johnson. He nodded to Maloney. Maloney flipped his cigarette into the fire, brought up his revolver, and shot Johnson three times in the chest. Johnson dropped his shotgun and reached out toward Bernstein with both hands. His arms were rigid, his eyes wild, his mouth open in shock. He pitched forward, flattening the coffee table. The blood pooled out from his chest, mingling with the whiskey that had stained the carpet. His legs kicked several times spasmodically and then he was still.

Bernstein looked down at him. Then rolled his body over and picked up the poker from the debris of the table and handed it to me. "A favor from an old man," he said. "My second for the

Cahills. Back when I was young, I shot that river pirate who drowned your father. He was getting in the way of business. Looked him in the eye and shot him six times, and then set him and his boat afire. It was in all the tabloids."

He took a step forward and kicked Johnson once, but the man did not move. "A drunk who talked too much," he said. "I couldn't stand for that. He was a dead man the first time he talked to Frank Reno. I kept him around until I needed him and here we are."

Bernstein sat down in the armchair and looked over at Johnson's body. "The last of a long line," he said, and he leaned forward and closed the man's staring eyes.

Then he turned to me. "At least he died by the rules," he said. "Drunks usually don't. If anybody should know that, it's you."

"You knew I had a gun?"

"Of course. But killers never hesitate. I knew if you didn't start firing when you walked in the door, you wouldn't do it at all. Go tell your smart boy he's got what he wants. Johnson's the jailbreaker. And now he's shot while trying to kill the warden, and Maloney's the hero. It's a great story and it's almost true."

"What about the warden?"

"Ralph understands how simple it is. He keeps his mouth shut, he gets to live. Street will play it that way too. In his business, appearances are all that matter. But he can't know Maloney's with us. You and I need him next to Street until the day he dies. That should be about two years from now. After I've squeezed everything I can out of him and he's an ex-governor. Then nobody will care a damn. Let the vermin in the fields feed on him."

Bernstein walked to the door and opened it, and the wind whistled in. He breathed the winter cold in deeply and turned back to us. "One thing for sure," he said. "Our sergeant always hits them clean," he said. "Isn't that right, Aloysius?"

Maloney lit a cigarette, his face impassive. "Whatever you say, boss."

Into the Light

November, 1996

*M*y *father's breathing is ragged and faint. He lies in the Stryker bed and stares at the ceiling, and his chest rises and falls irregularly. He is at the edge of life, but I must ask.*

"Why do you think she did it?"

He reaches up to wipe the tears from my face. The dam within me has burst and I am weeping, choking back the sobs with my clenched fists. He smiles at me, that warm, winning smile he used with every jury he ever charmed.

"It's all right, Francine," he says. "Your mother told me everything. She came home early that morning from visiting your grandmother and walked upstairs. She saw him from the bedroom door. You were there, Francine, you were there. Your mother backed away from the door and ran down the stairs. She waited for him in the kitchen with the iron poker from the fireplace set. When he walked through the kitchen door, she crushed his skull. Then she called me."

"He made me do it, those things. He made me." My voice is a groan, the words a dirge.

"Of course he made you. Your mother knew that. And she had to stop him."

We sit in the darkened room. I am suspended, lost. I cannot move. I cannot think. I cannot speak. Finally my adopted father, my real father, says to me, "Dying is not for weaklings and neither is living. What your mother did, she did for you. And what I did, I did for her."

"How could you go back to her, after she had been with Street?"

He rolls his body toward me and his eyes moisten. "I realized it didn't matter a damn. No one's pure in this life, Francine. Everyone lies and nothing is as it seems. But you have to live it anyway, as best you can. And that's what we did. We lived it, as best we could."

I cannot, I will not speak. My father turns his face to the wall and drifts into that dreamy gray world that lies near the end. The candle flickers in the quiet, deadly hours before dawn when hope is lost and life ebbs. Past becomes present, appearances have no meaning, and reality is an illusion. He tosses in the bed and whispers his commands, rallies his men, and leads them off the beach and up the cliff, through the yellow morning mist. He stiffens as he sees the wire and then the awful emptiness of the bunkers. Then he cries out in agony as the pain courses through him.

But in time he passes through the shadows. The ghosts that people the room fade with the sun. He slips into sleep and his chest rises with a slow rhythm. I know that he will awaken and it is time for the accounting.

He has cast me as a victim, but I was more than that. He has spread his story out in front of me, but there is one secret thing left, one last buried shard of guilt. He does not know that I, too, had another part to play. He saw a gulf between my mother and me. But it was a bond, sealed in violence and then kept in silence. We made our conspiracy without voice. Beyond words. Beyond thought. Beyond the law and wholly unrelated to it.

Yes, my mother and I made our pact and yes, we kept it across the years of her life. We kept it even from the man who became her husband and my father. He said there was enough guilt to go around and he was more than right.

Oh yes, there was death in the morning that day. Charles Cahill, tarnished knight-errant, thought my mother had killed that man. But it was not her hand that brought that poker down. He believed in her and believed her guilty. But I was the one who delivered that man to eternity.

Yes, with what he had done with me, I had thought myself destroyed. But I was not. Then too, I could not speak. I could not think. But I could move, ever so quietly. I floated down the stairway without a sound, behind him. Past the fireplace in the living room with its iron poker and then on into the sunny kitchen. The room was filled with light, warm and bright. The light dazzled me and for a moment I was blinded.

He sensed me behind him then, in the morning light. But I was too fast for him. Too feral in my fear. Too strong in my hate. I struck him with that iron talon, and when he fell to his knees, I hammered his skull from behind, over and over, until the blood pooled, thick and grainy red on the shiny linoleum of our kitchen floor. Yes, I sent him on his way into the dark. I took away every-thing he ever was and everything he ever would be. And then I felt an aching, soiled release.

My mother came into the kitchen, into the sunlight. She saw me kneeling there, smiling and sobbing. And she walked to the phone to call for help. To call the man who now lies so peace-fully before me. He thought he was rescuing her. But it was me he saved.

My mouth tastes of the rust of old rage and the salt of new tears. I have kept that rage frozen deep within myself all these years. No one who lives today knows that the frail, quiet girl I once was killed with no mercy and no regret on that beautiful autumn day. I am without conscious thought, but the past is fully with me now, scratching at the sealed windows of my soul. I await his verdict. Let him be my confessor, my judge. "Charlie," I whisper. "Charlie, it was me. I killed him." Finally I have spoken the words, and they hang suspended there in the air like icicles in the dead of winter, frozen sharp and clear. Does he hear? Can he understand?

His eyelids flutter, once, twice, and he turns his head slowly, an inch at a time, to the sound of my voice. His mouth is open with the effort and his breathing is a whistling rattle. His eyes are wide now, staring, accepting.

"Sarah," he says. "At last."

ACKNOWLEDGEMENTS

On the surface, the creation of a book would appear to be a solitary task, a writer painfully pecking away, night after lonely night, at a typewriter or computer. But, as with many things, surface impressions are far from reality. In truth, I have found, creating a book and bringing it to publication is actually a collaboration. And so, my heartfelt thanks and sincere appreciation to my collaborators: my wife Stephanie, my first reader, my toughest critic and my biggest fan, who gave me that most precious of gifts, the gift of time; Linda Peckham who encouraged me as I was starting out on this journey; my agent Gary Heidt who stayed with me throughout the mysterious process of finding a publisher; my publishers Marty and Judith Shepherd of The Permanent Press who, once we found them, gave me enormous help and encouragement throughout the entire process; Joslyn Pine who provided not only excellent line editing but kind words as well; Bill Castanier, my publicist who has worked tirelessly on my behalf; and my friend and confidant Mark Hahn, whose photography and cover art we have happily utilized.